Meant for Good

(A Novel)

JANENE RYAN

Meant for Good

(A Novel)

ANOINTED ROSE PRESS™

ANOINTED ROSE PRESS™

The Anointed Rose Press name and logo are registered
Trademarks of ANOINTED ROSE PRESS™

MEANT FOR GOOD©

JANENE RYAN

E-mail: JanenetheWriter@yahoo.com

ISBN-13: 97809826841-4-6
ISBN-10 0-9826841-4-2
© 2011 by Janene Ryan

Anointed Rose Press™
P.O. Box 21371
Philadelphia, PA 19141
E-mail: anointedrosepress.@gmail.com

Library of Congress Control Number: 2011902177
Library of Congress Catalog-in-Publication Data

Ryan, Janene

Meant For Good / Janene Ryan
p. cm.

ISBN 0-9826841-3-4 (trade pbk.: alk. paper)

1.   Fiction 2. Romance

Cover Design:
THE PRINTED WORD, INC.
Philadelphia, PA (215) 224-5500

...DEDICATIONS...

First and foremost I would like to thank Yahweh for giving me the strength and sustainability to handle life and all of its uppercuts. You have been my foundation!

Second, I would like to thank my family, especially my daughter, for loving me, supporting me and dealing with me – in spite of. You guys keep me sane.

Last but not least, I would like to thank everyone who bought, read, and recommended this book. You guys have made my dreams come true. Blessings!

Janene Ryan

...*FOREWORD*...

"Meant For Good" is an absolutely "must read" book. If this was a gourmet meal, and I was asked to use only one word to describe it – that word would be "scrump-ti-deli-umptuous" (as in scrumptious and delicious). This first time author has surely demonstrated her creative writing ability and a wonderful imagination.

Janene Ryan has definitely achieved a high standard with her very first published book, both in content and in presentation. The story, though a work of fiction, is completely timely and realistic for all adult readers; for the mature as well as young adult, and for male and female alike. Because there are some places in the book where the language is risqué', in keeping with the sub-culture of many college aged students, it would not be appropriate for very young readers.

The author has reached deeply into multiple societal issues that young people face as they seek to make their rites of passage from home to independence; including their personal spiritual development. "Meant For Good" follows a young woman through her metamorphous process from caterpillar to butterfly, and ties your heart to hers as she struggles to gain the victory. As the great author, Maya Angelou has said, *"We delight in the beauty of the butterfly, but rarely admit the changes it has gone through to achieve that beauty."* As you read this book, you will be truly inspired, and you will be captivated by the richness of the characters.

To the author I say, "Job well done, and I anxiously wait to see it on the top sellers list." God Bless you, Janene, for taking courage and writing such a powerful book.

September Summer
Pastor, Author, Radio Show Hostess
www.septembersummeronline.com

...SYNOPSIS...

LaTasha Daniels had a great life – a supportive family, great friends and an unmovable faith. However, when her father has a heart attack, this "always on point" young woman allows the smooth talk of vulnerability to catch her off guard.

Uncertain of the future of her father, LaTasha is sacked with more life-changing news. Soon her attempt at hiding a damning secret and living a life of falsehoods spiral out of control.

Adding to the mix of all that has erupted in her life are three men with three different purposes – all of which open her eyes to what love is supposed to be and what it actually is. Despite the support of a fiery tempered home-girl and prayer-warrior grandmother, LaTasha knows she will have to deal with her self-created struggles single handedly. Now on a journey to reclaim her spirit and redeem her vitality she meets the woman and the God she thought she knew so well.

Meant for Good is a coming of age novel that exposes the ups and downs, the ins and outs and the failures and rewards of life – leaving everyone involved to know love, grace and forgiveness are the only things that will keep us standing!

This is the first novel by author Janene Ryan.

CHAPTER 1

If I had one wish in the world it would be to disappear; to just vanish into thin air without even my scent left behind to be traced.

Frustrated and confused Tasha knew she had to make some changes in her life. As she lay in her bed staring at the white bland ceiling, all she could think about was the turmoil she had been through in the past five years; the stuff juicy novels were made of. With one burst of energy Tasha jumped up and began moving things. She headed straight for the bureau. She pushed and pulled until every piece of furniture in her bedroom was not in its original place. She pushed and dragged dressers from one side of the room to the other. She moved the television and its stand to the back wall where her full sized bed once stood, Tasha had enough! She was tired of the same old nothing going on in her life. Although she had no money to redecorate, she needed and wanted a fresh start. So, what else was there to do but rearrange some things in her life - starting with her apartment?

A sudden reflection of herself in a mirror hanging on one empty wall brought Tasha to a complete halt. She gazed at the face that gazed back – almost like a dog when it notices something unfamiliar. All she could do was stare. She frowned at her light dull skin. Growing up, the neighborhood children would tease her and call her "cracker" because she was so light skinned. The dark pink freckles that highlighted her cheeks were the main reason for the teasing, but thankfully they disappeared as the furious sun of Florida had given her some color. Only half of the children knew her coloring was because her father was half white. Even he, himself refused to admit it. The secret conversations between her parents let Tasha know her father's past was not one openly discussed. Even the way he dealt with family led her to believe he probably had an issue with his own.

She then focused on her wavy reddish-brown shoulder length hair that was pulled back in a ponytail. When she ran her hand across it, she noticed she had worn it in that style everyday for over a month. Moving her eyes downward, she took notice of her stomach and the way it poked out. Her weight was like the weather – it fluctuated. It was never a problem while she was growing up because she was always thin until she hit puberty. Then, her slight weight gain filled her out in all of the right places causing no one to doubt she was indeed a black woman. Three things Tasha was always satisfied with were her height, her smile, and those strikingly beautiful green eyes. Her 5' 7" worked perfectly for her. She figured she was neither too tall nor too short, and her smile and eyes could always brighten a room. Her striking features were certainly passed on by her father. He seemed to be the only black man in the south with green eyes. The reflection caused her to get angrier than she already was. The sound of a police siren racing past her window broke her from the visual trance.

By the time Tasha was finished with the bedroom she still had enough energy for another go-round so she headed for the living room. Before taking a hold of anything, Tasha stood back against the far left wall and looked around. She looked at the furniture her mother had given her when she moved out three years ago. She looked at the shading of her curtains along with the tone of her wallpaper and became disturbed at her choice of colors. *Why would anyone want navy blue curtains and taupe walls with navy blue furniture*, she thought as she scanned the room. She looked at her carpet and was instantly disgusted with its taupe complexion and dozens of dirt spots. She scrubbed the carpet numerous times, but how clean can you keep a carpet with a four-year-old running around with juice, ice cream, tootsie pops and everything else sticky? The only things Tasha was satisfied with were the two paintings on the adjacent walls her mother had given her as a birthday gift, her first year in the apartment. One painting portrayed a group of black woman playing in an orchestra. The women were all faceless but dressed in an array of colorful gowns. Tasha knew the meaning of the painting. She thought even though these women were faceless, they were dressed as important women. These women knew who they were and what they stood for even if no one else did. This hurt Tasha because she knew in her heart she would never feel the power these faceless women felt. She had been through too much in her life to think she would

3

one day be able to play in the orchestra of life and be noticed. The other painting was of a celebration – African kings and queens at a wedding. The looks on the faces of these men and woman were of pure joy. They gloried in the occasion of loved ones being married and the hope a new life would bring them. Although smiling while looking at the painting, Tasha became angry; angry at herself for her own life. She had dreams that were never fulfilled and made promises to herself she had never kept. Tasha was sick and tired of being sick and tired.

Without another thought, she grabbed the sofa and pulled it into the middle of the living room. She grabbed both end tables and put them in the kitchen to give her more space to move around. Tasha pushed and pulled, slid and dragged, lifted and moved everything in the living room until it looked like someone else's apartment. Tasha's heart was racing so fast at all she had done, she hadn't noticed her daughter standing in the doorway of the bathroom until she heard a voice say, "Mommy, what are you doing?" Startled, Tasha turned to see Chanelle looking at her mother with a confused look.

"Mommy, why are you moving everything around?" Chanelle asked before her mother could answer the first question.

For some reason, Tasha wanted to explain to her daughter what was going on but how could she possibly explain failure and frustration to a four-year-old? She wondered how she could talk to her daughter about what had been going on in her life without making her daughter feel any less for her as a mother. As Chanelle and Tasha stood there staring at each other, Tasha began to cry.

"Mommy, why are you crying? Did I do something wrong?" Chanelle asked her mother as she walked over to give her a hug.

All Tasha could do was to hug her daughter as the tears poured from her face. She wept for herself and all that had not gone right in her life. She wept for her daughter and all she had put her through by not having her life together.

She wept even harder when Chanelle said, "Mommy, it's gonna be all right."

Tasha wept and wept until she burst into laughter.

Confused, Chanelle looked at her mother and said, "Mommy, are you play crying?" Laughing even harder at what her daughter

4

had just said, Tasha squeezed her daughter until she said, "Mommy, I can't breathe!"

As they both laughed together and tickled one another, Tasha told her daughter to go put her shoes on and get ready to go to the park and to get some ice cream. As she watched Chanelle run away doing her happy dance, Tasha thought, *"why spend a beautiful Saturday afternoon confined in the house feeling sorry for myself when I have a life to save?"*

CHAPTER 2

Unlocking the door to the apartment, Tasha could hear the telephone ringing. Fighting with the key, she managed to get the door open in time to pick up the phone on the fourth and final ring before the answering machine was to pick up.

"Hello," she said trying to catch her breath.

"Hey, what's up?" she heard a man's voice she was unfamiliar with.

"Who is this?" Tasha said.

"You don't know who this is?" the man said with a slick voice.

"No, I don't know who this is," she said beginning to get angry at the game the man was trying to play.

"Think for a minute who this might be," the man said still trying to get a response from her.

"Look, who do you want?" Tasha said, angered by the man's unwillingness to make himself known.

"I'm sorry; I'm looking for LaTasha Daniels. My name is Curtis Martin and I am an old friend of hers. Is this her home?" the man said.

Was Tasha awake or dreaming because she was almost certain the man said his name was Curtis Martin? Curtis was Chanelle's father who refused to admit he had even gotten Tasha pregnant; let alone left her without any support or telephone number and address to contact him.

"Sorry, you have the wrong number," Tasha lied; now trying to disguise her voice. She could hear the pause in his voice before he spoke again.

"Okay, I'm sorry for disturbing you. Have a nice day," he replied; and just in time before he heard the sound of a dial tone.

*   *   *   *   *

La Tasha and Curtis met in college – Coppin State. He was from South Central Los Angeles and she from a small town in Florida called Dunbar – right outside of Jacksonville. They had come from two different backgrounds but seemed to meet at one certain place - Baltimore. She was from a huge family and he …well, let's just say "he was". Although she was an only child, she had tons of cousins she grew up with. All she knew was family and the love they had for her. Growing up in an atmosphere like that, she had no idea everyone didn't get the same care she had received. No, Tasha wasn't naive and her life wasn't perfect. She had her share of ups and downs; thankfully more ups than downs, but she had them. However, she was unfamiliar with people who were abused and neglected as children, even by their own parents. When she met Curtis in school it was no big deal. She didn't look at him and see the future; all she saw was a tall, lean, and bright eyed man with the gift of gab. Not really her type, but something about him caught her attention.

From the first semester in school she had seen him get comfortably adjusted to the new environment and the new women. It seemed to her every weekend that she saw a new girl coming from his dorm room. It didn't affect her in the least bit until one day, while leaving class, Curtis asked her if she wanted to take a drive with him. "A drive?" she thought. This wasn't the norm of asking a woman out to dinner or to the movies, but he asked her to ride to the mall with him. She was so shocked by what he asked her that immediately, without thinking, she said yes. After she heard the word leap from her lips, she wanted to kick herself. How could she want to be seen with a man like this – a player? As they talked and walked back to the dorm, they set a time to go on their first unofficial date.

Not long after Tasha got back to her dorm room, her best friend Lenora – who preferred to be called Lee because she felt her name was so old-fashioned – came to the room asking about Curtis. Like a nosey friend, she wanted to know why Tasha was walking and talking with Curtis Martin. Didn't her friend know what type of reputation this man had? Tasha told Lee what she and Curtis were planning to do. Lee just stared at her with a disagreeing look on her face. "All I'm saying is be careful," Lee said leaving Tasha's room. Tasha pondered about every possible thought Curtis was thinking when he approached her. Was he just trying to make her another booty call? Was he trying to get familiar with her to get to another one of her friends? Or was he just trying to be friendly? "I have a good reputation on campus; everyone knows me as the cool girl, a "one of the boys" type of girls", she thought while still going over the reasons for his interest. She had yet to come up with a reasonable answer. One thing she knew for sure – she would uncover his motives once they went out.

Glancing at the clock radio sitting on her desk, she noticed the time – 6:25! Only the growl of her stomach and the slight headache she felt coming on prompted her to take notice of the time. Immediately she jumped up, slid on her shoes and headed for the cafeteria with only five minutes till the end of dinner.

"The cafeteria is closed," one of the aides said as Tasha grabbed a tray and got in line.

"I know, I know Mr. Biggums, but I was studying and didn't know what time it was. Can I just grab something real quick?" Tasha asked in a solemn voice.

Staring at Mr. Biggums, Tasha began quietly chuckling at his appearance. He was a short brown round man, about three hundred pounds and five of his front top teeth were capped in gold. He was dressed in his normal get-up; an all white uniform with an apron that was originally white but covered with splattered food, and a knit stocking that covered his Gerri curl. He almost reminded her of a ghetto version of Boss Hog from the Dukes of Hazard. A few of the boys would publicly laugh at him, making comments like, "Be careful before you do a Michael Jackson on us," referring to Mr. Biggums' Gerri curl possibly catching fire while he worked with the hot stove. She tried not to laugh out loud when he bit into a sandwich, so he would know she was serious about getting something to eat. But she couldn't help it; especially when he began talking and some food flew from his mouth.

"Sorry, the cafeteria is closed and all the food is put away," the aide again replied with a nonchalant attitude and a mouth full of bread.

Tasha left the tray where she was standing and walked away without another word being said. On her way back to her room she spotted Lee and a few other friends.

"Hey Tasha, whatchu about to do?" Lee hollered out from across the campus track field. She and three other girls had been sitting on the benches talking about God knows what.

8

"Nothing, I'm hungry," Tasha yelled back while jogging over to the field to join the other girls.

"Why, what y'all finna do?" Tasha asked the girls now in arms reach.

"Wanna go get some ice cream from Double T'?" one of the girls asked while munching on a bag of Doritos.

"Yeah! Double T's got the good grub too and I'm starving," Tasha warned the girls.

"I didn't see you in the caf; did you eat dinner?" the girl with the bag of Doritos asked Tasha.

"Nope, I missed it. I have a biology exam tomorrow afternoon and I was studying and forgot what time it was. When I went to the caf, Mr. Biggums wouldn't let me get nothing to eat, talking 'bout "the caf is closed," Tasha said filling the girls in on what had just happened.

"Mr. Biggums ain't no joke, especially since he just got his curl redid," Lee jokingly said.

The girls continued laughing getting a visual picture of Mr. Biggums.

"Well, I'm ready when y'all are," Tasha said interrupting the laughter.

As the five girls loaded into Lee's car, Tasha could hear a man's voice calling her name.

"Is someone calling me?" Tasha asked, looking around.

"Yeah, Curtis is," one of the other girls in the car said pointing as he ran across the track field.

"Hey, what's up?" Curtis said once he was standing in front of Tasha.

"What's up?" Tasha said with an uncertain tone.

"I thought we were going to the mall?" Curtis asked with his eyebrows raised.

"Oh, that's right; I forgot," Tasha replied with a surprised look. "We finna go to Double T's and get something to eat. If you want, you can meet us there?" Tasha was giving Curtis the option.

"Nah, I'll just check you out later," Curtis said as he turned and began walking away.

"Sorry," Tasha said with a sympathetic tone letting Curtis know she honestly forgot.

While at the diner, the girls noticed a handsome, chocolate and tall man walk through the door. "Don't he go to the school? I've seen him around. I think he's on the basketball team," one of the girls said while they stared at him following the waitress to a seat. Not too long after the waitress handed the man a menu, the door swung open again and in walked Curtis and a few of his boys.

"Now looka-here, looka-here," Lee said with a sly tone.

"Tasha, what'd you do to that man?" one of the girls questioned.

"What? I ain't do nothing to him," Tasha exclaimed.

As Curtis and the rest of his friends took a seat with the handsome chocolate man, he exchanged eye contact with Tasha. Throughout the rest of the girls' dinner, she and Curtis caught eye contact on a number of occasions, exchanging sly grins. After the girls got up and left the restaurant, Curtis ran out to meet them in the parking lot.

Nodding his head for Tasha to come over to him, she walked up and said, "What's up?"

"You," Curtis said staring into her eyes.

"Me? Why me?" Tasha said.

"Look, I'm not gonna beat around the bush 'cause that ain't my style, so check this out. I have been watching you and I'm really diggin' you. I see how you carry yourself and how others react to your presence. You have a style I have never seen on a female, and baby you wear it well; and I just wanna know how I can be down, up and all in ya flow?" Curtis said with complete confidence.

"Oh, I see," Tasha said with a flattered look. "Well, I'm not looking to be in a relationship with anyone right now; and to be honest, you seem to be very familiar with the ladies, if you know what I mean," Tasha said in a non-jokingly tone. Curtis just stood there with a smirk on his face.

"But, we can chill and hang out sometimes if you would like that," Tasha said walking towards the car where her friends had been waiting patiently.

"I would like that," Curtis said walking in the opposite direction, back into the restaurant.

*   *   *   *   *

Throughout the first two semesters in school, Tasha and Curtis became very friendly. They were seen around campus together, and even out in the city having romantic picnics in the park. He taught her things she was unfamiliar with, and likewise she taught him things he had no clue about. She exposed him to love from a relationship and Godly perspective, being she grew up in church. She tried to explain to him that they could not have a physical relationship because it was outside of the will of God – a sin. She almost had to explain things like that to him as if he were a child because he was what they considered "unchurched". He couldn't understand what the big deal was with sex. Often, when the issue of sex came up with him – and it almost always did – she would try to explain biblical stories to him like David and Bathsheba or Samson and his lustful way. She never could get through to Curtis because he only viewed those stories as just that – stories. In her efforts to expose him to what she was familiar with, he in turn tried to show her the ins and outs of urban life. He conferred with her in a way he had never done with any other woman. He told her his most hidden secrets and his wildest dreams and exposed his heart to her, hoping to let her know just how special she was to him. He offered to take her to clubs but she refused to go. He tried to show her that with a good woman on your side, a man could change – or so she thought.

Time and time again, she was tired of the rumors of him being seen sneaking out of other girls' dorm rooms in the middle of the night. She was tired of the sly comments from other girls like, "That chocolate stick is too big and too good not to get some," or "He ain't really her man if he was licking my snatch last night." She was tired of asking his friends had they seen him, and getting the answer, "No," when he told her he had been playing ball with them all day. Once when Tasha was on her way to choir practice, she noticed Curtis talking with one of the girls who had a bad reputation for being loose. Curious, she watched the two from afar. Anyone watching would have assumed the two were a couple because of the body language between them. A number of times he reached over and pushed the girl's flowing bangs from her face as the wind blew it. In return, she would grab his hand and suck and lick his pointed finger as he glided it across her lips – giving

11

him an illustration of what she would do to him later. Tasha just shook her head. She wanted to trust him, but it was literally impossible with the evidence of his unfaithfulness.

There were many times she caught him with other women, either kissing them or grabbing them, but the final straw was one night as Tasha was returning late from a gospel concert she had gone to with a couple students from the Saved Students Association. She caught Curtis coming from Monica's room – the "campus Ho." As black as he was, she still could notice the dark black passion marks decorating his neck. All he could do was make up some lie about how a football game earlier that day had gotten too rough, but they both knew he was caught. It was becoming too much for Tasha to handle, especially since her grades were beginning to slip. Why had she not listened to her friend when she told her to be careful? Tasha knew the summer break was soon approaching and decided to break it off with Curtis.

The time and energy spent with him was something new for her. It was almost an awakening that she would never have expected to happen, or even know it could happen. Even with all the drama he was bringing to the relationship, she tried to see the good in him; the good she had seen when he originally began to pursue her. The good she saw when they spent intimate time together. The good that she knew every person possessed in some form or another. But, it was causing her too much pain. Although she knew by now she was deeply in love with him, she still had to do the break-up before she was hurt any more. Tasha wanted a man like her father, upstanding and honest, not the very opposite – and that's what she had.

Over the summer Curtis called Tasha periodically, but she tried her best to keep it neutral – that they would only speak as friends. He would occasionally bring up the point that he missed her and asked if she would give him another chance once they returned to school, and that he would prove himself. But Tasha was consistent with her point of not getting back together. It crushed her to have to tell him no, but she had to hold her ground. One night they had a phone conversation of him begging and pleading for them to get back together. The next day while at work, she received a dozen red roses with a note that read, "Nothing has ever felt like this." Those words belonged to Tasha's favorite song; the song she told Curtis about in intimate conversation that would one day be her wedding song. The thought not only impressed her, but caused her to reconsider his sincerity.

For the next week, her mind thought only of him. She pondered the thought that this time he would be different. This time she would give him what he needed. This time it would work, but she quickly snapped from that illusion after he promised to call her several times and never did. His inadequacies of not keeping his word caused Tasha to realize he was who he was and that he may never change. She told herself she could not continue riding that merry-go-round with him because only her emotions were the ones that wound up restless and unstable. One night, when she knew he would be calling, she refused to answer the phone. She just let it ring until it stopped. After five straight days of that, Curtis completely stopped calling. Tasha figured he had finally gotten the point and left it as it was – over.

*　　*　　*　　*　　*

When August rolled around Tasha began packing her stuff to return to school. A few days before Tasha was to leave for school, her parents surprised her with a car. They told her they were proud of what she was doing with herself and how they knew God would continue to bless her while she was away. Tasha was shocked and happy at the same time. After Tasha thanked her parents, she went to her room and prayed, thanking God for his continued blessings. All summer she had been praying for a car. Her father would always tell her, "Faith without works is dead," so she worked to try to get enough money for a car. One day in July while waiting for her father to pick her up from work, Tasha noticed a car in the parking lot of the mall displaying a "For Sale" sign in its windshield. She took the number down and stuck it in her purse. When her father arrived, she pointed out the car to him. He took a look and told her to pray about it. Her father would always tell her to pray about anything she wanted or decisions she needed to make. "The Holy Spirit in you will let you know if it's the will of God or not," her father would always add. She guessed it was the will of God because this was the same car in the parking lot of the

13

mall. But how did her father get in contact with the people who owned the car when she never saw him take the number down? After Tasha prayed, she came down stairs and asked her father how did he get in contact with the people who owned the car if he never took the number down? "I can't explain it, but when you become a parent, than you will understand," her father said with a big grin on his face. "Daddy, I think you love me," Tasha said to her father while giving him a big hug. "I think you're right," he added as they both laughed together.

A few days later, Tasha packed up her car, kissed her parents and headed back to Baltimore, but not before her mother laid hands on her. This was a familiar ritual Tasha had gone through while growing up. When she left home for over a three-day period or took a long trip somewhere, her mother would anoint her head with oil, pray for her, rebuke the devil off her life, and begin speaking in tongues all in the same breath. She had gone through this so many times; she was no longer embarrassed if friends or relatives were present during the prayer. Actually, the older Tasha got, the more she welcomed the prayer. She knew her mother was a godly woman and if anyone could get a prayer to heaven, it would be her.

Before she left, her mother had gotten her a calling card so she wouldn't need any money while using the payphone in case of an emergency. Thankfully, her eleven hour ride back to Baltimore went smoothly. It was better than taking the Greyhound; besides the twenty-six hour bus ride, it was no telling who you would be sitting next too. All types of people rode Greyhound, from illegal foreigners to folks going across country who were afraid of flying. Because her parents had brought the car, she was able to use the money she made while working during the summer to get anything she needed when she got back to school. Tasha was determined to get to Baltimore as soon as possible. Around the ninth hour, she began to get tired of driving and decided to pick up the speed a little. Not paying attention to the speedometer, she heard the sound of a police siren. When she looked in her rearview mirror, she noticed the police car was flagging her to pull over. After sitting in the car for over fifteen minutes the officer finally got out of his unit and walked over to Tasha's car.

"License and registration please," the officer asked with both hands on his hips.

Tasha reached in her glove compartment and handed the officer the information. She was so glad her father had gotten all of her car issues situated before she left home.

"Miss, do you know why I pulled you over?" the officer asked glancing over her information?

"No sir I don't," Tasha replied in a humble tone.

"Miss, I clocked you in at 90 mph in a 65 zone," the officer said while looking Tasha directly in the eyes.

"I'm sorry officer; I was unaware of my speed. I'm on my way to Baltimore – Coppin State, coming from Tallahassee, Florida and I'm starting to get a little tired. Plus, I have to use the bathroom really bad."

"Miss, how long have you been driving?" the officer asked Tasha.

"So far, about nine hours," Tasha said with her eyebrows raised hinting for pity. "I promise to slow down and take my time officer," Tasha said.

"Well Miss, I'm going to give you a break. We here in Washington, DC are very concerned about our roads and we want everyone on them to drive safely. Everyone!" the officer stressed.

"Thank you, officer!" Tasha proclaimed with glee in her voice.

As Tasha pulled off slowly, the officer got back in his unit and made a U-turn going the opposite way.

Glad to be back in school Tasha headed straight for the admissions office. She had only fifteen minutes to get her room assignment, keys to the laundry room, picture ID taken and to register; and to speak with the financial aid counselor before the office would be closed for the day. The office was packed. School started in two days and Tasha still had to handle some important matters. She noticed her Biology teacher, Mr. Burns from last semester sitting behind one of the registration tables reading a newspaper. Tasha smiled within when he adjusted his Mr. Peabody glasses that were sliding from his nose. As always, his bowtie was slightly crooked and he needed a haircut according to Tasha and a few of the other students; because his mini Afro was played out like an 8-Track. Many of the students laughed at Mr. Burns behind his back because of his too short trousers and suspenders, but they all knew he was a brilliant man and respected him as such. Without any other choice but to ask the teacher for help Tasha headed straight for him.

"Mr. Burns, how are you?" Tasha spoke to the teacher as he read a newspaper.

"Welcome back Miss Daniels," the teacher said glancing up from his reading.

"Mr. Burns, what are you doing in here?" Tasha asked trying to probe.

"I'm just helping with registration and picture ID's," the teacher said plainly.

"Mr. Burn's, may I ask a favor?" Tasha asked with a puppy dog look.

"Sure, Miss Daniels, what is it?" the teacher asked looking back at Tasha.

"I know I only have fifteen minutes to get everything taken care of before the office closes for the night, and I don't even have my room assignment or anything taken care of. So, I was wondering if you could take my picture and register me while I wait to get my room assignment and other keys," Tasha asked the teacher with a humble voice.

"Miss Daniels, I'm not sure if I can do that. This is the last stop after you take care of all the other stuff," the teacher clearly let Tasha know.

"I know, Mr. Burns, but if I don't get this taken care of then I won't have anywhere to stay tonight," Tasha admitted to the teacher.

"Ok, Miss Daniels, but don't tell anyone what I'm doing for you. As a matter of fact, when we're finished here, I will take you up front so you can get everything else situated before the office closes."

Tasha was so excited, she wanted to jump in Mr. Burns' arm, but settled for a vivacious, "Thank you Mr. Burns!"

Once Tasha had everything situated, she headed straight for her dorm room. She was moved from Kyle Hall to Bakers Hall since she was now a sophomore. Walking down the hall of the second floor, Tasha heard a loud voice scream her name, "TASHA!" Before turning around, she knew who that voice belonged to. It was her best friend, Lee. Lee was considered a ghetto girl from Philadelphia. She reminded Tasha of her cousin Lisa, but not so childish. She was thin and brown-skinned and had strikingly amazing hazel eyes – no one knew they were contacts. She stood 5' 4", wore her hair in micro mini braids and had a shape out of this world. As always, she was dressed sharp enough to put even the most super supermodel to shame. She had a confidence Tasha had never seen before. Lee told her it was because of how she was raised. She had gone through tremendous difficulties as a child and she wasn't going to allow anyone to stand in her way. She didn't take anything from anyone. She and Tasha had become really close during their first semester after officially meeting during orientation. Tasha knew right off the bat that she and Lee would be really good friends.

"What's up girl?" Tasha asked Lee as the two hugged like childhood friends.

"Nothing, girl. When did you get here?"

"Yesterday," Lee said in her ghetto fabulous voice.

"I thought you would have been back by now but I guess you wanted to parlay a bit longer!" Lee said still being critical. As Tasha began to tell Lee about her ride back to school and the possible speeding ticket, Lee interrupted with a, "Guess what girl?"

"What?" Tasha said not sure of what would come from Lee's mouth.

"Guess who is in the room down the hall from me?"

"Who?" Tasha asked anxiously.

"That Ho – Lola."

Standing with a blank stare, Tasha had no reply to what Lee had just said. Lola was one of Curtis' other girls. Actually, she was the main girl Tasha had heard about. She was the one he would run to each time he and Tasha got into it.

"Oh well, me and Curtis ain't together no more so it don't matter," Tasha said even lying to herself.

"Well, I'm glad you see it like that. By the way, what room are you in? I got that silly girl Jean as my roommate this semester; and she better not try talking me to death, 'cause I don't want to have to put her in her place," Lee said in her always jokingly voice.

"Let's see, I'm in room 211," Tasha said looking down at the folder she had gotten from the registration office.

Without another word said Lee placed her hand on Tasha's shoulder and shook her head.

"Now you sure you left all your feelings for Curtis behind last semester?"

"Yeah, why you say that?"

"'Cause that's Lola's room," Lee whispered.

All Tasha could do was laugh. She knew this had to be a set up in some way. How on God's green earth did she manage to get the same room assignment as her competition?

"Well, like I said, I ain't sweating it," Tasha reassured Lee and herself at the same time.

As Tasha walked down the hall to her assigned room, she began praying. "Lord, I need your help. I need you to step into the situation even before I do. I need you to shine through me so that your name may be glorified. I know I haven't always lived the way you wanted me to (her mind taking her back to the times she and Curtis had gotten into heavy kissing and petting matches), but I am still your child." As she concluded the small prayer, she grabbed a hold of the doorknob, took a deep breath and opened the door. There inside was Lola and Curtis sitting on Lola's bed having a conversation. Of course Tasha's heart stopped, but she refused to let it be seen on her face.

"Hello," Tasha said as she walked through the bedroom door not making eye contact with either of them.

"Hello," Lola responded but Curtis didn't.

"I believe we will be roommates this year, Lola," Tasha informed everyone present. As Tasha placed the material she had received from the registration office on the empty bed, she could feel the eyes of Curtis staring at her from behind.

"Well, I don't want to interrupt you two, so I will leave and start to get my things," she said as she stopped moving about and faced the two of them. Tasha noticed that Curtis' hair had grown quite a bit over the summer and his braids were now hanging just above his shoulders. She also couldn't help notice the fact that he was looking better than ever. He had obviously been working out and his chocolate skin was so clear and smooth. Lola was looking quite appealing herself. She sported freshly twisted burnt-orange colored locks that worked great with her golden brown complexion. She had obviously learned to wear make-up over the

18

summer because the natural colors in her blush, eye shadow and lip gloss agreed nicely with each other. She too had been working out because her arms, thighs and belly showed no evidence of flab; as she wore a sleeveless burnt orange tank with a faded jean mini skirt with traces of burnt orange swirled through it.

"It's nothing going on here, so please come in and out as many times as you need to. As a matter of fact, Curtis was leaving anyway," Lola said alerting Tasha and Curtis. Not saying another word, Tasha walked out of the room.

After the initial shock of being roommates with her "competition," all had gone well with Tasha and Lola. They were not the best of friends, but they did have a mutual respect for one another; after all, they were roommates. Occasionally, they would talk in the middle of the night about how and where they grew up. They would discuss what type of future they wanted and why they chose Coppin State even though both were from the south. In spite of how friendly they became, they never once brought up Curtis – almost as if he were off limits to each other. All was going well between the two roommates until Tasha left a class early one afternoon with a splitting headache; only to come back to the room and find Curtis with his head buried between Lola's legs giving her pleasure that would last all night – had Tasha not interrupted. Startled at what her eyes were witnessing, she quickly slammed the door as she backed out of the room. Angry wasn't the word for how she was feeling – hurt was. She heard the rumors but refused to believe them. Not in a million years would she have thought that the two of them would disrespect her so that they would bring their lewdness back to the room knowing it was her room too.

As Tasha walked down the hall in a fit of rage she decided to turn and go back into the room. She wanted them to know how she felt, and how dare they do that to her. Turning the knob, she could feel someone else on the other side of the door turning it with her as if they were coming out. When the door swung open, it was Curtis wiping his face.

Tasha pushed him. "Yo, what's up wit dat?" he said turning his face up as he fell back into the room. Lola just sat on the edge of her bed buttoning her jeans. When Tasha shut the door behind her she leaned on it to let both Curtis and Lola know they weren't leaving until she said what she had to say.

"How dare ya'll disrespect me like this! It really doesn't matter to me that ya'll are doing ya'lls' thing, but don't bring it back here! I thought you would have had enough decency in the fact that you knew he and I had something, but I guess bitches are still classified as dogs," she shouted looking at Lola.

"And you! You just a straight up dog because you know we're roommates! Even if ya'll was creeping last semester or whenever, you still should have handled yourself better! Couldn't you take her to your room?" she demanded staring Curtis in the face.

Tasha was hurt but she didn't want them to see this, she only wanted them to see anger; anger that would motivate a woman to get indignant even when she didn't want to; anger that would cause her to still feel for a man even if they weren't together. She wanted to let them know how selfish and childish they had carried themselves; but she knew they only heard words and not the breaking of her heart. Tasha had never loved any man the way she loved Curtis and for him to be doing this to her was a kick in the face as well as the heart. As she stood there and glared at the two of them with unperturbed looks on their faces, she wondered why either of them had done this to her. Did Curtis do it because she had ended their relationship or was it because she had refused to share a physical romance with him? Or was it simply because he was a dog of a man?

And why had Lola done this to her? Was it something Tasha had done to her that wasn't obvious or was she just being a scandalous "ho" that was only out for hers? Whatever the reason behind the triangle, Tasha was the only one who was coming out with the short end. After saying her piece, Tasha shook her head, sucked her teeth and exited the room leaving them both to finish what they were doing. Walking down to Lee's room she fought the tears back from rushing down her face. It was only one thought that penetrated her brain – she wished she had taken Lee's advice when she told her to be careful, but it was too late – she was already in love.

*   *   *   *   *

From the way the week was going Tasha knew somewhere, somehow, more heartache and pain was on its way. That Valentine's Day, after catching her roommate and her ex-boyfriend intertwined in a sexual encounter; Tasha received a disturbing phone call from her mother. She told Tasha that her father had a heart attack in the middle of the night and he was now in intensive care. She told Tasha not to worry, but how was that possible? Tasha and her father were as close as any father and daughter could be – even like best friends at times. Tasha was distraught by the phone call. She could hardly concentrate or talk without stuttering. Her first impulse was to go home, but her mother told her not to. Her mother asked her to stay until the Thanksgiving break which was only a week away, but Tasha couldn't possibly wait that long to come home. She wasn't sure how bad off her father was and she wasn't willing to take the chance of not seeing him if, God forbid, he was worse off than she thought. While sitting on her bed, Lee came to the door.

"Hey girl, you going to breakfast?" Lee asked, walking into the room without knocking.

Tasha just sat there staring at the ceiling without answering.

"What's wrong?" Lee asked with an obvious look of concern on her face.

"My mom just called me. My dad had a heart attack last night and now he's in intensive care."

Lee could hear the concern in her voice. "Wow! What are you going to do?" Lee asked.

"It's nothing I really can do. I want to go home but my mom told me to wait until Thanksgiving so I won't miss no time from school. But that's a whole week away, and you know me; I can't let stuff fester for too long before I go nuts and lose my mind."

"Look, if you can't wait that long, go home. Let your professors know the situation and they shouldn't have a problem letting you make up the work."

"I think I will go home. I can't sit here and do nothing," she said, jumping up and grabbing some clothes from her closet.

CHAPTER 3

Walking into the hospital room Tasha tried her best not to break down and cry. She had never seen her father so vulnerable. He was always a big man, tall and handsome. He had been a military man until he met her mother during his last tour in "Nam" – and thankfully for both of them the war was ending.

Coming from a very religious background, Cilla's family was totally against her and Jared's courtship (that's what it's called in "the Church"). They felt like he wasn't the man for her since he wasn't "saved". Priscilla's father, being the town Pastor, refused to marry them. The decision was crushing to Priscilla but she knew with all her heart that Jared was the man God had for her. With much fasting and convincing, her prayers had been answered and the wedding was set for a hot summer day in August.

In the beginning Priscilla and Jared tried to have children but they couldn't. They didn't understand why they weren't getting pregnant. Back in those days, they didn't have the many doctors who could diagnose the cause for infertility like they do today, so it was very difficult to understand the barrenness. On many occasions, Cilla would tell Jared that she may have sinned and that's why God was punishing her with not being able to conceive; but he would quickly shoot down her pity excuses and encouraged her that God would indeed give them a child. One day during a week-long revival the speaker for that night took his text from I Samuel Chapter 1. That night, in her heart, Priscilla knew God would surely give her a child. Six years later, LaTasha Marie Daniels was born.

*   *   *   *   *

"Hey sweetheart," Tasha's father said in a solemn voice hearing someone creep in the room.

The smell of pinesol gripped Tasha's nostrils and she instantly became dizzy. The gloominess of the dull white walls gave the sense of a psych unit even though they were in the ICU. Just being in the hospital and the particular reason paralyzed all feeling in her legs. Tiptoeing over to her father she whispered, "Daddy, you awake?"

Jared didn't respond. Just the grin that eased across his face let Tasha know he was still a man of honor.

"How are you feeling?" Tasha asked, speaking in a low voice not to alarm her father of her fears.

"God is good," Jared said with the peace of the Lord in his voice. "What are you doing here sweetheart? You should be in school." Jared's eyes were not fixed on his daughter.

"School can wait!" Tasha said.

"Tasha?"

"Yeah, Daddy?" Tasha answered her father in a voice he hadn't heard since she was five years old.

"Do me a favor?"

"Sure Daddy, what is it?" Tasha asked willing to do anything her father would ask.

"Get my word and read Psalm 91 for me," Jared again closed his eyes, allowing a slight smile to effortlessly ease across his face.

Tasha knew that was her father's favorite scripture. While she was growing up, whenever the family would go through hard times, Tasha's father would always ask her to read that scripture to him. He would sit with his eyes closed and a smile on his face while Tasha read. When Tasha would finish, her father would say "Selah" even though the scripture didn't end with it.

By the time Tasha reached verse seven, "A thousand shall fall at thy side, and ten thousand by thy right hand; but it shall not come nigh thee," Jared was asleep. Tasha laid the bible down on the steel food tray still opened to the passage of scripture, kissed her father on the forehead and walked out of the room.

  CHAPTER 4

Back in school, Tasha was relieved her father was out of danger. With his speedy recovery, she was able to get back to school and catch up with her schoolwork. Her first day back was hard. Her body was in Baltimore, but her mind was in Dunbar. She constantly thought about her father and how he would get back to his normal routine. She wondered if he would be able to read his morning paper or if he would even have the strength to continue in the ministry. Since the attack he had not been back to church, but the saints had been by the house to visit. They brought food and anything they thought he needed including plenty of anointing oil for prayer. Knowing her father, he welcomed everyone with a good heart. As the days went by Tasha tried to get back on track. She studied even harder trying to keep up with what she had missed. Her best medicine was being with her friends. Lee was a big help simply because she kept Tasha laughing. Even when Tasha wasn't in the mood to laugh, Lee knew what to say, when to say it and how to say it to make Tasha feel better.

Although Tasha didn't want to admit it she longed for the presence of a man in her life. This was the time Tasha needed to be held, kissed and caressed. Her girlfriends were fine and they understood, but only a man could whisper in her ear and tell her it would be all right. Her father was always the man to comfort her, but with him being the one on her mind, she needed someone else. She had seen Curtis around and on occasion they spoke, but it never went beyond that. When Curtis heard about Tasha's father he came and asked her if he could do anything to help. Of course Tasha said no, but it meant a lot to her for his concern. One night while taking a walk Tasha noticed Curtis sitting on the bleachers in the track field. She hesitated before walking over to him but she decided to go for it.

"Is everything ok?" Tasha asked Curtis walking up to him.

"Yeah, I'm fine. I should be asking you that," he said glancing into her eyes.

"Well, I'm fine. My daddy is doing ok, thank the Lord," Tasha said trying to convince herself.

"Well, I'm glad to hear that."

As silence filled the air, Tasha glanced over at Curtis' chocolate skin and wide smile and her mind immediately reminisced to good times between them. While she was chuckling to herself, Curtis asked her what was so funny.

"Nothing."

"Come on, you can tell me," he said with a sly tone.

"Well, I was just thinking about that time me and you, well you know," Tasha said pausing.

"Which time?" Curtis said letting out a giddy laugh.

"The time we were in the park – 'cross town'."

"Oh yeah, I remember that. Matter of fact, I was thinking about that the other day," Curtis said.

While they looked in each other's eyes Tasha longed for the touch of Curtis. It had been almost a year since she had been held by a man and just as long since she had been kissed by one and now she needed it. She wanted the warmth of a man's arms and his touch. She wanted the comfort only a man could give. Tasha wanted Curtis. Before Tasha could speak another word, Curtis stood up and walked over to her. Tasha, not sure of what he would do, stared him in the face. As they stood face to face, Curtis said to Tasha, "I am here for you." Tasha broke out in tears. She cried until she fell into Curtis' chest. The feel of his chest made her miss him even the more. While she cried, he held her as tight as he could. He wanted her to feel the concern he had for her. He wanted to be there for her. He wanted her. Embarrassed at her tears Tasha collected herself and began walking away.

"Tasha, where are you going?" Curtis asked grabbing her hand.

"Thank you for being here for me but I don't want to get too comfortable," Tasha said pulling away.

"What are you talking about?"

"Lola is what I'm talking about. I don't want to come between you two," Tasha said looking Curtis in the eyes.

"Tasha," Curtis said pulling her chin upward to look at him, "I have nothing to do with Lola. She and I have not seen each other since last semester. You are the only woman I have ever loved and will ever love."

Tasha needing to hear that gazed into Curtis' eyes. She so desperately needed to know that because Curtis was indeed the man she had fallen in love with. As they stood there, Curtis pulled her closer to him. He softly held her face and kissed her lips.

"I need you Tasha, I need you," Curtis whispered in her ear as he continued to kiss her ever so gently.

Tasha had dreamed about this meeting since last semester. Tasha did all she could to release Curtis, but she couldn't – both her body and her heart were saying "Yes". As they walked back to Tasha's room hand and hand, the campus seemed to be a ghost town. The faces of those around were unfamiliar. When they reached room 211 Tasha searched for her key. Lola had left for the Christmas break – three days before the official end of the fall semester, so Tasha knew they wouldn't be interrupted. All she could think about was having Curtis lie next to her. As she slid the key in the door she got a whiff of his cologne, Issey Miyake, her favorite. He would always wear it when they went out. As she walked in the dark room, he was close behind. Tasha knew where this could lead and wanted to be faithful to her faith and to her God but right now, all Tasha knew was she needed to be held and caressed. She needed someone to remove her burden and since Curtis was there when she needed him, why couldn't he just stay for a few moments? Standing in the middle of the floor they stared at each other with a burning lust.

"Tasha, like I said, I am here for you if you need me."

The sound of those words brought tears to Tasha's eyes once again. Before she knew it, they were embraced in a passionate kiss – the type she missed. As they kissed harder and longer Curtis gently laid Tasha on the bed. Without a missed beat he began kissing her neck and down her chest. Engulfed in the serenity of it all Tasha went with the flow of things. She could feel his hands massaging her breast as he continued kissing her. As the two lay on her twin sized bed kissing passionately, all Tasha could think to do was repent for what she was about to do. She knew fornicating was against God but right about now she had too much on her mind to think about not falling into sin. All she knew was that she

26

needed to be with a man and who was better to be that man besides Curtis?

"Curtis," Tasha said applying pressure to his forearms as they leaned over her body.

"Yeah baby," Curtis managed to whisper past his heavy breathing and constant kisses.

"Please forgive me," Tasha said as she began unbuttoning his Wu Ware jeans.

Curtis never budged even though he had no idea why Tasha was asking him to forgive her, but Tasha knew why she was asking for forgiveness. She knew she would regret this act later so she was not only asking Curtis to forgive her for not portraying a Godly woman, but she was also asking God to forgive her because she knew He would not be pleased with her sin.

Later that night as they lay in the bed, Tasha felt an overwhelming rush of guilt when she felt Curtis' hand glide up her thigh. Earlier his hands felt like a life jacket coming to rescue her, but soon after they felt like the anchor that had tried to drown her. She knew she had done wrong and was ashamed. As she lay there tears began to run down her face.

"What's wrong?" Curtis asked as he turned to look at her.

Tasha refused to answer.

"Tasha," Curtis continued to call out as he tried to pull her face towards his.

"Curtis, please leave," Tasha asked pulling away from Curtis.

"Why? Did I do something wrong?" Curtis asked with a confused tone.

"Please just leave," Tasha begged.

"Tasha, I love you, why are you doing this?" Curtis continued to ask.

"Get out!" Tasha yelled without turning her face from the wall.

Without another word said Curtis put his clothes on and left the room. Tasha just lay there crying. Tasha felt dead. She repented and repented but nothing would lift the burden. Her friends noticed how she was quiet for the past week but they paid it no mind. They figured it was still from the heart attack her father suffered so they tried not to pressure her into talking about it. But Lee knew it was more than that. She asked Tasha constantly if she needed to talk, but Tasha refused saying she would be all right. Lee figured the month long break would do her friend some good. She was probably just exhausted from the long semester and the ordeal with her father.

CHAPTER 5

When everyone returned for the spring semester they all had fresh new looks. That seemed to be a ritual for college students – look different at the beginning of each semester. All was well for the first couple of weeks until Lee noticed her friend falling back into the slump she left in. One Sunday morning Lee came to Tasha's dorm room as she did every Sunday morning to pick her up for church but Tasha still lay in the bed with her night clothes on. As Lee knocked, Tasha refused to answer. "Tasha, I know you're in there. You better open this door before I come through the window," Lee screamed jokingly but Tasha refused to answer. Lee being the prankster she was, managed to locate Lola in the bathroom and got the key from her. When the door opened and Lee walked in, Tasha let out a sigh.

"Honey, what's going on with you?" Lee asked Tasha walking over to her desk.

Immediately tears filled Tasha's eyes.

"Let me guess, you slept with Curtis," Lee said in a nonchalant tone.

Tasha continued to cry.

"I already knew that."

"Then why didn't you say anything to me," Tasha asked now looking at Lee.

"Look Tasha we all make mistakes. Like you always tell me, if we repent, HE is faithful and just to forgive us from all unrighteousness. Baby, you have to forgive yourself," Lee said in the tone of her mother.

Instantly Tasha felt better. She took a deep breath and sat up out of the bed.

"That's right girl, pick yourself up and dust yourself off," Lee said.

As Tasha stood to her feet she shouted "This is the day the Lord hath made, I will rejoice and be glad in it!"

After church the two decided to go to dinner but first they came back to the dorm to change into something more comfortable. As Tasha walked into her room, she saw Lola sitting on the edge of her bed. Not thinking anything of it Tasha said hello. When she didn't get a response from Lola, Tasha stopped digging in her closet and looked over at Lola.

"Girl are you all right?" Tasha asked with a voice of concern.

"No I'm not alright."

"What's the matter?" Tasha said, standing by Lola's side.

Tears began to stream down her roommate's face. As Tasha began rubbing her roommate's back, Lola blurted out, "I'm pregnant!"

Tasha froze. She had no words for Lola. Tasha knew it was nothing she could possibly say that would change the situation. She just continued rubbing Lola's back as she sobbed.

"Lola, can I ask you a question?" When Lola didn't answer, Tasha asked, "Whose is it?" With a faint voice she heard Lola say Curtis. Tasha's heart immediately began racing. She wondered how they could have been together when she had never seen them together. She wanted to know when and how long they had been seeing each other – again. Not alerting Lola of her anger Tasha continued consoling Lola while she wept.

"Is there anything I can do?" Tasha asked with an honest concern.

"No," Lola responded.

"Have you told Curtis yet?"

"Yes," Lola said.

"And what did he say?"

"He said he needs some time to think about it," Lola continued to talk. "How could I be so stupid to get pregnant again?" Lola blurted out in anger slapping herself upside the head.

Did Tasha hear right? Did she just say again? Had she and Curtis already been through this or was she referring to another man?

"So what are you going to do?" Tasha asked in a questionable tone.

"Get rid of it of course!" Lola said, wiping her face and fixing her clothes. "I can't let no baby stop me. I've done it before and I'm gonna have to do it again!"

30

Tasha didn't have a response to that. All she could do was stand there. With a knock on the door, the conversation was interrupted. As Tasha opened the door knowing it was Lee, Lola got herself together. As Lee walked in the door, Lola walked out. Before she shut the door, Lola turned and looked at Tasha and with a wink of the eye said, "Y'all girls have fun," and
walked away.

CHAPTER 6

Tasha tried not to worry about Lola because it was nothing she could do or say to change Lola's mind. As a matter of fact, Tasha knew Lola had already gone through with the abortion because she had taken a few days off from school to go home for a family emergency or that's what she told Tasha. Tasha wondered how someone could do a thing like that but one thing her mother always taught her was to never judge another; because unless you've been in that person's shoes, than you could never understand how they feel. Tasha had seen Curtis around the campus and in class but she hadn't spoken to him since that night. She felt she couldn't look him in the face because she was too embarrassed. Even after she found out he and Lola had still been seeing each other, she really had nothing to say to him. She wanted to know why he lied to her that night they slept together but at that point it really didn't matter either way. She remembered vividly how he told her he wasn't seeing anyone else and how he loved only her. Tasha was still hurt about that and like a soldier, she never allowed it to show but it ate her up inside.

A couple weeks later Tasha woke up with a splitting headache. She didn't know why and really didn't pay it any mind. As she got out of bed to get some Tylenol, she instantly felt ill. Without another thought Tasha was racing to the bathroom with vomit in her hands. She had gotten sick without warning. In the bathroom as she heaved and brought up everything she had eaten in the past two days, a few of the girls in the bathroom asked her was she alright.

"Yeah, I'll be fine," Tasha said wondering what had made her sick. "Did I eat something sour?" she thought to herself as she cleaned up the stall and began washing her face in the sink. As Tasha walked back to her room, Lee met her in the hallway.

"Girl are you okay? Jean told me you were throwing up."

"Yeah, I think so," Tasha informed Lee.

"What got you sick like this?"

32

"I don't know, maybe it was something I ate," Tasha said still thinking of everything she had eaten in the past two days.

"Maybe some of Mr. Biggums' drip drip fell in the food and you got a scoop of it," Lee said as the two of them laughed hysterically.

"I don't know what it was, but I'm fine now."

As Tasha went on with the rest of her day she continued to have a headache. She had taken some Tylenol twice that day but the headache kept coming back. Later that night Tasha decided to take a shower before going to bed. Maybe that would help her feel better and relax her enough to get rid of that headache once and for all. As Tasha walked in the bathroom, Lee was standing at one of the mirrors putting on make-up.

"Missy, where do you think you're going this time of night?" Tasha asked Lee in a motherly tone while one hand made its way to her hip.

"Girl, I got a date."

"A date at this hour! I would say more of a booty call at this time of night," Tasha said to Lee looking her straight in the face.

"Well you know," Lee said with the look of guilt written all over her face. As Tasha stood there shaking her head it was nothing else she could say to Lee. She knew her mind was already made up and thought the guy was probably already out in front of the dorm waiting for her.

"Big head Michael I bet," Tasha said as she walked over to a shower stall and turned on the water.

"Of course, who else?" Lee asked knowing Tasha already knew. As Lee put the finishing touches on her make-up and Tasha jumped in the shower, Lee began singing. "You make me feel, you make me feel, you make me feel like a natural womannnnn."

"Okay I'm out," Lee shouted letting Tasha know she was leaving.

"Be careful," Tasha hollered out from behind the shower curtain.

"Always," Lee yelled back as she skipped out of the bathroom.

*　　*　　*　　*　　*

Early the next morning Tasha woke from her sleep suddenly. Her first reaction was to look at the clock; it read 5:12. Because it was early spring, the sun was already beginning to peek its beams through the night sky. As Tasha sat up she felt her heart racing at a speed of about ninety miles an hour. She couldn't understand why she was feeling this way. She knew she hadn't had a dream so her mind automatically went to her father. Just yesterday she had spoken to him and everything seemed to be fine. He told her that he was doing much better and had even gone to bible study that Wednesday night. Her mother also assured her that her father was making a full recovery. Still, Tasha couldn't figure out what the problem was. Where was this instant panic coming from? As she sat there watching the clock advance from 5:12 to 5:33, her mind continued to race. She looked around her room as if to see if anything was out of place. She looked over at her roommate who hadn't flinched at all since she woke up. The only sound Tasha could hear was the radio playing the Body and Soul CD Lola had put on the night before. The girls usually slept with music playing so for Tasha to wake up and hear the tunes was nothing out of the ordinary.

As the sun began to bully its way through the clouds, the morning was becoming alive. Still confused as to why the sudden awakening, Tasha noticed the clock again; 5:59 it read. Since it was Monday morning and her first class was at 8:00, she decided to take her shower now before the bathroom began to fill with women scrambling over shower stalls. Tasha decided to sit on the edge of her bed another few minutes to think of what she could wear that day. Just like any other woman her mind focused on what she knew was clean and not just what she needed to iron.

As Tasha stood up, she instantly got sick. She could feel her mouth filling with a horrible thickness which automatically caused her to grab her mouth and head for the bathroom. The slam of the door as Tasha swung it open and ran down the hall caused Lola to pop her head up and see what the problem was. Luckily only two other girls were in the bathroom when Tasha finally made it to a stall and continued throwing her guts up. Tasha could hear one of the other girls ask from outside the stall if she was okay? "Yeah, I'm fine," Tasha managed to get out in between heaves. Tasha knew something was really wrong because why on earth would she get sick like this? When it happened last week, she figured she must have just eaten something bad but this had happened three times since then. As she sat on the cold bathroom floor wiping her mouth with her nightshirt, a thought popped into her head. "Isn't today the 24th?" she thought to herself? If it was, Tasha knew she had a major problem. Her period was five days late. Staring at the brown tiled floor, all Tasha could do was shake her head. She instantly began praying to ask God not to let this be happening to her. Before she could get too deep into the prayer she forced herself to get off the floor when she heard two more girls come into the bathroom. She walked over to the sink, splashed some water on her face and walked out of the bathroom as she said "uh-huh" to the original voice that asked her was she alright again. Tasha headed to her room with tears streaming down her face. Before she turned the knob of her dorm room door, she wiped her face and walked into the room.

"Girl, what happened?" Lola asked as she heard the door shut.

"I don't know. I had to *run* to the bathroom. I hope I'm not coming down with this flu. I hate getting sick when the weather begins getting warm," Tasha said in a nonchalant tone.

She hoped Lola didn't hear the real expression behind her lie.

*   *   *   *   *

For the rest of the day Tasha couldn't concentrate. Her mind was all over the place. Half the time she thought about what would happen if she was pregnant and the other half of the time she tried not to think about it. When her final class was over at 3:50, she headed straight for Lee's room. She hoped her friend would be there being as though Lee's next class didn't start until 6:00 PM.

"Come in," a voice said as Tasha knocked on the door.

"Hey girl," Lee said before Tasha had a chance to speak; but even after the initial greeting, Tasha still didn't respond. She just headed for Lee's bed and lay down.

"Oh boy, what test did you fail this time?" Lee asked as she watched Tasha bury her face into Lee's pile of stuffed bears. When Tasha still didn't respond, Lee walked over to the bed.

"Tasha, what happened?" Lee asked in her most concerned voice. The only response Tasha gave was a heave of tears.

"Okay, you don't have to talk, just nod your head if I'm right," Lee said as she sat on the edge of her bed rubbing Tasha's lower back. "Is your father alright?"

Tasha's headed nodded yes.

"Did you sleep with Curtis again?"

Tasha's head nodded no.

"Is this about when you slept with him last semester?"

Tasha's head nodded yes.

"Tasha, please don't tell me you're pregnant," Lee said with a disappointed tone.

Tasha just began to sob.

"Oh, Tasha. Are you sure?"

Tasha nodded her head no.

"Then why do you think you are? Are you late?"

Tasha nodded her head yes.

"Okay. Okay," Lee said as she stood up and got her thoughts together. "This is what we're going to do. I have a class at 6:00 but screw that. You and I are going to go to Wal-Mart and get a pregnancy test and put an end to all this madness." With a pause of silence, Lee yelled out, "Do you hear me?"

Tasha just nodded her head yes with her face still buried in the pile of stuffed animals on her best friend's pillow.

CHAPTER 7

At 5:40 that March afternoon, the two girls drove down Arnold Street on their way to Wal-Mart. The air was filled with silence except for the sound of breeze blowing into the rolled down windows of Tasha's 1995 grey Honda Accord. After the initial conversation in the dorm room, Lee told her friend to get herself together before they headed for the store. She wanted to make sure she was stable enough to go through with it. As the two walked from the dorm room towards the front entrance, the pay phone in the hall rang. Neither girl paid it any attention until another girl who had answered the phone said "Tasha, it's for you." Tasha wasn't sure what to do because she didn't feel like talking, but she grabbed the phone anyway.

"Hello?"

"Hey baby," an elderly woman's voice said from the other end of the line.

Tasha knew it was her grandmother.

"Hey, Nana," Tasha said trying to pick up the emotion in her voice.

"How you doing, baby?"

"Fine," Tasha said in a more upbeat voice.

"You were on my mind so I decided to make sure everything was alright with you."

"Yeah Nana, I'm fine. How are you?" Tasha uttered trying to get the topic of discussion off of her.

"I'm doing well. God is still good," her grandmother added.

Before Tasha could get another word out, her grandmother began rambling on about what she'd been doing over the past two weeks. All Tasha could do was sit and listen to her every word. She turned to see where Lee had disappeared to after she took the phone. That's when she saw her friend sitting in the lounge with three other girls who had already been there watching Jerry Springer. She leaned against the wall continuing to listen to her grandmother talk. Because her mind was so preoccupied she only caught a few things here and there that her grandmother was saying. One thing that certainly caught Tasha's attention was when her grandmother mentioned she had had a dream about fish the night before. Tasha knew that when someone had a dream about fish that meant someone close to them was pregnant. Her grandmother automatically made mention that she thought it was Tasha's cousin Lisa who was too fast and too furious for only being fifteen years old. Although Tasha considered her grandmother as her best friend, besides Lee, she didn't have the nerve or the guts to admit to her grandmother that she may be the one causing the fish dream. Twenty-three minutes after the conversation between Tasha and her grandmother began, it ended with her grandmother saying, "I just wanted to make sure you were doing okay."

"Love you Nana," Tasha said as she hung up the telephone.

"You ready?" Lee hollered out over the noise of the fighting on the television and the other girls in the lounge laughing. Tasha simply shook her head "Yes" and began walking towards the door. Without even asking Lee to drive, she simply handed her friend the keys and walked towards the passenger side of the car.

CHAPTER 8

Pulling up in the parking lot of the Security Square Mall, the two sat there for a minute with the car still running. After two deep breaths Tasha grabbed for the handle on the door and got out of the car. She turned to look at her friend, who was following her lead, and said with a jolly tone, "It's a nice day". All Lee could do was laugh at her statement.

"Hey, that's my job," her friend said with eyebrows raised high.

"What is?" Tasha asked with a confused look on her face.

"To make jokes during sticky situations," Lee said as the two of them let out a relieved chuckle.

Walking through the mall Tasha's senses seemed to be wide open. She could smell almost any and everything within a two mile radius of where they walked. She could smell the salt from the fries that came from McDonald's and the lotion from the Victoria Secret shop they passed on their way to Wal-Mart. She could even smell the fragrances of three different colognes on the teenage boys who walked pass her and Lee. It was weird to Tasha because her senses had never been this alert. As the two continued to walk through the mall to their destination, Lee seemed to be the only one talking even though Tasha would answer her with an "ah-huh" or "uh-un" or just a simple laugh at whatever her friend was talking about. The walk to Wal-Mart seemed to take forever. While walking past a Tower Record, the song "Emotional Roller Coaster" was bumping from the speaker right outside the store. An emotional roller coaster was exactly what Tasha was on right now and not until she got the results of that test would she be able to know when the ride would end. Wal-Mart's sign was big and blue. Not until that moment did she realize what was about to happen. Either way, her life was about to change. She just hoped the change would be in her favor.

"Well, you ready?" Lee asked her as they entered the store. Before Tasha got the chance to respond she heard someone call her name. Even before she turned around she recognized the voice. It was Lola.

"Hey," she said turning around and not alerting Lola that anything was wrong.

"What you doing here?"

"Just figured we would get out and get some air," Tasha said looking over at Lee.

"Well, had I known ya'll was coming then I would have just caught a ride with ya'll."

Just as soon as she said that, Curtis came from around the corner of the store. Tasha's eyes immediately got big. She tried not to look at him but she couldn't help it because she knew he and Lola was there together.

"Well, we gotta go," Lee interjected pulling Tasha's arm to get her away from the conversation. Tasha didn't even have an opportunity to get upset because Lee was upset enough for the both of them. Tasha wasn't sure what was about to happen. She tried to slow the racing of her heart, but all she could think was how stupid she had been. She actually allowed a man to use her. She felt even stupider because she had talked to so many of her friends about not letting themselves get in these situations and here she was. "Don't even trip," Lee told Tasha looking at the obvious hostility on her face. Tasha just shook her head in disgust as her and her friend continued reading the signs above the aisles looking for the one that read *personal* or *medication*.

Looking down one aisle, Tasha noticed an older black woman standing very close to the shelves. The position of the woman made her a bit suspicious but Tasha wasn't there to catch shoplifters -- she was there to get what she needed and get out. Trying to mind her own business Tasha just shook her head when she saw the woman slip a few small picture frames and three hand-held clocks in the duffle bag slumped over her shoulder. Her parents had always taught Tasha to do the right thing when she saw wrong but she was in no position to throw stones at someone else's house when she was surrounded by glass windows herself. The sound of Lee yelling her name caused Tasha to ignore the woman and continue her search. When they found the aisle, they began looking over all the choices the store offered. EPT, First Response, even American Fare had a pregnancy test on the market.

There were so many to choose from, but Lee made the decision when she grabbed the EPT and headed for the cash register. Tasha couldn't even keep up with her friend and she wasn't sure she wanted to. All she really wanted was to make sure those two were out of the store. Lee approached the counter, allowed the clerk to scan the test and pulled out a $20 bill when the clerk said $14.23. Tasha tried to hand her friend the money but Lee just ignored her as if the test was for her.

As the two walked from the store, Lee turned to her friend and said, "This is what we're going to do." "Since I'm hungry and I know you are too, we are going to go to the public bathroom and take the test – just to calm your nerves and mine," Lee added. Tasha didn't say anything, she just followed her friend as if she was a camper lost in the woods and Lee was the counselor who knew the way home. Tasha was glad that only one lady was in the bathroom when they got there, and she was washing her hands which meant she was about to leave. So, Tasha went in the stall as Lee took a seat on top of the sink. Even before Tasha could read the directions on the box, Lee began telling her what to do as if she had written them herself. Tasha just listened and followed instructions.

"All you have to do is pee in the cup: sit the cup on the floor to free up your hands. Then, open the package with the test. Take the test tubie thing and squeeze it so that you get enough pee to wet the blank white window."

"What?" Tasha asked with confusion in her voice.

"Did you pee in the cup yet?" Lee asked walking towards the stall.

"Yes," Tasha said opening the stall door knowing her friend was coming over. When Lee saw everything spread across the bathroom floor, she bent down and commenced to performing the test for her friend. She filled the test tube with pee, squeezed it in the appropriate blank window and sat there for three seconds.

"Now we wait," Lee said as she backed away from the stall.

"How long?" Tasha asked.

"About five or ten minutes." Tasha began cleaning the mess up off the floor. She dumped the cup of pee in the toilet and grabbed all the paper from the floor leaving the test itself there.

"Let's go get something to eat," Lee said walking towards the bathroom door.

"How, when I need to find out what this thing is saying?" Tasha asked with a hint of annoyance.

"We can hide the test behind (looking around the bathroom) the trash can. No one will find it, plus we will only be gone about twenty minutes. By that time the results will be clear. Plus you need to get your mind preoccupied," Lee said trying to calm her friend.

Tasha didn't say a word. She just put the test behind the trash can – out of eye sight - walked over to the sink, washed her hands and left the bathroom. By the time Lee had come from washing her hands, Tasha was in line at the Popeye's Chicken stand. When Lee heard Tasha order enough food for the both of them she went and found them a seat. As the two sat there and ate, Tasha mentioned anything not relevant to what was happening. She talked about how Michael had made a fool of himself when he walked into a pole on his way to the caf, while hollering at one of his friends for not calling him to smoke. "That's what he gets, 'cause I already told him to leave that stuff alone," Lee said noticing Tasha looking at her watch for the fourth time in ten minutes.

Even during her rambling Lee dare not mention that she took a peek at the test before leaving the bathroom and saw that pink line sitting there just as plain as day. After ten more minutes of Tasha picking over her food and Lee rambling, they decided to head for the bathroom. As they walked Tasha felt herself dragging her feet along. She wanted to get it over with but she was scared to death. When they got to the bathroom door, Lee grabbed her hand and said, "Let's go."

Tasha didn't need any explanation. She could look in her friend's eyes and know exactly why she said what she said. The two just kept walking – straight past the bathroom and out to the car. During the ride home not a word was said. When they pulled up in the dorm parking lot Tasha looked at her friend.

"Thanks".

"No need to thank me. Just be ready by 9:00 tomorrow morning. We need to be positive before we do anything," Lee said getting out of the car and walking towards the dorm with her friend.

"Okay, I'll be ready," Tasha said, headed for her room while her friend went towards the opposite end of the hall. Thankfully Lola wasn't there when Tasha got there because she didn't feel like talking to anyone; especially since she had seen Lola and Curtis together earlier. All Tasha wanted to do was to get in her bed and fall asleep – fast.

CHAPTER 9

Tasha had trouble sleeping but she managed to make it through the night. When she woke up, the clock read 6:22. She looked over and noticed Lola was not in her bed. Of course she started wondering where she could be but her mind just pulled up to one particular spot and parked – probably in Curtis' bed. She didn't have time to think about those two. The only thing important to her right now was being certain of what that test would say. Tasha lay there until she heard a knock at the door. It was 7:20 and she had no idea who would be coming to the room this early in the morning. Maybe it was Lee making sure she was awake or maybe it was Miesha from next door asking to borrow another bar of soap. "One minute," Tasha yelled getting up from the bed and walking towards the door. When she swung the door open it was Lola.

"Sorry to wake you, but I forgot my key last night and couldn't get in," Lola said walking past Tasha and over to her closet to get some clothes.

"I was already awake," Tasha said without a bit of animosity in her voice.

As Tasha sat on the edge of her bed hugging her pillow, Lola just continued grabbing clothes to get dressed. Neither girl said a word. After Lola left the room and headed for the showers, Tasha decided to get her clothes ready too. She didn't want Lola to come back and still see her sitting there. When Lola returned to the room Tasha made her exit. She felt like she couldn't be in the same room with this girl – at least not right now.

By the time Tasha was dressed and ready to go it was only 8:25, so she decided to go and grab some breakfast from the cafeteria before they left. Although she wasn't a bit hungry, she just wanted to occupy her time until Lee was ready. On her way out the front door, she noticed Lee coming out of her dorm room and rushing towards the bathroom. Tasha knew from the way Lee was scurrying she had overslept.

"Just give me thirty minutes and I'll be ready," Lee shouted down the hall when she saw Tasha.

"Take your time; I'm gonna go get some breakfast anyway." Tasha yelled back.

As Lee disappeared into the bathroom, Tasha headed for the cafeteria. On her way she spoke to a few others on their way to their classes. When she walked up the stairs to the caf, she heard a group of guys laughing from a distance. She just kept walking and got in line for a hot breakfast. As the line began to move she heard someone behind her say "hello". Not catching the voice Tasha turned around to respond – it was Curtis.

"Hi," he said again as she turned and looked at him.

"Hey," she said in her matter-factly voice as she turned her back and commenced to ignore him.

It was obvious where she stood. She didn't want anything to do with that man, and when she found out the results of the test she could finally bury whatever they had. Although Tasha only had a scoop of eggs, a scoop of fried potatoes and two strips of bacon on her plate that was all she needed – anything to get out of that line. On her way to an empty table she decided to go another direction. She saw John, a guy from her Sociology class and decided to sit with him. That way Curtis wouldn't try sitting with her.

"Hey John," she said as she headed his way.

"Hey Tasha," he said pulling out a chair next to him for her to take a seat.

"You finish that paper yet?" John asked as he wolfed down his bowl of Corn Pops.

Tasha's mind drew a blank because she had no idea what paper he was talking about, but she lied and said, "almost."

"Well, you know it's due at 3 o'clock," John said with his eyebrows raised.

"Yeah, I know," Tasha said still lying.

"Thank God I finished it this morning. I pulled an all-nighter working on that thing," John said with glee and exhaustion in his voice.

"Yeah, I just have to finish typing it and I'll be done," Tasha said as her heart began to race.

"Well, let me go. I have a 9 o'clock and it's already 5 after," John said getting up from the table and walking to throw his bowl in the dispenser.

Tasha just waved. When she turned to see who else was around that she was friends with, she saw Curtis staring at her from across the room. She immediately picked up her tray, walked towards the trash, emptied the tray and headed for the door. She couldn't walk fast enough back to the dorm to see if Lee was ready yet. When she got there she headed down the hall to Lee's room. Before she got a chance to knock the door swung open.

"Just in time," Lee said to her friend as she finished rubbing lotion on her hands.

As the two girls walked to the car, Tasha broke the silence with, "You know that punk had the nerve to say 'What's up?' to me in the caf just now?"

"You lying," Lee said with the side of her mouth twisted in the air.

"Girl, you see how ni**as play?" Tasha said in her own ghetto voice but with her country accent.

"You darn right ni**as play. They play too much if you ask me," Lee said in her North Philly tone.

Just as the day before Tasha handed the keys to her friend and walked to the passenger's side. Lee was still shaking her head from what Tasha had told her.

"Check this out," Tasha said as they began pulling out from the parking lot. "Your girl didn't come home last night either."

Lee slammed on the breaks.

"What? See, these mother******* is gonna make me hurt somebody," Lee said gripping the steering wheel extra tight. "They were probably out somewhere bumping nasties," she continued as she put her foot back on the accelerator.

"Oh well," Tasha said not wanting to seem hurt, but she was.

Lee just kept driving without saying anything. All she could do was shake her head in disgust and murmur under her breath something about "f'em."

CHAPTER 10

"May I help you?" is what the nurse behind the glass window said to Lee when she walked up and stood there. Lee already knew Tasha was scared to death before they had gotten inside, so she told her she would get all the papers she needed. The waiting room was painted in a soft yellow even though it was a clinic, and everywhere else always had white walls. The room was arranged like a living room. The furniture was made out of an oak wood but had navy blue cushions. The floor was hardwood without hardly any gashes or nicks. You could tell they had regular maintenance workers that cleaned the office every night. A large screen television was affixed to the wall with metal braces. On the center coffee table and the two end tables were rows of magazines – from Jet to Ebony. Had it not been for the walls covered with posters of pregnant women or warnings about STD's and HIV, the room would have simply looked like the personal practice of a rich black physician. It was a warm room, but Tasha didn't feel much like getting comfortable. When Lee returned to the seat next to Tasha's, she handed her the clipboard with the papers that needed to be filled out. While Lee, and the other three women that were already there, watched the Regis and Kelly Show, Tasha filled out the papers. Most of the questions were basic and trivial but she still wanted to take her time and answer each one precisely. After she finished filling out the papers she handed them to Lee, and in turn Lee took them back to the woman behind the window.

"You can have a seat and the nurse will call you shortly," she said to Lee as she stood there waiting for instructions.

As the two girls sat there and conversed amongst themselves, Tasha noticed the other women in the room. Two of the three were obviously pregnant but she wasn't sure what the third one was there for. Maybe she was there to get a pregnancy test too or maybe she was there to get a STD test. Tasha had not a clue, but it really didn't matter – all she could worry about was herself.

"La Tasha Daniels," a nurse called out while standing in a door leading to the rear of the building.

Tasha looked at her friend, took a deep breath and got up to follow the nurse. When Tasha emerged from behind the door twenty minutes later she looked pale. If anyone had a question of whether she was completely African American or mixed with some White or Hispanic blood they would be even more confused because she had gotten three shades lighter.

"So, what's the verdict?" Lee asked as Tasha walked over to her carrying a small piece of white paper.

"Guilty," Tasha said slouching down in the chair next to her friend handing her the paper.

It was nothing Lee could say. All she could do was rub her friend's back as she sat there with her face in her hands. After a few moments of comfort, Lee looked at the paper Tasha had handed her. It was on the clinic's letterhead and read:

Name: _La Tasha Daniels_

D.O.B. _08/17/84_

First Day of Last Menstrual Period: _December 13, 2002_

Changes in body: _Nausea, Dizziness, Sore Breasts_

Results of Test: [ ] Negative   [x] Positive

Expectant Date: _September 22, 2003_

* * * * *

The drive home seemed to be a familiar one – silence. Tasha didn't want to talk and Lee didn't know what to say. While Tasha sat in the passenger seat trying to slow her racing mind, she thought about the exact day she had gotten pregnant – December 16th. That was the first and only time she and Curtis had slept together – the first and only time she had slept with anyone at all. Suddenly, Tasha began saying something.

"Please don't think badly of me, but I can't keep this baby."

"What are you talking about?" Lee asked knowing darn well what she was talking about.

"This baby, I can't keep it," Tasha said with confusion in her voice.

"Don't talk like that. You're just saying this because you're scared."

"No I'm not. I know damn well what I'm saying and I'm telling you, I can't keep this baby," Tasha said raising her voice.

Lee knew her friend was very serious because she had never heard her curse before. She tried to find the right words to say, but what could she possibly say in a situation like this? Would she try to throw God up in her face and make her feel even worse or would she use another approach? As Lee pulled the car off the road, she turned to face Tasha.

"Sweetheart, I know you're scared, but I also know you want to do the right thing," Lee said in her motherly tone.

"And this is the right thing."

"Be honest with me, if this were me in this situation, what would you tell me to do?" Lee asked waiting for a response.

Tasha didn't respond. She just sat there looking away from her friend.

"Would you tell me to get rid of it or would you tell me that everything is gonna be alright?" Lee continued to ask her friend.

Still no response from Tasha.

"Sweetheart, I gotta be honest with you. Back in high school I was in your same situation."

Tasha's head swung around to face her friend.

"Yes, I got pregnant when I was in the tenth grade."

Tasha just sat there catching every word that fell from her friend's lips.

"And you know what I did?" Lee asked her friend but not expecting an answer. "I got rid of it. Yes, I had an abortion when I was fifteen years old. And because of that, I can't have children now. The doctors told me that the tools the abortion clinic used had not been sterilized properly and it gave me an infection. And because I had not told my mother when I did it, I let the infection sit too long. When I finally confessed to my mother about what I had done and got it treated, it was too late. The damage had

49

already been done to my body. As a result, I had to have a partial hysterectomy."

Tasha just sat there staring at her friend with the *"I'm-so-sorry to hear that"* look.

"Do you hear what I'm saying Tasha, I can't have no kids," Lee said with a medium case of scream in her voice.

There was nothing Tasha could say. On one hand she felt sorry for her friend but on the other hand she was scared. Scared of what her life would become. Scared of how she would disappoint her parents. Even somewhat scared of how Curtis would react when she told him the news – or would she even tell him?

"Look at me," Lee said grabbing a hold of Tasha's forearm. "Stuff like this happens all the time. Even to good girls like yourself. But, it's not the end of the world. You just have to get strong and do what you have to do. I know you're upset because you disappointed yourself but you also have to forgive yourself. Try not to look at this as a curse, which I know you are, but try to look at it as a blessing. I know you can't see the blessing right now, but you never know; maybe this is part of God's plan."

Half of what Lee was saying made sense and the other half sounded totally foolish to Tasha. How could she possibly see this as a potential blessing? Her mother had always told her that sin could never be a blessing – only a curse.

"Like I told you before, we will get through this. If you need me, honey, you know I'm here for you. Anything you need, just ask, and I do mean 'anything'," Lee said stressing the last part of her statement.

Tasha loved the way Lee continued to use the phrase "we" whenever she spoke about the situation. That let her know that her friend would be there for her no matter what. Tasha leaned over the car seat and gave her friend a big hug holding her very tight while whispering "thank you, Boo," in her ear. As Lee put the car in drive and began taking off, Tasha thought, *who said ghetto girls can't be classy?*

CHAPTER 11

That night Tasha just lay in her bed. She tried not to think about how her day had gone – but she couldn't help it. Her life had officially changed. When she and Lee had gotten back from the clinic it was only 10:30, so she decided to work on her sociology paper – anything to keep her mind occupied. Luckily Tasha wasn't a last minute person, so she had already started the paper when the professor gave it out ten days before but the twist of events over the past week had carried her mind away from school. She decided not to go to any of her classes that day, which was only two because it was Tuesday, and just solely work on the paper. When Tasha went to the library to get all the books she needed to complete her project, she thought of staying there but ruled against it just in case she broke down and began crying; she didn't want anyone asking her what was wrong. She got all the right books and headed back to her room. When she got there she spread the books out on her desk and began looking for a CD to listen to as she did her work. She wanted to listen to Fred Hammond's "Purpose by Design," but ruled against it because she felt guilty. Gospel music always lifted her spirits but she didn't even feel worthy enough to listen to the music. After the debate, she went for Jahiem's CD, "Still Ghetto."

As she began to read over the articles in the books she got caught up in the lyrics of the music. She listened to Jahiem talk about this woman he lost acting foolish. As she sat there and continued listening to the songs she realized all he basically sang about was this woman he treated wrong. He was admitting that he was the cause of their love lost. It was probably so easy for him to admit to his guilt now because he was making money, but was he really sorry for breaking that woman's heart? Was he man enough to even now, after these apologetic songs made him big bucks, willing to go back to that woman and apologize for what he's done – even if they weren't together anymore? Breaking herself from the trance, Tasha realized an hour had passed and she still hadn't gotten any further then when she begun. She got up, took the CD out and went with her original choice – Fred Hammond. But, it wasn't just "Purpose by Design"; it was a mixed compilation of all Fred's worship songs she had burned onto one CD. The very first song on the CD was "Give Me a Clean Heart." Tasha just sat there as the words of the song brought tears to her eyes. Tasha wanted desperately to ask God to give her a clean heart but she didn't feel worthy. She felt like God would never forgive her.

As the songs continued, she listened to Fred ask the Lord to "Breathe into Him" and thanking Him for being a Prodigal Son. Although her guilt was overwhelming, the words of the songs and the spirit behind it were even more powerful.

CHAPTER 12

The next several weeks for Tasha were dreadful. Besides preparing for finals, she had a list of other things that needed to be taken care of before she was to go home for the summer. She still hadn't told anyone about her being pregnant. The only person who knew was her best friend. She wasn't ready to expose herself just yet – not even to the one who had helped create this problem. Tasha had seen Curtis many times throughout the weeks, but she did everything in her power to keep her distance. He tried to talk with her but she refused. Lee tried to convince Tasha into telling Curtis but she just told her friend she wasn't ready to tell him yet. She managed to keep her composure around Lola even though they were roommates. A time or two while she and Lola were talking late at night, Lola managed to bring up Curtis. She talked about how she missed him sometimes and how weird it was for two of his ex-girlfriends to become roommates. Tasha just listened and hardly spoke. She knew it would just add more fuel to the fire if Lola knew the real truth.

With just a few days 'til finals, Tasha was able to get her thoughts together. She had done pretty well with keeping up on her school work regardless of the situation. Once she received all of the reviews from her professors, she knew she had to focus. Nothing else mattered right now except for Tasha A'cing these finals and keeping her GPA up to its typical 3.5. She knew within a matter of days she would be on her way back to Florida and that she would have to face the music. She still hadn't told her parents yet – not even her grandmother whom she trusted to keep the secret. Things were going so well back at home. Her father made a full recovery. He was back at work and church participating in his normal routine. Her mother had just gotten a promotion at the bank where she was now the supervisor. Tasha knew she couldn't drop a bomb like this on them – not yet. Right now, Tasha was just confused. When she thought about it she had to be at almost four months pregnant or more. Besides the initial visit to the clinic for the test, she hadn't been to see a doctor yet. Baltimore wasn't the place for that. She wanted to wait until she had gotten home and discussed the situation with her parents before she saw a doctor. Tasha so desperately wanted to talk to her mother about this because she knew she would give her good advice, but she just couldn't break the news to her that way. Even though Tasha felt like the biggest punk in the world, she still wanted to be respectful and woman enough to tell her parents face to face. That was one rule Tasha had remembered her father teaching her – always talk with people face to face and not hide behind anyone or anything. Right about now, Tasha wanted to crawl under a rock and die.

*   *   *   *   *

It was the first day of finals and Tasha was pumped. She hadn't been feeling good for the past two days but she just attributed it to morning sickness. Her symptoms were finally starting to dissolve, although they should have been long gone according to Lee. She wasn't throwing up in the mornings anymore nor were her breasts as sore. One thing Tasha noticed was that she had been extremely tired. She figured it was from the late night studying, but even when she took a nap during the day she was exhausted again by 10 o'clock. She noticed herself eating a lot of junk food but quickly cut it down; she didn't want to pick up too much weight. Regardless of what was going on in Tasha's body, she had a plan – to stay as normal as possible. As Tasha walked to her first class that Monday morning, she heard someone call her name from down the hall. Before she even turned around she recognized the voice.

"Good morning, Miss Daniels."

"Good morning, Mr. Burns, how are you?" Tasha said in her most pleasant voice.

"I'm fine, thank you. I wanted to ask you a favor."

"Sure Mr. Burns, what's up?" Tasha continued in her pleasantries.

"My church is having a special service for the young people Friday night. Because my wife and I are the Youth Pastors we are in charge of putting the service together. Last night, the speaker

54

we had booked called and canceled leaving us in a bind. I mentioned to my wife what a godly young women you are and in prayer this morning, the Lord put you on my heart. So, I'm asking if you would be willing to speak to our young people."

Tasha froze. All she could do was stand there in a panic mode and hope Mr. Burns couldn't read her body language. Before Tasha could even open her mouth to respond, Mr. Burns continued in his spiel.

"It's not much, Miss Daniels. Maybe you can hit on a few points of maintaining a holy lifestyle as a young person yourself, and the promises God makes to His people when they obey Him and His will. Don't let me tell you what to say, just pray about it; I'm sure the Lord will give you what to say – that is if you are willing to do it."

Tasha couldn't believe her ears. Was this man actually asking her to come and preach a message of holiness when she herself had not been living holy? If this man only knew what was going on in Tasha's life at the moment, he would have her on the front row of the pew come Friday night instead of behind the pulpit.

"Well Mr. Burns, I'll have to decline. I planned on leaving for Florida on Friday night," Tasha said knowing she hadn't planned on leaving until Sunday morning.

"Aw," Mr. Burns said with half a frown on his face.

"Yeah, I'm sorry. But, if you don't mind, I can recommend someone to you?"

"Who?" Mr. Burns said in anticipation.

"Do you know John Samuels?"

"The one from the basketball team?" Mr. Burns asked, not sure.

"Yes. He's in my sociology class and we got the chance to talk on a few occasions; and he tells me that he is one of the youth ministers at his home church in Atlanta and at Second Baptist on Arnold Street."

"Oh, yeah? I would have never known had you not told me. I just thought he was quiet. I never knew he was involved in the ministry," Mr. Burns said in a pleasant tone.

"Yeah, and from what I heard, he's staying for summer school so he can graduate next May," Tasha said.

"Well, thanks for the recommendation. I'll go and talk to him and see if he can do it," Mr. Burns said, bidding Tasha a good day.

As the professor walked away leaving Tasha standing in the hall, she was still in shock. In a way she felt flattered that someone she respected looked at her in a positive way, but the instant turning of her stomach let her know she had no right to be flattered at all. When Tasha came to she took a glance at her watch and realized it was 8:58. In a hurry she ran down the hall and into her class as the Professor was closing the door and handing out the final.

"One down and four more to go," Tasha told herself confidently walking from the room she had just finished taking her exam. It wasn't as bad as she thought. Luckily those study sessions with a few of her classmates had prepared her for what was on the exam. Tasha was always good with taking tests. She pretty much knew the strategy to studying and preparing herself for the process. She also had enough sense to space her exams out for the entire week. When everyone else scheduled all of his or her exams within a three day period, she had scheduled hers for one exam each day. It didn't matter to her that she would be one of the last students to leave for the summer. Besides that, everyone thought she was crazy when she decided to take 18 credits for the semester, but she knew exactly what she was doing. Tasha knew she had the will power to buckle down and do it, but she would have never known that her rapid start would end in a fizzle.

CHAPTER 13

The last few days weren't all that bad, Tasha thought as she continued packing. She had managed to pass all of her exams with a 90% or higher which brought her GPA above the 3.5 to a 3.8; her grades were one thing she could feel proud of. Lola had already taken all of her exams and left for the summer. As Tasha sat on the floor of her half empty dorm room continuing to pack her clothes, she thought about Lola and how earlier in the week they both happened to be in the coffee shop one night. When Tasha walked through the door of the shop, she noticed Lola sitting over in a corner reading a book. From her positioning, Tasha figured her roommate didn't want to be bothered. When Tasha looked around to find an empty booth on the opposite side of the café, she noticed Lola waving for her to sit with her. For a minute Tasha hesitated but she didn't want to seem rude, so she headed towards Lola and took a seat.

"Hey girl, what are you doing here?" Tasha asked as she sat down waving to a few others in the room she knew.

"Just reading a book I've been wanting to read the entire year but never had the time," Lola said turning the book so Tasha could read the title.

""The Coldest Winter Ever', huh? Good book," Tasha added as she looked around the café' trying to avoid eye contact with Lola.

"You all packed?" Tasha asked keeping the conversation friendly.

"Yup, finally. I didn't know I had so much junk until it was time to pack it all up," Lola said jokingly.

"I know what you mean. I've already got two suitcases and I've only emptied one dresser. I haven't even gotten to my closet yet," Tasha said as the two girls shared a laugh together. After an entire year Tasha still didn't have any gripe with Lola, even after what had happened between their "threesome." Sure, Tasha could have been angry at Lola for lying to her about Curtis but there was no need for that. Tasha always wondered why girls fought over men. Was it because women were always trained that to not have a man meant something was wrong with you? Whatever the case was, Tasha didn't feel a need to compete with Lola. It wouldn't do any good for her to fight over a man she would never wind up with in the end anyway. During their chat they did everything in their power to avoid the topic of Curtis but it was impossible. His name had to come up in the conversation sooner or later.

"Let me ask you something?" Lola said looking Tasha square in the face.

"What's up?"

"What ever happened with you and Curtis?" Lola said catching her roommate by surprise.

"Nothing. Why?"

"Well, I know ya'll were seeing each other for a minute there and I didn't want to seem like I was barging in on what you and he had," Lola said with a hint of slickster in her voice.

Taking a deep breath, Tasha felt an almost sigh of relief. All this time she thought Lola had slept with Curtis over something Tasha might have done.

"Nah, it wasn't much between me and Curtis," Tasha said lying through her teeth. "Let me ask you, what was up with you and Curtis?"

"To be honest with you...nothing. We just used to...uh, how can I say this... 'get down,' if you know what I mean. After he told me you and he were over, I just figured he was up for grabs. The thing that messed me up was that I got pregnant in the process – but you already knew that."

Tasha just sat there with her eyes glued on Lola. She wanted so badly to tell her that she had messed up too, but she knew that wouldn't be a good idea; especially since she hadn't told Curtis yet.

"Are you and him still seeing each other," Tasha blurted out.

"No. Last time me and him was together was a few weeks ago."

"You mean that time I saw ya'll in the mall" Tasha asking pressing for answers.

"Uh, yeah, I think so," Lola said trying to remember. "Speaking of the mall, what was up with you that night? I felt like you had a beef against me or something," Lola asked.

"Not at all. Lee and I were just out shopping for some things and we promised ourselves we wouldn't be out there all night; that's why Lee pulled me away like that. Trust me, it had nothing to do with you," Tasha said.

"Okay, cool," Lee said in a nonchalant attitude as she looked around the café as not to pay her roommate any attention.

When a moment too long of silence between the girls fell, they both sat looking around the room as if they were both seeking out the same person. They began commenting on some of the other women's clothing in the room.

"Can somebody tell me why she got those shoes on with a dress like that," Lola said looking cockeyed at one girl from across the room.

All Tasha could do was chuckle because she agreed wholeheartedly with what her roommate was saying.

"One of her friends must have told her it looked nice," Tasha said trying to give the girl the benefit of the doubt for her clothing creation.

"Well, they must not be too much of a friend if they told her that."

While the two girls continued in laughter, Tasha thought of how badly she wanted to tell Lola about her being pregnant. Tasha wanted to ask her roommate about the abortion she had only a few months prior and how she felt about what she had done. There was so much Tasha wanted to say, but she was too embarrassed. She was always the one who did the comforting and now she was the one who needed to be comforted. As the girls sat there and continued to chat about other things and people in the café, Tasha turned and looked at Lola with a peculiar look.

"Can I ask you a personal question?"

"Sure," Lola said focusing on Tasha's lips and the words that were coming from them.

"I know you said you and Curtis were only 'getting down,' but did you have any type of feelings for him?" Tasha asked with nervousness in her tone.

59

"Not really," Lola said in her matter-of-factly attitude. "See, the thing with me and Curtis is that we became friends because we come from similar backgrounds. We both come from the ghetto, so we think and live ghetto. Look Tasha, we didn't have it like you growing up. We didn't have the supportive families and friends that were down for us no matter what. We, or at least I, learned at a young age that if you want something you take it! And if something is in the way of what you want, you get rid of it. That's why I had that abortion. I have goals and dreams, and I'm not gonna let nothing stand in my way – and I mean nothing. Curtis is just like my father; and all he ever did was make babies, run women, and gamble. I knew he wasn't gonna be no real support or help with that child, to be honest."

All Tasha could do was stare at Lola. What her roommate was talking about was foreign to her. She knew nothing about using people to get what you want or not caring about people so much that hurting them was always the outcome. In a way Tasha was sad. Sad that people had been raised with that mentality. Sad that people didn't grow up with a loving environment like her and especially sad that maybe one day they would have children of their own and teach them the same animal like tactics their parents had taught them. On the other hand, Tasha was glad. Glad that she wasn't one of those people – but who was she to judge?

Placing one hand over Tasha's folded hands, Lola looked her in the face. "I'm not trying to scare you or make you think that the world is all bad because you already know that it's not. But I am trying to let you know that people these days are more concerned with themselves than they are for others. Girly, if you don't understand that now, you're in for a life of hell."

Tasha's eyes began to fill with tears.

"Did I say something wrong?" Lola asked rubbing the back of Tasha's hand.

"I'm pregnant," Tasha blurted out before she even had time to think.

Lola's eyebrows went up as if what was said had been a shock.

"I figured that but I wasn't too sure. I mean, I noticed you have been filling out your clothes a little more. And, it was kind of obvious because of the morning sickness you were having a few months ago. I immediately thought you were pregnant, but then I thought she can't be because she's too "good" to get herself in a situation like that. But, I guess it happens to the good girls too."

"Why didn't you say anything, if you had a hunch?" Tasha asked.

"Girl, I was pregnant too and I had to worry about what I was doing with myself before I could worry about anyone else."

Tasha wiped her face with a napkin she had taken from the dispenser.

"Let me guess – it's Curtis'"?

Tasha just shook her head yes.

"And what is he saying about all of this?"

"I haven't told him," Tasha said unable to look her newfound friend in the face.

"You haven't!" Lola asked in a slightly raised tone. "Are you even going to?"

As Tasha moved around nervously, Lola asked another question.

"Tasha, are you going to get an abortion?"

Tasha didn't say a word. She stared at the cover of the book Lola had originally been reading. By that time the book was laying flat on the table as if someone had left it there by accident. Tasha's eyes traced the contour of the lips on the cover of the book. She stared so hard, she could probably have drawn an identical sketch of the cover of the book without a line out of place.

Lola just sighed, "Well girl, do what you gotta do."

Tasha didn't know what else, if anything, to say. She just sat there holding inside the tears that so desperately fought to fall, but she held them back, almost with steel cages.

Again, silence filled the space between the two girls until Lola let out a fierce laugh. "Girl, we've been played!" Tasha's heart began to race knowing the statement just made was the God's-honest truth. Her mind swirled. How could she have been so foolish to get caught up in the mess and drama?

"It's no big deal, girl. It happens to women everyday, all over the world," Lola added. "We just happened to be next on the list," she continued in laughter. Looking at Tasha, Lola knew this was

61

her first heartbreak. "Never thought you'd be involved in anything like this did you?"

Tasha just shook her head no. "Well, I'll tell you like my mama always told me, suck it up." Tasha had no rebuttal just an uneasy exhale.

"Well Tash, I have to go because my ride is going to be here in a few minutes to take me home. I wish you luck and I hope to see you next semester." Lola said squeezing Tasha's hands that she had been holding. Just before Lola got up to walk away she stuck the book she had originally been reading, but which was now lying on the table, in her purse, pulled out a piece of paper and began writing some numbers.

"If you need me for anything or just wanna talk," Lola said handing Tasha the sheet of paper.

Tasha stood face to face with her one time rival and gave her a hug whispering in her ear, "Thank You!"

"I know you'll do the right thing," Lola said as she winked and walked away.

Tasha sat back down; she wanted to leave but she didn't want to walk away with tears in her eyes. So, she just sat there for a few more minutes until she got herself together. Taking a deep breath Tasha knew what her next mission was – to find Curtis and let him know what was going on.

CHAPTER 14

Just to clear her mind Tasha decided to take a walk. Since the air was clear and most of the students had gone for the summer, Tasha figured she would stay on campus. Heading towards the football field Tasha noticed the many banners arrayed along the perimeter of the field - 1975 State Champions, 1983 Regional Champions, 1988 State Champions, 1992 State Champions, 1996 State Champions, and 2000 Regional Champions. Tasha thought of how beautiful the banners looked in the way they blew in the wind. The yellow and red mingled with passion, while the white and blue overlapped in splendor. The twinkle of the stars added majesty to the already lit sky. A full moon only illuminated peace as the sky embraced its elements. This was truly a beautiful May night, Tasha thought as she inhaled and strolled in consecutive paces. From behind her she could hear the laughter of a man and woman. When she turned to see who it might be, a smile glided across her face when she heard the laughs escalate.

From afar she noticed her best friend Lee in an intimate embrace with Michael, her boyfriend. Obviously, they had also been taking a stroll when Tasha noticed the laugh. As Tasha propped herself against one of the lighted field poles, she watched the two playfully wrestle in the evenly cut field grass. She wanted to call out to them but she didn't want to be the cause of ruining their evening. Just from the laughter she knew they were happy together. Sure Michael was considered a thug from West Baltimore but he had potential and that's what Lee saw in him. She saw he could one day be a great man if he only kept his mind and his will focused on his goals. Many times Lee would tell Tasha about how she and Michael talked about one day getting married and having kids. Tasha chuckled when she thought of how Lee shared with her the fact that Michael wanted to be a lawyer. Not that she thought it was impossible for him to strive for such a position, but that he even had his eyes focused on such a prize. That let Tasha know that no matter where you came from or who you came from, you can still go on to be better. Even with Lee, she had dreams and goals of her own that would take her out of the normal ghetto state of where she came from, to the fabulous state of where she was going. As Tasha stood there and thought for a minute, she had to shake herself from the thoughts because she felt as if she were comparing herself to them – almost as if she was a bit jealous and that's exactly what she didn't want to be. Tasha didn't want to seem too obvious in watching them so she began looking up at the hanging banners and singing. When she heard them within earshot she turned and flashed them one of her big bright smiles.

"Hey ya'll!"

"Hey," they both said with synchronized voices.

"What ya'll up to?"

"Nothing, just out here taking advantage of this good air," Lee said as she and Michael stood hand in hand.

As the three of them stood looking up at the banners blowing in the wind, Michael asked Tasha how she was feeling.

Tasha immediately looked over at Lee with her eyes wide as quarters.

"I'm okay," she said replying to Michael's question but still staring at her friend.

"Like he didn't already know," Lee said in her matter-of-factly tone of voice.

"Whatever," Tasha said sucking her teeth and rolling her eyes.

"So, did you tell him?" asked Lee.

"No, I ain't tell him yet," Tasha replied with a pinch of erk in her voice.

"What you waiting for!"

"Dang! If you so eager for him to know then why don't you tell him and save me the hassle!" Tasha said.

"Can I suggest something?" Michael said trying to bring calm to the storm about to erupt between the two friends.

They both looked his way waiting for him to give them the highly anticipated answer to the forbidden question.

"Tasha, I think you need to let him know what's up. I mean, he needs to know now before you get too far along and then he try to question you about it being his or not. You know what I'm saying?" Michael implied in his West Baltimore accent.

"True," Lee added.

"I hear you," Tasha said as she folded her arms across her chest.

"Sweetie, I just wanna make sure you're alright when all of this comes out, because I don't wanna have to bust nobody's ass for dissin' my girl. I know how these Cali fools can be – shit, ni**as in general and they like to act like they don't need to be responsible; but they do – we all do. Look, I know you a good girl because I have seen the way you carry yourself and from what Lee tells me too. I got people's like you that I grew up with in the hood, and I have seen them get played when they didn't deserve it, and I don't wanna see it happen to you," Michael said as he rubbed Tasha's left arm.

Tasha stared at Michael dressed in his navy blue Phat Farm jeans, blue and white PF embroidered tank, half laced Tims and a red and white "P" cap cocked to the side of his head. Tasha knew Michael was a strong man because he was very athletic and built like the next Mike Tyson, but she didn't see him as a violent man. Nonetheless, she had never had that kind of response from a guy. She and Michael were always cool because of Lee but she never thought he saw her in that light nor would he have made a comment like that. She immediately had a newfound respect for him. Tasha knew Lee was right – he did have the potential to be a great man.

*   *   *   *   *

Tasha's mind raced as she stood at Curtis' dorm room knocking. It had been weeks since she had spoken to him although she saw him constantly in class and around campus. Not wanting to tell him anything about the baby, she was persuaded by Lee's constant pleas and Lola's final comment. Tasha couldn't believe she was in this situation. Never in her wildest dream or nightmare would she ever think she would be an unmarried pregnant teenager. She had been raised better than that. Her parents had taught her better and she certainly knew God required better.

After the third knock she began to walk away from room 219 when she heard the door creep open. "Yeah?" she heard a man's voice ask as if awakened from a peaceful dream. She walked back in eye's view so the man who opened the door could see her face.

"Oh hey, what's up?" Curtis asked her as he rubbed the sleep from his eyes.

"I'm sorry. I didn't mean to bother you. If you're busy then I'll come back a little later."

"Nah. I'm up now. What's up?" Curtis asked opening the door wider extending an offer to come in.

Walking through the door, Tasha stood in the middle of the floor careful not to touch anything. "We need to talk."

"Uh oh, what'd I do?" Curtis asked taking a seat on his perfectly made bed.

Tasha was still standing there. She was extremely nervous, but the fact that Curtis' roommate wasn't there gave her some comfort. She didn't want anyone or anything to interrupt her confession. Tasha took a deep breath and began talking.

"You remember last semester when we had sex?"

"Yeah," Curtis replied waiting for the rest of the story.

"Well, somehow, I got pregnant."

Not a word was said. Curtis just sat there staring Tasha in the face as if she hadn't just told him she was pregnant.

"Well?" Tasha said waiting for a response.

"Well what?"

"What you mean 'Well what'?' I just told you that I'm pregnant!" Tasha's voice had now escalated to a scream.

"Look, that was a while back when we fucked so how am I supposed to know you wasn't sexin' somebody else? Ya'll know ya'll good for that!?

Tasha's mouth hung open. Did this man, this boy, this punk stand here and tell her that she was in essence a "ho"? Did he just tell her that the baby she was carrying wasn't his?

"So what are you saying Curtis?

"I ain't saying shit!"

By this time Curtis was lying back on his bed with his arms underneath his head and Tasha still stood in the middle of the room. She dare not budge. She tried her best to hold the tears that formed in the corner of her eyes but they fell – they had to. They were too heavy for Tasha to hold back.

"Don't try that crying act cause that shit don't work on me. I know that's not my baby 'cause when I came I pulled out. Even if it was, why you just coming to me now? Why you ain't tell me before? Oh, I know what it is; you probably told some other nigga it was his and he sent your ass away, so now you up in my face with that bullshit. I ain't trying to hear it!"

Tasha couldn't believe the way Curtis was talking to her. She had never been so disrespected in all her life. Tasha knew she didn't deserve this, nor did she understand why or how he was accusing her of being scandalous. Everyone who knew Tasha knew she wasn't like that – even Curtis.

"Look you stupid asshole. If you don't wanna stand up to your responsibilities, then that's on you, but just know this is your damn baby!"

Without another word Curtis stood to his feet and walked over to a dresser. He pulled the top drawer open and handed Tasha a wad of money and went and lay back down on his now slightly ruffled bed.

"What is this?" Tasha asked holding the money up in the air.

"It's $300. Go handle your business."

Tasha just closed her eyes and dropped her head. It was getting worse by the minute. She wasn't queen of the streets or their slang but she knew exactly what Curtis meant.

"You bum motherfucker!"

Tasha just dropped the money and headed for the door. As the door slammed behind her she could hear him in the background yell, "Don't tell me I don't take care of my responsibilities!"

Running down the hall with tears streaming down her face Tasha plowed into David, Curtis' roommate. Luckily he hadn't been in the room when all of that went down, but she still had a grudge against him – just because he was a man.

"Whoa, Whoa, slow down," David said grabbing a hold of Tasha's hands.

When he noticed Tasha was crying he asked her what was the matter. Tasha couldn't reply. She was crying too hard.

"Tasha, what happened?" David said with an obvious look of concern on his face. "Is it your dad again?" he continued.

Tasha just cried even harder. She and David weren't the best of friends but she knew him because of him and Curtis being

67

roommates. David was always a good guy. He seemed to be polite and treated her with the utmost respect. David was one of those "cool kat brothers." He was from Brooklyn, New York and knew all the tricks of the trade. As long as you treated him with respect he treated you with respect; but if you crossed him then he would let you know he didn't appreciate it, in no uncertain terms. David had heard about Tasha's father, probably through Curtis and had even asked her if she needed anything. He even went as far as to say her father was in his prayers.

"If you don't wanna tell me what happened than I'll leave you alone," David said trying to catch eyes with Tasha.

She just fell in his chest and sobbed. In a way she felt relieved to be able to cry like that. Most of the dorms were empty because of summer vacation, but the remaining few guys that were on the second floor came to the door when they heard the voice of a woman crying. After David yelled for them to mind their business they returned back into their rooms.

As Tasha began getting herself together David asked her again what was wrong.

"Ask your boy," Tasha said as she pulled away and ran down the staircase.

Then, from the hallway window he just watched her disappear across the walkway.

CHAPTER 15

4:32 AM is what the clock read when Tasha looked at it the last time. Since about 12:20 she had paid close attention to the time because it seemed as if it weren't moving. She didn't want to, but she couldn't help it. Her aim was to go to sleep as soon as possible so she could awake and realize the day she just had was a dream, but Tasha knew better. She knew it was not only an unfamiliar dream but a horrible nightmare she hoped to soon awaken from. Lying in her bed she stared at the walls. Most of them were empty because Lola had already left, thoroughly cleaning her side of the room, and she was almost completely packed and ready to go home herself. Home - now that sounded like the best place to be right about now. Even though she still had to deal with her parents, she was more willing to take their bashes instead of Curtis'. Tasha wanted so badly to do something – anything because she was far from sleep. Her first thought was to go find Lee and talk to her but she knew her friend and didn't want to get her riled up. She hadn't told her about what happened although she desperately wanted to. She knew Lee would break his neck after she cursed him out, but she didn't want her friend to handle her problem. Her next thought was to go for a jog because of the anger she was holding on too but quickly ruled that out. When she was a child her father would tell her to go somewhere and cool off when she got too upset to handle things rationally.

Hour after hour she replayed the conversation between her and Curtis in her mind. She went over the words and the looks that were exchanged. Most of all, she went over the insults. How could he even think she was trying to use him? How could he talk to her that way when she was just being honest with him? Her mind raced as she tried to calm it but it was no use: she knew nothing else to do except let the thoughts run wild until her body eventually gave way and she fell asleep.

Hours later Tasha opened her eyes. Although they felt glued she managed to get them open and focused. Her immediate reaction was to look at the clock because her body had already told her it was way past the normal awake time of 7:00. She was right, it was 11:30. As she lay her head back down on the pillow she heard a knock at the door. "Who in the world could that be?" she thought to herself before she asked who it was. After the second knock she heard a man's voice call her name – "Tasha?" Unfamiliar with the voice she didn't answer. Again, the voice called her name but she refused to answer. By the third knock she heard another voice call her name. It was certainly louder than the first voice and this time it belonged to a woman; she knew just who that woman was – Lee.

"Girl, I know you in there! Open this door!" her friend yelled out.

Although hesitant, Tasha got up from her bed and opened the door. Outside were Lee and David. Neither one of them said a word. Lee just pushed her way through the door and David politely followed her lead. As Tasha crawled back under her covers, David took a seat on the empty bed, while Lee stood in the middle of the floor with both hands on her hips. From the look in her eyes Tasha knew she was furious.

"Why you didn't tell me?" Lee asked.

Tasha didn't answer; she just looked at her friend as if she were a stranger. Tasha noticed the outfit her friend was wearing. A navy blue Gap jean skirt that ended right above her knees with a navy blue halter top with the word "superstar" etched in white across the front. To top off the outfit, she wore a pair of white Prada sandals as she clutched a white Prada handbag. All Tasha could think about was how well her friend's outfit matched to a tee and how flawless her makeup was. Lee had superb taste and she knew exactly how to coordinate her clothes and her attitude. The more Lee talked, the more Tasha tried to ignore her but she couldn't. David just sat on the empty bed staring at Tasha with puppy dog eyes as if to apologize for being a man.

"David told me what happened last night," Lee told her friend.

"I'm sorry if I got in your business but I figured you had already told her, I guess you didn't," David said referring to Lee.

"Tash, why you ain't tell me?" Lee pleaded.

Tasha couldn't move. She just sat there as her eyes went between the two now sitting on the vacant bed.

70

"I can't believe that ni**a went there. He actually had the unmitigated gall to say that ain't his baby. Who the hell do he think he is with his ugly ass?" Lee yelled out. "That mother****** lucky he ain't nowhere to be found because he would have some serious shit coming to him."

Tasha immediately looked over at David. She wanted so badly to ask where he was but didn't want them to think she still cared, although in the bottom of her heart she knew she did. In the middle of Lee's fit of anger a knock at the door interrupted them.

"Who it is?" Lee screamed out even before Tasha had the chance to.

"It's me, Mike."

When Lee swung open the door she was boiling. Mike could tell by the look on everyone's faces that something was wrong.

"What happened?" Mike asked looking at all three to see which one would answer first.

"That bum-ass punk is what happened," Lee yelled out.

"You told him?" Mike asked looking at Tasha. She just shook her head yes.

"And what he say?"

"Yeah Tasha, tell Mike what he said?" Lee added as they all looked her way.

"Basically, he said the baby wasn't his and that he ain't want nothing to do with it. Then he gave me $300 and told me to handle my business."

"Handle your business! Handle your business! That punk-ass nigga gonna tell somebody to handle 'dey' business when he don't even wanna handle his. He got some f'in' nerve!"

Lee was so upset she couldn't help but curse and Tasha knew that; that's why she never asked her once to watch her mouth. Most of the time Tasha would look at Lee as a hint for her to tone down the profanity but this wasn't a time for ethics or morals; this was a time for everyone to speak their mind. Even the night before Tasha had used a few choice words to express her anger towards Curtis so she had no right to tell anyone else to watch their mouth.

When Mike grabbed Lee's arms and told her to calm down he looked at David and said "Where he at?"

"He left for the airport already to go home. I took him about an hour ago."

71

"What time his flight leave?" Mike asked.

"I don't know. Probably around 1 or so," David suggested.

"Okay," Mike said as he pulled out his cell phone and headed for the door.

"Where you going?" Lee yelled.

"Didn't I tell you that I wasn't playin' with that nigga?" Mike said as he walked over to Tasha's bed. "I told you that I didn't want to hurt nobody and I see that's what I'm gonna have to do. If you're hurt than that means that Lee is hurt which hurts me!"

Tasha sat up.

"Mike, please don't. He ain't worth it," Tasha said pleading with Mike. "It's okay. Really, it's okay."

"You sure? 'Cause you know all you gotta do is say the word and the shit will be handled," Mike said holding up the phone and staring Tasha in the face.

The glare in his eyes let Tasha know he was very serious. All she had to do was give the word and the man who in essence had called her a whore, broke her heart and disrespected her to her face would be taken care of physically – if not death. Tasha had no idea she had that type of support from her friends – that they would go as far as to make sure no one would hurt her again. But, Tasha just couldn't give the okay. Although Mike would be the one handling it, she still didn't want another man's blood on her hands.

*   *   *   *   *

After everyone left her room, Tasha tried to get up and do some more packing but was unable to. All she could think about was how she would go through with the abortion. One thing Tasha did manage to do was get out of her old clothes and put on some new clean ones. Not until her friends left her room did she realize she still had on the same clothes from the day before – somehow she fell asleep without taking them off.

By the time the clock read 3:15 Tasha was about to lose her mind. She knew if she didn't get out of that room and do something, she would go nuts and that was exactly what she didn't want to do. While sitting on the floor fooling with her suitcases Tasha thought of what she could possibly do with her afternoon.

Thousands of ideas crossed her mind, but she wanted to be sensible and not just do whatever she wanted – that's what ended her in this situation to begin with. With one quiet moment of her thoughts, the Blacks in Wax Museum popped in her mind –almost as if someone or something had whispered it in her ear. Wherever that idea came from was beyond Tasha, but it was a great option. She hadn't been to the museum since the beginning of her college career when a few kids from the freshman class went to check it out. Some of the older students had bragged about its history and artistic genre. Tasha could hardly remember what the museum offered and at that point it really didn't matter to her, all she knew was that it was something to do. Her first consideration was to find Lee and ask her if she wanted to go, but then ruled against it just because she wanted some time to herself to think things over. Tasha quickly slid on her shoes, fixed her hair and headed for the door. On her way to the car she noticed David talking with a few other guys in the parking lot. It took everything in her not to look his way but she had no choice when he waved to her. Tasha managed to get in her car and pull off without anyone else noticing her.

Headed down Arnold Street, Tasha's mind raced. So many things crossed her mind that she didn't know what to think about first. Everything was so jumbled. With the heat of the dry air of mid-May, Tasha could smell the atmosphere. Ever since she found out she was pregnant her sense of smell had been like never before. She was able to smell things from inches and sometimes blocks away. She could smell when someone was perming their hair in the bathroom down the hall and she could smell if someone was on their menstrual cycle while she was in the bathroom. The potency of her senses intrigued her and yet scared her all at once. Her body had never reacted to anything like this before. Not only were her smelling senses awakened, but her sight, hearing and tasting senses had emerged from an embryonic slumber – she felt incarnated. Everything dealing with her instincts came alive as the weeks went by. Because she had never been pregnant before, she wondered if this happened to all women or if something was wrong with her. This was one of the many times she wanted to call her mother but she knew she couldn't – not yet.

73

Pulling up in front of the museum Tasha glanced at the clock on her dashboard. Not seeing any people going into or coming from the museum she wasn't sure if it had already closed, so she parked the car, grabbed her purse and headed for the door. The beige and brown building looked plain from the outside, but when she swung the doors open and an oversized wax statue of Thurgood Marshall met her face to face; she knew she was in for a treat.

"How many?" a woman sitting behind a glass window asked Tasha as she walked over.

"One please," Tasha said handing the woman a ten dollar bill.

When the older brown skinned woman handed Tasha back four one dollar bills and told her the museum closed at 6:00, she could smell her breath through the small circle that was an opening for talking. It carried the scent of alcohol trying to be concealed by a mint. Tasha just stood there and stared at the woman for a moment saying "thank you" after throwing the change in her purse. For some reason the woman looked familiar to Tasha but she wasn't sure how. Her smoky grey eyes and her salt and pepper curly hair matched perfectly as only God could do. The wrinkles under her eyes and the coarseness of her hands let Tasha know the woman had to be at least sixty years old. As Tasha strolled away she felt the woman staring at her from behind but she dare not turn around, she just kept walking towards the double doors that led to the displays.

Walking slowly through the exhibits Tasha tried her best to pay close attention but she couldn't. Too many things were on her mind and another had been added when she struggled with the clerk's identity. She wandered through the slave ship display onto their escapes and then into the huts the slaves slept in on the plantations. By this time she was upset. She tried not to react to what she was watching but it was hard for her to act like it had never happened. So many obstacles those people went through when they were captured and stolen from their home land. It crushed Tasha when she thought about one preacher she heard preach a sermon on why God brought Blacks from Africa and that it was a blessing. She just couldn't understand that concept no

74

matter how she looked at it. The silent anger Tasha was beginning to feel prompted her to skip the rest of the slave summaries and move onto a more positive account of Black Americans. The mirrored faces of Frederick Douglas, Fannie Lou Hammer, Martin Luther King Jr., Malcolm X and a list of other superb African Americans brought a sense of pride to Tasha as she walked through reading the inscriptions of each and every silhouette.

Unaware of the time, Tasha was startled by the sound of a bell ringing. She knew the ringing of the bell meant the museum would be closing shortly. Picking up her pace, she quickly began walking the opposite way looking for an exit. Going down a flight of stairs she realized the museum was in the shape of a maze. As she turned corners and walked past familiar sights, she ran into a display that featured a black woman hanging from a tree while a white man cut an unborn baby from her womb. Tasha stood there in horror. She wanted to scream but she couldn't; all she could do was stare at the image with tears running down her face. She tried to walk away but her feet felt like they were glued to the spot she stood. The sight was undeniably wicked and that was the last thing she needed or wanted to see being herself, carrying a baby. How could anyone do something so cruel she thought as her heart raced at maximum speed and she began to sweat?

Again, she heard the ringing of the bell which gave her the opportunity to detach herself from that horrible scene and exit the display. Walking swiftly through the double doors and into the lobby she continued wiping the tears from her face as she searched for her car keys. She felt the glare of the clerk's eyes attach themselves to her once again and this time Tasha looked her way. She eyeballed the woman back as if to let her know she wasn't scared or ashamed. Tasha wondered what the woman was thinking. Was she staring because she knew Tasha from somewhere or was she just staring because the liquor altered her vision? Whatever the case was Tasha wanted to put it to an end.

She gathered herself, walked over to the window and asked the woman if she knew her.

"I don't think so," the woman replied.

"So why are you staring at me?"

"Sweetheart, I stare at everyone that walks in and out those doors to make sure ain't nothing being stolen," the woman answered in a nasty tone.

Suddenly, something in Tasha leaped and she recognized the woman. She was the woman from the mall whom she had noticed stealing from Wal-Mart that day her and Lee was there to get the pregnancy test. Tasha knew from the moment she saw the woman's face she was someone who had left an impression – and it wasn't good.

"Well, I ain't no thief; and you might wanna watch who you call a thief when you got dirty hands yourself," Tasha said to the woman as she exited the building.

When she walked to her car with keys in hand a conviction hit Tasha in the heart. She knew she was wrong for talking to the woman like that – even if she was mistreated. She couldn't allow her emotions to alter the way she was raised or what was right. Removing the key from the car lock, Tasha walked back into the museum towards the window in which the woman was sitting behind. The woman just stared at her with hate in her eyes.

"I apologize for the way I spoke to you. It was wrong and I ask for your forgiveness."

The stiff eyebrows of the clerk softened as a half grin glided across her face.

In a slurred tone the woman rudely responded with, "Fine."

Walking from the building towards her car Tasha felt relieved. A heavy weight had been lifted off her shoulders and she knew that regardless of whatever would be on her mind that night, that would be one less thing she would have to wrestle with.

CHAPTER 16

Tasha heard the sound of a blasting radio from down the hall blaring the tunes of 50-Cent. She knew it was the girls in room 220 celebrating their last night together before the semester was finally over. Lee had told her that one of the girls wouldn't be returning because she decided to transfer to Rutgers University in Newark, New Jersey where she was from. She figured it would be cheaper if she remained in state – that way she would receive more financial aid. Any other time the noise would interrupt Tasha because she would be studying, but she wasn't moved at all. As a matter of fact, the music broke her from the constant trance of pondering her dreadful situation. How and when was she going to get the abortion were the thoughts that penetrated her mind throughout the day? She didn't know anything about where she could go through with the process. Sure, she could look in the phonebook but would that give her enough variety? She thought about asking her friends who had gotten abortions, but she didn't want to alter their opinion of her.

As she lay there, her cousin Lisa popped in her mind. "Of course, Lisa would know," Tasha thought. As the music got louder her mind raced even faster. Where would she get the money to get the abortion and how much did it cost to begin with? Maybe it wasn't more than the $300 Curtis had offered her? If he had already gone through it with Lola, then he probably knew how much it cost. The more she deliberated the more she wanted to tell her friend. She knew Lee didn't approve of Tasha going though with the abortion simply because of what she had been through, but she also would support her either way. As Tasha thought of her friend she wondered where she had disappeared too. She hadn't seen her since earlier in the evening when the two of them sat in Lee's room chatting. That thought quickly ended when she heard the song "P.I.M.P" pounding from the speakers. Mike had played that song about ten times a day since he brought the CD when it was released back in February. It was obvious Lee was spending her last night with her man.

*   *   *   *   *

Early the next morning Tasha heard a knock at the door. She immediately wondered who it could be because she wasn't expecting anyone, but she still decided to answer.

"Who is it," she yelled out as she took notice of the time – 7:12 AM.

"It's me, Lee."

Wiping the crust from her eyes, Tasha got out of bed and opened the door. "What's up girl?"

"Nothing. I came to take you to breakfast before we both left for home," Lee said strolling in the room and shutting the door behind her.

"This early?"

"Well, I just got in, so I figured I better catch you before you leave or I crash".

"You just getting in from last night?"

"Yup," Lee admitted with a look of guilt on her face.

"And what were you doing that you just getting in at 7am?"

Lee just turned her head and began whistling.

"Uh, huh," Tasha said shaking her head.

Lee lay stretched out across the empty bed that had been Lola's.

"You packed yet?" Lee asked taking the focus off of herself.

"Yup, finished last night," Tasha said grabbing her toiletry bag, towel and wash cloth and heading for the door.

"I'm not, but I don't have to drive as far as you so I have some more time,"

"True. Be right back," Tasha added leaving the room.

"Be right here," Lee shouted out as the door closed.

When Tasha returned to the room Lee was fast asleep on the empty bed. Obviously, she had taken Tasha's pillow off her bed because she had it comfortably propped underneath her head. Tasha tried not to make too much noise and wake Lee, so she crept around the room getting her clothes she had hung up to wear after she finished packing everything else the night before. As Tasha sat on the edge of her bed naked and lotioning down, Lee suddenly lifted her head up when she heard a loud crash.

78

"Oops," Tasha said picking up the bottle of lotion she had dropped, from the floor.

When Lee looked over at her friend's naked body, her eyes got slightly large.

"What?" Tasha asked.

"Your boobs are getting big, girl," Lee said in her North Philly tone.

A bit embarrassed, Tasha covered herself with the towel she had been drying herself with.

"Sorry Boo, I didn't mean to say that."

"I know," Tasha said as she walked over to the mirror hanging on the back of the door and dropped the towel around her waist.

Her breasts were getting big she thought as she stared at them. Her nipples were also becoming dark brown as the nurse from the clinic told her they would.

"I can't believe this," Tasha said in a tone of frustration while covering herself back up with the towel.

"Well," her friend said as if she didn't know what else to say.

As Tasha continued to dress, the room fell quiet. Neither girl knew what to say regarding the situation. It was what it was and they both knew that.

"Ready?" Tasha said lightly tapping Lee. She had managed to fall back asleep after the last comment and the room got quiet again.

"Yup," Lee said rolling off the bed and onto her feet. "I gotta go brush my teeth and wash my face so I'll meet you at the car in ten minutes," she said heading for the door.

"Okay."

Walking to the car, the morning sun and humidity of the mid-May day was already speaking volumes. She thought if it was already hot in Baltimore and summer hadn't come yet, than she knew it would be scorching in Dunbar by now. Even though she broke out in an instant sweat and it was only 8:15 am, Tasha didn't mind because summer was always her favorite time of year. The sound of a man calling her name interrupted her thoughts. When she turned to see who it was, John was running towards her.

"Hey, Tasha."

"Hey John," she said creating a smile to come across her face.

"I talked with Mr. Burns..."

"I hope it's okay with you that I gave him your name," Tasha interrupted him.

"Yeah, it's fine. Matter fact, I was coming to thank you."

"Thank me? What for?" Tasha asked.

"For giving Mr. Burns my name. I'm always willing to serve the Lord and I know you are too."

Tasha just stood there with a bleak look on her face.

"Mr. Burns told me that he originally wanted you to speak, but that you were leaving for Florida last night... or is it tonight?"

"Actually, I had planned on leaving last night, but I was too tired and decided to leave this morning," Tasha said. She realized her lying was starting to become a bad habit.

Before John could ask any more about her travel arrangements, she interjected with, "So how was the service?"

John's eyes immediately lit up when he heard the question and a smile danced across his face, "It was awesome!"

"I bet it was," Tasha said as she glanced over John's shoulder hoping Lee was coming.

"God really moved and two people got saved," he continued.

"That's excellent! See, I knew you were the one for the job," she exclaimed as she watched her friend walk over to the two of them.

"Hey," Lee said interrupting the conversation.

"John, this is my best friend Lee Dickinson, Lee, this is John Samuels," Tasha said introducing the two.

"Nice to meet you," they both said in unison while shaking hands.

"You ready?" Lee asked.

Tasha couldn't be happier to hear those words. She wanted so badly to run when she saw John coming, but she wasn't raised to be rude or arrogant. The excitement she heard in his voice when he talked about the Lord caused her to be both ashamed and jealous. She remembered the zeal she once had when someone mentioned God or church, but in her current situation, she didn't want to hear about either.

"Sure am," she said to her friend while bidding John a goodbye.

*   *   *   *   *

80

"Who was that?" Lee questioned while swiftly switching lanes on I-76.

"Who? John?"

"Who? John?" Lee said mimicking her friends' response.

Tasha just laughed. "That's John Samuels."

"I know his name, but who is he?" Lee inquired in her matter-of-factly voice.

"He was in my sociology class last semester."

"Does he like you?" Lee probed.

"What?" exclaimed Tasha.

"Does he like you?" Lee asked moving her hands as if she were speaking sign language.

"No!"

"I think he does," her friend urged.

"How you figure that?" Tasha asked now curious.

"Because of the way he was looking at you."

"And what way was he looking at me?" Tasha continued.

"With all teeth."

"He was just excited because we were talking about the Lord, that's all" Tasha stated.

"Well, he might have been talking about the Lord, but he surely wasn't thinking about the Lord by the way he looked at you," her friend said jokingly.

"You are so wrong."

"Whatever! I know a look when I see one and that man gave you a look," Lee slyly suggested, coming to a stop at a traffic light.

Tasha didn't respond to her friend's observation. She just turned her head and began looking at the faces of the people on the streets. Her mind began to think back to the conversation between her and John, and tried to remember any odd looks he may have given her but she couldn't remember any. To her, it was just basic conversation. With that thought, her mind took her back to other conversations she had with him but still couldn't pick up on any awkward looks. Pulling into the parking lot of Double T's broke her from her thought. Getting out of the car and walking to the entrance of the restaurant, Tasha shook her head at her friend.

"Don't shake your head 'cause you know I'm right," Lee said holding the door for her friend to walk through first.

"Whatever, bighead," she said as the two laughed.

After finishing their meal the two girls stepped outside. The blazing heat caught them by surprise because it had gotten about fifteen degrees hotter than it was before they walked into the restaurant.

The drive back to campus was filled with much laughter. They talked and drove with all four windows down and the radio blasting – just like typical college aged girls. Both girls felt an uncertainty in the air but neither one spoke of it. They just acted like all was perfect.

Pulling in front of the dorm, they saw it was crowded with people. Not only was it check out day for those who remained, but it was also graduation day. Tasha noticed the time. She figured, since the commencement ceremony was beginning, she would take a few minutes to pack her car up and leave before everything was over and the roads would really be crowded.

Walking side-by-side to her room with her friend, Lee asked, "How many bags do you have?"

"Four," she said unlocking the door and walking into the room.

The room was stifling from the heat. Tasha had turned the air conditioner off and closed all of the windows before she left for breakfast. The warmth immediately caused the two girls to back up and stand in the hallway.

"I'll be right back," Lee said walking down the hallway.

After a few moments of preparing herself to enter the sauna that was once her room, she caught her breath and was able to walk back in and began grabbing bags. She could hear the sound of heavy feet walking down the hall towards her.

"Let me get that," a man said.

When she turned to see who it was, John, Lee and a short, dark skinned, chubby college-aged guy were standing in the doorway.

"Yeah, let him get that," Lee said with both eyebrows raised and a giant smile etched across her face.

As the two guys loaded the car, Tasha and Lee stood by talking and laughing. Tasha spoke of the dreadful ride home while her friend continued making subtle comments about her and John.

"Finished," John said as he closed the trunk of Tasha's grey Honda Accord.

"Thank you," both girls said in unison.

The other guy walked away after saying, "you're welcome" but John still stood there.

"Well, I guess you're all ready to go" he said standing in front of the two girls.

"I guess so," Tasha replied.

"Be right back," Lee said running into the dorm. John and Tasha just stood there watching her run.

"Wow, she's fast!"

"Yeah. She ran track all through high school," Tasha explained. As quick as Lee was gone, she had returned with a camera in hand.

Catching her breath, she asked John, "Can you take a picture of us"?

"Sure," he said grabbing the camera and focusing on the two girls, both with humongous smiles planted on their faces.

"One more," Lee asked after the first flash.

Repositioning himself, John flashed the camera a second time after the girls posed in a "jail-house portrait."

"Now, let me take one of you two," Lee said grabbing the camera.

Tasha's eyes got big but John just said, "Okay" as he walked over and put his arm around her.

"That's beautiful," Lee exclaimed from behind the camera as she snapped the picture.

Tasha knew her friend was up to no good, but she just tried to ignore her hoping John wasn't catching on to what was happening.

"Well guys, I'd better be going before it gets too late because I have a long drive ahead of me," Tasha said reaching for her friend.

As the two girls hugged tightly, tears began to form in Tasha's eyes. She wasn't sure if she would see her friend during her college years again or not, but she wanted to cherish that moment. Her friend just whispered in her ear, "You know I got your back, right?" Tasha didn't answer; she just shook her head "yes" because she knew exactly what she was referring to. When the two finally separated they were both wiping tears from their faces. John smiled.

"Tasha, do you mind if I pray before you leave?" John asked.

Her eyes wanted to get big but her friend beat her to the punch.

"Sure," she said.

As John prayed and the three held hands, Tasha could feel her friend squeezing her hand extra tight. She knew it was because she was making fun of John and his praying, but Tasha didn't mind one bit. As a matter of fact, she welcomed and appreciated it.

When John concluded the prayer he reached over and gave Tasha a hug. Both girls were surprised because neither one of them saw it coming. Lee had a half smirk on her face as if to say I told you so. After telling her friend she would call her when she got home, Tasha got in the car and drove off honking the horn and waving. Both John and Lee waved back. As she looked in her rear view mirror she smiled at them standing there. Then she sent up a small prayer – "thank you Lord for giving me a best friend like Lee and hopefully one day I will be thanking you for giving me a husband like John."

CHAPTER 17

When Tasha pulled up in her driveway, the clock on the dashboard read 10:15 PM. The eleven hour drive felt more like three hours because her mind raced the entire way. She thought of what would happen once she got home and had to tell her parents about her being pregnant – or would she? Her first task was to call Lisa and ask her the abortion information, but she didn't want to seem too anxious. She knew anxious people usually got caught because they were too sloppy and hurried in what they were doing. She knew she was further along than the average woman seeking an abortion, but her research had given her a time period of when she could still have the procedure done. Therefore, she still had time to get the information, make the arrangements and go through with the process before anyone knew anything.

When Tasha walked through the back door that led to the kitchen the house was dark and quiet. She knew both her parents were home because she noticed both of their cars perfectly parked in the garage when she pulled up. The bark of Coco - the chocolate brown Labrador-Retriever startled her when she clicked on the light in the kitchen. Her parents had gotten Coco when Tasha graduated from 8th grade and began her freshman year in high school as a gift for her honor roll status all through middle school. The dog had brought a much needed enjoyment to the sometimes dull and quiet home. The bark not only alerted Tasha, but also her parents. She could hear at least one of them walking across the bedroom floor, down the hall and towards the staircase as she stood in the kitchen petting the energetic dog.

"Is someone there?" she could hear her father yell from the top of the stairs.

"It's me Daddy," she said as she hurried through the kitchen over to the bottom of the staircase so her father could see her.

"Hey honey," Jared barked with enthusiasm – almost as loud as the dog.

Tasha just stood at the bottom of the stairs with a bright smile impressed across her face. The dog had followed her into the living room where she stood and continued sniffing and licking her feverishly.

"Come say 'Hi' to your mama," her father insisted when he could hear her mother in the background asking was that Tasha.

"Hey Mama," she sang in her teenagery voice while bouncing up the stairs towards her parent's room.

The room was half lit by a table lamp and the T.V. Her parents had been watching TBN. Both their faces had gleaming smiles that let Tasha know they were elated to see her. As she reached over and kissed them both on the lips, she carefully flopped across the foot of the bed and took a comfortable position.

"So, tell me how the semester ended," her father said nudging her with his foot from under the covers.

Tasha knew exactly what he meant – how were her grades? Education was always stressed in the Daniels household letting Tasha know she must do good no matter what. When she thought about it, she had made the honor roll every quarter since first grade and had only missed ten days of school since kindergarten. Because of her father's strict diet and exercise routine he had acquired in the military, her mother had always prepared meals that were nutritious; which therefore, gave little room for a poor immune system. And, since she lived in the south, there were never any snowstorms, so that was not a reason to stay out of school; as opposed to some of her cousins that had moved to New York or Ohio and had horrible winters. Therefore, only a common cold would be the reason for her to miss a day.

"The semester ended well. I did really well on all of my finals and ended with a 3.8," she said with the confidence her father had instilled in her.

"That's my girl," Jared exclaimed.

Tasha's stomach began throbbing after she realized the way she landed on the bed but brushed the pain off. Thinking about her condition was the last thing she wanted to do. As the three of them sat and watched the featured preacher work up a sweat, Tasha's mind immediately took her to John. For some strange reason, he reminded her of the Bishop when he said the word God. It had a twang. A smile glided across her face as she listened to her mother

86

praise the Lord in a quiet tone from behind her. It was almost impossible for her mother not to get involved when she heard the word of the Lord being preached. She was either going to wave her hands, shuffle her feet or let out a rambunctious hallelujah! Tasha didn't even look her way; she just continued to watch the tape as if everything was completely normal – because to Tasha, it was.

CHAPTER 18

The morning was beautiful. The birds were chirping, the sun was shining and the bacon was frying. The smell of bacon aroused Tasha's nostrils as well as her hunger. As she lay there for a minute, she realized she had not eaten since she and Lee went out to breakfast the morning before. She had not even bothered to stop for food during the ride home. She was not hungry. The longer Tasha lay there, the more her stomach began to ache. By this time, it wasn't just from being hungry, but she had begun to feel a bit queasy. Since she found out she was pregnant, she had only gotten morning sickness a few times. But she knew from the turning of her stomach, this morning would be added to one of those few. Heading towards the bathroom, she knew from past experience to take her time and walk slowly; she didn't want to pass out on her way. When she opened the door to her bedroom, Coco ambushed her in a plea for attention. "Move Coco," Tasha yelled as she pushed her way to the bathroom. Luckily, she made it before yesterdays' breakfast decorated the inside of the toilet. As Tasha washed her face, she could hear her father knocking on the bathroom door.

"Honey, are you alright?"

"Yeah Daddy, I'm fine."

"You sure?" Jared said with concern in his voice.

"I'm sure," Tasha replied trying to calm her father's worries. When Tasha opened the bathroom door, she could hear her mother calling her name as she walked up the stairs. She knew her father had told her mother about her throwing up, and like any other concerned parent, Cilla was coming to make sure all was well.

"Tasha, you okay?" her mother said as she followed her daughter to her bedroom.

"Yes."

"Are you sick?"

"No. I probably just ate something bad," Tasha said as a quick answer while taking a seat on the edge of her bed.

"You gotta be careful eating at those fast food restaurants. That food ain't always fresh," her mother added.

Tasha didn't answer; she just grabbed her pillow and tried to cover what her nightgown didn't.

"You just need something solid on your stomach. I'm gonna make you some tea and toast," her mother continued.

"Yeah, that sounds good. I'll get dressed and come right down."

"Alright sweetheart," her mother said walking from the room.

Tasha didn't want to get up until she heard complete silence in the hallway. She didn't want to take the chance that her parents would walk past her bedroom and notice her mildly protruding belly or swollen breast from underneath her nightgown. As she stood to her feet, she heard taps coming down the hall. Immediately, she hurried to shut the door and ran back to her bed. Scratches on her door let her know it had to be Coco and not her parents. Tasha felt bad for not responding to the dog's plea for attention, but right about now, she didn't feel much like being around humans *or* animals.

*   *   *   *   *

By mid-afternoon, Tasha was feeling much better. She had unpacked some of her clothes, talked with her father about his time back at work, and had lunch with her grandmother. While on her way home later that evening, she decided to take a drive around the city. Dunbar was always a beautiful city. It was a middle class suburb known for its blue velvet night skies. Because the city was along the gulf, the seaports were loads of fun during the summer months. Tourists would rent beach houses for the summer and some local celebrities would rent out the docks and have mega parties. Only those from Dunbar and surrounding cities knew of these private getaways. Being a small town was not so bad after all, especially when you were only two hours south of Jacksonville and four hours north of Orlando.

Strolling down Morgan Boulevard was a sight Tasha had missed while away at school. Saturday nights always attracted residents out to either Smoky Joe's for seafood or Mick's Mega

Rama Conglamour for skating, bowling, and pool. Skeet's was a well known, highly talked about underground hotspot for the men.

As the sun began to set and the muggy air began to cool, the city began to light up. It was officially summertime in the city. The neighboring town of Wilson was considered the "gutter-butt". It was ghetto. The men, women and children that lived there acted like they didn't know any better. Reports of murders, robberies, muggings, rapes and drug activity were constantly on the nightly news or in the newspapers; but people who weren't from the town somehow found it exciting. All of the hyped parties, ghetto fabulous men and women, and best drugs in Florida were said to be there. Because Tasha wasn't involved with the "worldly" life, none of those things ever appealed to her, but she had indeed heard of them – it was inevitable.

The blistering sound of a car horn was startling. However, Tasha paid no attention to the sounds of the beeps. She kept her face straight – looking at the light waiting for it to change. Again, she heard the horn. Not sure of whom was beeping or why, she stared at the stoplight after it had changed. "Tasha!" she heard someone call her name. When she looked around, she noticed someone in a car in the left lane – it was her friend Nicole from Kingston High. When Tasha noticed Nicole pulling over, she followed her lead.

"Hey girl," Tasha said as they hugged.

"Dang, I haven't seen you since we threw that cap in the air."

"I know. How have you been?" Tasha asked.

"Just fine, girl. You know I had a baby right?"

"What!"

"Yeah girl," Nicole said as she pointed through her car window.

A car seat was neatly positioned in the back. Tasha stared in amazement. The baby was peacefully sleeping -- not moving one inch. From the size of the baby, he or she was probably around six months. Nicole just continued to talk but Tasha's focus was on the child. Not to seem rude, Tasha paid just enough attention to answer when a question or funny comment popped up. As the two girls leaned up against the car and continued to catch up, the baby began to cry.

"May I? Tasha asked as Nicole opened the car door to pick up the baby.

"Sure."

From the blue, Tasha knew the baby was a boy. "What's his name?"

"Marcus. Marcus Anthony Powell, Jr."

"Marcus Powell? As in Snooky?" Tasha asked with both eyebrows raised.

"Yeah, girl. Me and Snooky hooked up right after we graduated. We gettin' married too," she said as she held up her left hand.

"Oh, my goodness. Congratulations!"

Both girls smiled. As Nicole continued to fill Tasha in on what happened with everyone in town over the past two years, Tasha couldn't help but focus on the baby. He was so handsome. So soft. And he smelled great. She could almost feel the kinship between the baby she held and the one she carried.

Nicole interrupted Tasha's thoughts with "Enough about everyone else, How are you doing"?

"I'm doing okay. Nothin' much goin' on with me. Same 'ole, same 'ole. School, work, you know how it is." Tasha dare not mention anything about her condition. Even after Nicole commented on her slight weight gain.

"I sure do."

When the baby began to wiggle and whine, Nicole looked down at her watch. "Oh my, its dinner time – again" she said. When Tasha passed the baby over to be placed in the car seat, her friend just continued to talk.

"Give me your number so we can hang out sometime."

"Yeah, that would be cool," she said as she passed over a piece of paper.

"I'm gonna be callin' you," Nicole said as she pulled off beeping the horn.

        *   *   *   *   *

"Hey Aunt Viv, is Lisa home?" Tasha said as she walked in the backdoor watching her aunt cooking at the stove.

"Yeah babe. She should be in her nasty ass room."

"Okay," Tasha said as she chuckled and headed for the staircase, but only after hugging and kissing her aunt.

Knocking on the door, Tasha could hear the radio blasting the song "Ignition" by R. Kelly.

"Come in," Lisa yelled over the music.

Sitting on the floor with her back against the bed putting a fresh coat of polish on her fingernails and toes, Lisa was looking grown up. She was a light caramel complexion and wore a honey-blonde wrapped weave that flowed over her caramel candy shoulders. The pink pastel sleeveless sundress she wore brought much attention to her size six waist and perky 40C breasts. The older she got, the more she resembled her mother who resembled Felicia Rashad from the Cosby's. Everyone knew Lisa was gonna be a beautiful woman – if only she could carry herself as one.

"What's up, cuz?" Lisa said as she slightly turned down the radio.

"Nuffin. Just came by to holla at ya."

Although Tasha was four years older than Lisa, they were pretty close. Lisa had tried to teach her older cousin so many things about boys, petty girls and how to handle herself in the streets, but Tasha didn't seem to take to the lessons. She felt people couldn't be as bad as Lisa was making them out to be – but she had learned they were just that – and worse. While the two sat and chatted about everyone and everything, Tasha began to get a little edgy. She wanted so bad to get to the point of why she had come over there in the first place but again, she didn't want to expose herself.

"What's up, cuz? You look a bit worried."

"Nah. Just thinking 'bout one of my girls," Tasha said trying to act nonchalant.

"Who, girl? I know her?"

"Nah. I don't think so. We went to Kingston together and I bumped into her last night. She told me she was pregnant but wants to get an abortion," Tasha uttered as her eyes darted in Lisa's direction.

"Oh."

"What you mean, oh?"

92

"Just oh. It ain't no big deal," Lisa commented as she searched for a new CD to play.

"Well, she asked if I knew of a place, but I told her no." Tasha's eyes carefully followed Lisa's reaction.

"It's places all over she can go to," Lisa said as she bumped her head to Lil' Jon and the Eastside Boys.

Tasha listened intently as her eyes traced her cousin's bedroom. The room was a mess. Clothes were spread all over the bed and floor. Shoes were scattered from one side of the room to the other. Any place shoes or clothes weren't thrown, CD's were. A huge poster of Snoop Dog with a full length white mink coat, white hat with his curly permed hair draping his shoulders, and white three piece suit, holding a gold mug that said P.I.M.P covered the wall behind her bed. On another wall was a poster of LeBron James completely naked holding a basketball that only covered his genitals. Her pale yellow curtains gently blew as a slight breeze came threw her opened window. Her oak dressers were covered with several perfumes, powders and make-up cases. The room portrayed that of a typical teenager.

"They got this new place out in Polk one of my girls was tellin' me 'bout."

"What place?" Tasha questioned

"I don't know. Some spot that's supposed to be highly confidential or some shit like that."

"Hey!" Tasha said letting her cousin know she was offended by her language.

"My bad, cuz."

The conversation between the two girls came to a halt. Only the sound of screaming "To the window, to the wall," came through as noise. Lisa answering her mother when she hollered "Telephone" broke the silence of both girls. When Lisa said "hello" a smile followed. Tasha could tell from her giggles it was a boy on the line. She didn't say anything. She just got up, waved and exited the room.

CHAPTER 19

"Doctor's office, Cyndi speaking, how may I help you," is what an even toned, southern, almost obviously white woman on the other end of the telephone line said after the second ring.

"Morning ma'am. I would like to make an appointment."

"Are you over the age of eighteen?"

"Yes ma'am".

"When was your last menstrual period?"

"Um, December thirteenth."

""Ma'am, you are a bit farther along than most of our patients. Are you sure about this?"

"Yes," Tasha quickly blurted out.

"Okay. Do you have a particular doctor in mind?" the woman asked.

"No ma'am."

"Would you like a male or a female?"

"Uh"... Tasha paused for a minute to think, "male please."

"Okay. How does Thursday, June nineteenth at 10:00 am sound?" the woman asked.

"June nineteenth!" Tasha said with dread in her voice. It was only June first which meant she had over three weeks to wait.

"Yes. June nineteenth is our first opening. Would you like that date?"

After letting out a huge sigh, Tasha answered – "That will be fine."

"May I have your name and the last four digits of your social security please"?

Again, Tasha froze before responding. "Lisa Jackson, 1024," she blurted out before even realizing what she had said or done.

"Okay Ms. Jackson. I have you penciled in for Thursday morning, June nineteenth at 10:00 AM. Do you know where we're located?"

"I'll find it."

"Any questions?" the receptionist asked.

"No, ma'am."

"I must warn you. This is a highly confidential medical facility. Everyone who enters the building must go through a metal detector. The security guards will ask you to remove your shoes and place all personal material, handbags, book-bags, items from your pockets, jackets, etc., on the monitoring belt. Make sure, and I stress, make sure you have someone to pick you up and drop you off before and after your appointment. The anesthesia will make it impossible for you to drive. Only those with appointments are allowed to enter the building – even if you're married. No spouses, children, boyfriends, parents, unless the patient is a minor and has parental permission, or other friends – No One! Once you are finished with the security process, take the elevator to the third floor and sign in. The entire procedure will take about two hours and that includes check in, anesthesia, etcetera. Any questions?"

Although Tasha's heart was racing at five hundred miles a minute, she answered with a calm, "No ma'am."

"Are you sure?" the woman asked with apprehension.

"I'm sure," Tasha replied.

"Okay Ms. Jackson. I will see you..."

Tasha interrupted the woman's closing comments as she remembered one important question: "Can you tell me the cost please?"

"Sure Ms. Jackson. The cost is $427.39. Will that be okay for you?" the receptionist asked.

Tasha wanted to scream out "four hundred dollars!" but remained composed – "That's fine."

"Any other questions?"

"No ma'am. I think that's it," Tasha said letting out another huge sigh.

Hearing the fear in her voice, the receptionist asked, "Do you mind if I gave you a word of advice?"

"Not at all, please do."

"I know the waiting period sounds dreadful, but it can also be helpful. We often tell clients, the time allows them to know for sure if they want to go through with the procedure. One thing I've realized is that almost a fourth of the women who make

95

appointments never show up or call and cancel because they have had a change of heart. Then there are other women who are too far along – twenty eight weeks or more, which you may be. We can't be sure until we complete an ultrasound once you get here. Then we either recommend you to another facility or make exceptions to the wait time."

Tasha remained as silent as a mouse as the woman spoke.

"Just think about it – okay?"

"Yes ma'am, I will, and thank you," Tasha said as she and the receptionist ended the call.

CHAPTER 20

The past couple of weeks for Tasha had been dreadful. She tried not to think of the situation she was in, but couldn't help it. It was a constant reminder each time she got dressed and felt her clothes hugging her body as they had never before. She was always tired or hungry and her nose was getting wide. Even her mother had made a comment about how her hips and butt were spreading. One thing Tasha tried to do was act as normal as possible. She didn't want her parents to suspect anything. The fact that she had already made the appointment for the abortion brought her some form of comfort because she knew it was only a matter of time she would have to continue lying.

She managed to get her job at Ashley Stewart back shortly after returning from school. Her plan was to work as much as possible – for two reasons. To get the over four-hundred dollars needed for the abortion and to stay as far away from her parents. She did not want them to see her ballooning. Since her mother was promoted at the bank Cilla offered her daughter a summer job, but Tasha quickly refused. She knew it would be impossible to be around that much without her mother noticing her body changes. It was bad enough they were going to be in the same house but she wasn't taking the chance of being on the same job. She knew her mother was a bit offended when she turned down the position, but Tasha gave her a good reason. She told her Laura, the manager from Ashley Stewart had promised her the Assistant Manager position when, and if, she came back for the summer. Cilla couldn't argue with that. Promotion was always what the Daniels strived for; that and the perfect will of God. At least Tasha had accomplished one of the two.

She had also spoken with Lee a few times telling her everything was fine, and although she had not told her parents as yet, she had decided to keep the baby. Tasha felt bad for lying to her friend. She felt like if she couldn't even tell her best friend the truth then anything was possible. Lee tried to convince her friend to tell her parents as soon as possible, but all Tasha could say was – I am, I am. Lee knew better. She had been in the same predicament once before and knew exactly what her friend was thinking and about to do – no matter what she had told her.

*   *   *   *   *

A week before the nineteenth, Tasha had a dream. She dreamt she was in an abandoned building. She wasn't alone. There were hundreds of strange women all around, but she knew none of them. Some looked as if they had been dead for hundreds of years and the smell of the building reeked with bleach. As she walked down long dark hallways that led to other long dark halls, more strange women began coming from behind closed doors trying to grab her. As Tasha began running, she heard the sound of heavy footsteps behind her. She knew they were of a man because none of the other ghostly woman was that heavy. Suddenly, as she turned down another long dark hallway, she noticed a newborn baby lying in the doorway of an empty room. She was hesitant to approach the baby, but it was crying loudly. The closer she got to the child, the more she realized the child was growing before her eyes – from a newborn to an infant to an adolescent. Tasha wanted to walk away, but she couldn't because the child continued to cry and reach out for her. As she reached back for the child, a huge hand belonging to a man grabbed her. She tried to pull away but couldn't. She tried to scream for help, but the groans of the hundreds of ghostly women drowned out her voice. She didn't know what to do.

As she struggled against the man, she tried to get a look at his face but couldn't because it was covered with a doctor's mask that only revealed his pitch black eyes. All Tasha could do was scream, "God help me!" At that moment a little old white woman with mixed gray hair and green eyes peeked from behind a door. The woman calmly walked over towards Tasha and the man and simply held up her hand – as if to say back off! The man immediately released Tasha and began to run away. When the man reached the end of the hallway, he pulled the doctor's mask

98

from his face which revealed nothing. He had no mouth, no nose or any other facial features – except for those pitch black eyes. Once the man disappeared, Tasha turned to thank the woman for helping her but she was gone – everyone was gone and Tasha now stood there alone. No groaning sounds of other women, no baby crying, not even the heavy sound of footsteps walking. Everything was quiet and still. Suddenly, Tasha woke up.

*　　　*　　　*　　　*　　　*

Working at the store was a relief for Tasha. It kept her busy and also gave her time to waste as she sorted things out in her head. She opted for the noon to close position because she knew her parents would be out of the house working during the day. That way she could walk freely around the house during the day, and work in the evenings while her parents were home. She promised her parents she wouldn't work Sundays. That way, she could still make it to service every week.

Her father had gone back to work so she knew that would free the house from anyone lingering. All that was left were her and Coco. Most mornings, her growling stomach would wake her up between 5 and 8 am. But, not until the house was clear, after her parents had left for work around 9:00 am did she get up to satisfy her cravings.

One morning, Tasha felt hot. This could have been attributed to it being the beginning of the summer, but this was a different type of hot. She felt aroused. Once the house was clear, she headed for the bathroom wearing just her baby blue cotton nightgown. As she stood looking in the mirror, she could see the shape of her nipples poking through the pajamas. When she ran her open hand gently across the right nipple, her body tingled. She had not felt that type of tingle since she had been with Curtis. Immediately, her mind took her back to the night she made love for the first time. It was as if she were back in that place. She could smell his cologne and his breath close to her. Closing her eyes, she glided her hand up and down the inside of her thigh. Her body tingled even more. She remembered how he had unbuttoned her jeans and slid his long thin fingers across her pubic hair. As Tasha stood in the middle of the bathroom floor, she reenacted this adventure. She could feel sweat beads forming on her forehead as she softly glided her fingers across her clitoris and in between her vaginal lips. Silent moans escaped from her lips as she enjoyed the pleasure she was giving herself. As she continued to caress her clitoris, the moans got louder. By now drips of sweat were falling from her chin and nose as she rolled her head around in ecstasy. Suddenly, Tasha felt dizzy. She felt as if someone had set off a row of firecrackers underneath of her. She began shaking and twitching, and her hearing and sight were beginning to fade. She couldn't move – she didn't even want to. She squeezed her eyes and her pelvis as tight as they could be squeezed closed. She felt as if she had passed from her body to outside of herself. Seconds later, she released a huge breath as her chin fell to her chest. Everything she had been holding for the past half hour was released in that one exhalation. When she lifted her head, she was shocked and confused and embarrassed. She had never experienced anything like that before and she wasn't even sure what had just happened. When she removed her hand from between her legs, it was wet and sticky. Immediately, she turned on the faucet, grabbed for the soap and began scrubbing as if she had blood on her hands, blood from another person, blood she had possibly caused.

When she returned to her room and sat on the edge of her bed, she didn't know what to think or how to react to what had just happened. She had heard of people masturbating, but always believed it to be evil – or that's what she was taught in church. In sex education class, it had been taught and thought of in an entirely different way. They said masturbation was natural and nothing to be ashamed of. Whether it was or it wasn't, it damn sure felt good!

CHAPTER 21

The night before her appointment, Tasha couldn't sleep. After getting off work, she decided to take a drive before going home. She took a dry run to the clinic as she had at least twice a week since she made the appointment. The directions the receptionist had given her were perfect. She drove slowly pass the building as if she were staking it out; as if it had a secret inside only she knew about. Actually, it did.

When she returned home, it was after midnight. The house was dark and quiet. As usual, Coco met Tasha at the back door with excitement. Too anxious and nervous about her morning appointment, Tasha wasn't tired at all. After making a sandwich, she headed for the den to check her email. When she signed online and heard those famous words "You've Got Mail", she paid it no mind. She noticed four names on her buddy list but didn't much feel like chatting with any of them. Instead, she typed in the words "Testimony of an Abortion." Dozens of sites popped up. She double clicked on the first one and began reading. Like so many other testimonies she had heard and read, these women wrote of the overwhelming guilt they felt after the fact.

Most claimed to be Christian women but went through with the abortion because they found themselves in bad situations. Some of them were previously abused by their boyfriends and did not want to have a child for the man. Some had been sexually abused and gotten pregnant because they were looking for love in all the wrong places. Others had just "slipped up." Every woman's story was different with one common denominator – none were ready to handle the responsibility of the child. Continuing to read, Tasha was frightened by a message that suddenly appeared on her screen. It was an Instant Message that read "Hi there" from a screen name she was unfamiliar with. Instead of hitting the ignore button, she only x'd out the box. A few minutes later another message appeared. Immediately, she clicked "Ignore" and signed off. Tasha was making a life decision in the morning and didn't want anyone or anything to distract her mind. On her way from the den, Tasha turned out each light as she walked by it. With the house now pitch black, Tasha felt her way throughout the house. Reaching her bedroom, she shut and locked the door before turning on a lamp. She reached for the radio, but decided against it because it was after two in the morning and she didn't want to wake her parents. Instead, she turned on the television and hit the mute button.

After getting undressed, she sat on the floor, reached under her bed, and pulled out a shoe box. The shoe box contained five hundred dollars. She worked overtime just to save enough extra money. Her parents had always expected her to bank at least seventy-five percent of her paychecks. They figured if she wasn't paying any major bills, than she shouldn't be splurging her money on nonsense. That rule didn't bother Tasha too much because she knew she could get just about anything from her parents at any time – except for anything they considered too worldly, like secular music or slightly provocative clothes. Tasha knew her parents were over protective, but they had told her it was because they loved her so much and didn't want the devil to have his way with her. Plus, she figured, she would rather them care too much than not care at all, as she had seen with so many of her friends. As she sat on the floor, she counted the money five times. She wanted to make sure it was all there. The only preparation Tasha failed to make was getting a ride to and from the clinic. She didn't know of anyone she could trust to keep her secret; either that or anyone who would not look at her differently, and still respect her even after what she had done. Tasha could feel a ball forming in her throat. She refused to cry so she just swallowed hard until it disappeared. Before she could do any more thinking, she decided to go to bed and worry about a ride in the morning.

*   *   *   *   *

The day had come. The sun was shining bright and the temperature was already in the mid eighties by the time Tasha's alarm clock sounded. The moment she hit the clock, the telephone rang. Since it was after eight o'clock, she knew she was home alone. She didn't pay the phone any mind because she figured no one would be calling for her that early. After the fourth ring, Tasha knew the answering machine would pick up. Immediately, the phone rang again. And, again after the fourth ring, the machine picked up. When the telephone rang a third time, Tasha knew it was someone who was trying to get in touch with her. She had already told her job she wouldn't be in until Monday, so it wouldn't be a reason for them to be calling. Maybe it was one of her parents she thought, as she headed down the hallway to her parents' room to answer.

"Hello," she said with a groggy voice.

"Hey, cuz."

"Hey, wassup?" she responded knowing it was Lisa.

"You up yet?"

"Uh huh," Tasha said as she rubbed the crust from her eyes.

"I need a favor."

"What's up?" she responded, hoping her cousin didn't need the favor that morning.

"I need a ride to the DMV."

"What for?" Tasha was curious.

"To get my license," the teenager sang.

"Your license?"

"Yeah, baby girl. I turned sixteen yesterday, and if you don't remember, we here in Florida can get a driver's license at that age."

"Oh darn. I totally forgot it was your birthday. My bad. Happy Birthday, cuz," Tasha said.

"Tank ya, Tank ya," Lisa said imitating a Caribbean woman. "So what's up? Can I get a ride or what?"

"Yeah, but I gotta be somewhere by quarter to 10."

"No prob. You can just drop me off?"

Tasha took a moment to think. She knew she needed a ride to the clinic and who better to help but Lisa. She trusted her cousin enough - or she hoped she could. She had one of two things she could do, either tell Lisa what was going on and see if she would help her, or drive home from the clinic alone and possibly kill herself along with innocent motorists on the road. Either way, nothing was gonna stop her from making that ten o'clock appointment.

"What time do you have to be there?"

"It don't matter, but I wanna get there early to beat the crowd."

"Look, I need your help with something," Tasha said as her voice quieted.

"What's up, cuz. You 'aight?"

Tasha could feel another ball forming in her throat. "I'll tell you when I see you."

"Okay. You want me to meet you at the house or you gonna pick me up?"

"I'll pick you ... Matter of fact; meet me at the house 'cause I still gotta get dressed. Can you get a ride?"

"Yeah. I'll grab a cab and meet you there in like a half."

"'A'ight. See you when you get here."

"'A'ight cuz," Lisa said as she hung up the phone.

*　　　*　　　*　　　*　　　*

While anxiously waiting in front of the clinic, the clock on the dashboard read 9:45. Tasha had told Lisa the entire story during the drive there, of how she met Curtis and of how they spent time together. She even told her about the night they made love. For Tasha it was a painful reminder. She knew had she only been stronger, none of this would have happened. Now she sat in front of an abortion clinic, with only her sixteen year old cousin as support. One thing Tasha was grateful for was that Lisa showed no form of judgment – not even a look. Her face remained easy and gentle.

"So, what you wanna do?" Lisa asked breaking the silence.

Tasha didn't respond. She just stared at the clock as it turned 9:49, then 9:50.

"Tash, I know you really don't wanna do this. This ain't you. So what, you made a mistake – we all do, but don't do something that you're gonna regret the rest of your life."

Tasha knew Lisa was right but at that moment an abortion was her only escape. There was no way she could tell her parents and break their hearts. She knew Curtis wouldn't be any support – emotionally or financially. Plus, he was nowhere to be found anyway, so how could he be any help? As bad as she wanted to end this dilemma and make everything go away, she couldn't. All she could do now was make a decision. When she opened the car door, walked over to the entrance, and hit the buzzer, her decision was made.

"I'll be here when you come out," Lisa said as a guard opened the door and escorted her cousin inside.

*   *   *   *   *

After signing in and taking a seat, Tasha's eyes canvassed the room. The clinic resembled any other doctor's office. There were posters on the walls that advertised condoms and safe sex. There were rows of magazines lining the tables. Everyone working there was dressed in either a nurse's uniform or a white jacket. There were three other women in the waiting room besides herself, two White and one Hispanic. All of the women looked under twenty years old. The two white women were holding a conversation while the Hispanic woman watched the television affixed to the wall. The song to the People's Court was playing when Tasha heard a name being called – "Jackson. Lisa Jackson." After the second call, Tasha remembered she had given Lisa's name instead of her own. Immediately, she jumped up and walked towards the glass window.

"I'm Lisa Jackson," she said as the nurse slid the bulletproof window back.

"Miss Jackson, can you fill these forms out and return them to me when you're finished?"

Tasha just nodded her head and took her seat again.

The forms were trivial and basic. Simple information most doctor offices asked – Do you have any history of illness in the family; Are you allergic to any medications; blah, blah, blah. One question took Tasha by surprise; it asked, "How many terminated pregnancies have you had – None, 1, 2, 3 or more." Tasha wondered how many women actually circled the answer "more." When she finished filling out the papers, she walked back up to the nurse's station.

Once the nurse glanced over the papers, she said, "Okay Miss Jackson, that will be $427.39."

Tasha reached in her purse and pulled out a wad of twenties. She counted off four hundred and forty dollars and handed it to the

105

nurse. After the nurse recounted the money, she handed Tasha a receipt and her change.

"Just have a seat and a nurse will be out to get you shortly."

Before Tasha could take her seat, she heard a name being called – "Eileen Stein." One of the white girls got up and followed the nurse as she walked behind two revolving doors. Tasha watched every move made. The other white girl that had been sitting there now began talking to her.

"Hi, I'm Claudia."

"Hi Claudia. I'm Tasha."

"Tasha? I thought I heard them call you Lisa?" the girl asked.

Tasha wanted to grab her mouth because she knew she had slipped up, but just came back and said, "My first name is Lisa but my friends and family call me by my middle name which is Tasha."

"Oh. Cool," the girl said in a chipper voice.

Tasha turned her head and looked at the Hispanic woman. She had not budged one bit from watching the television show. Tasha glanced at the clock – 10:25.

"Lisa, you look nervous. Are you okay?" Claudia asked.

"I'm very nervous. I've never done anything like this before."

"Maria Gonzales" was the name that was called once the nurse reentered the room. The Hispanic woman got up and followed the nurse behind the revolving doors, just as the other woman had done only ten minutes earlier.

Tasha watched the girl's every step as she disappeared.

"There's nothing to be nervous about. It's not as bad as you might think," Claudia whispered interrupting the rhythm of Tasha's shaking leg.

Tasha's face immediately looked puzzled, but she quickly gave Claudia a fake smile, not to let on what she was thinking.

"Yes, I've done this before, if that's what you're thinking."

That was exactly what she was thinking.

"To be honest, I've done this a few times," the girl uttered as she pulled a pack of gum from her pocket and stuck a piece in her mouth.

That statement answered Tasha's question – *there was at least one person who had circled the answer "more."*

"Lisa Jackson?" the nurse asked as she walked over to where she and the white girl had been chatting. Tasha stood up. "Follow me," the nurse added as she began to walk towards those inevitable revolving doors.

"Don't worry. You'll be alright," Claudia yelled out as Tasha waved goodbye.

The room was brightly lit and cold. It smelled like ammonia. Tasha would say it resembled a GYN office, but she had never been to one. So, all she could relate it to was what she had heard. The nurse handed her a gown and told her to get undressed, and that she would be back in five minutes. While undressing, Tasha eyed the rolling table that held several medical utensils: gauzes and pads, scissors and small surgical knives, cotton balls and a white suction tube Tasha wondered about. Trying to calm her nerves, she took deep breaths. Her even toned breathing and heartbeat relaxed her enough to hear music. It had obviously been playing over an intercom system, but that was the first time she heard it since entering the building. It was Lionel Richie's *Rhythm of the Night*. The song ended and Celine Dion's – *My Heart Will Go On* began. The nurse and a technician entered the room. Tasha was sitting on the edge of the table with her legs dangling over.

"What will happen now is the lab technician will do an ultrasound to see exactly how far along you are. The information you provided said your last menstrual period was back in December; which means, if you have already made it to thirty weeks, then we will be unable to perform the procedure – according to the laws of Florida."

Tasha's heart began to race even the more.

"Do you understand so far?" the nurse asked.

"Yes, ma'am."

"Okay then, let's get started."

Tasha kept her eyes closed. She tried to keep completely still as they poked, prodded, and pushed at her stomach. Within seconds Tasha could hear the technician say, "Wow, twenty-eight and a half weeks – exactly. You just made it."

With that response Tasha was mentally numb, even before being physically numb. The nurse continued with her original spiel.

107

"Now that that's out of the way, let me tell you about the procedure. The anesthesiologist will come in to sedate you. He will place an IV in the back of your hand, and it will take about five to seven minutes before you begin to feel drowsy. During that time, we will begin prepping you for the procedure. I will be here the entire time for support; so, at any time you feel sick or scared, just let me know, and I'll do everything in my power to make you comfortable. Any questions?"

Tasha shook her head "no" as her eyes welled with tears.

The nurse began to rub Tasha's arm. "I know you're scared, but there's really not anything to worry about. Our doctors are highly trained and this is a well respected facility. Just try to relax and I promise you, it'll all be over very shortly." As the nurse finished talking, another nurse and the anesthesiologist walked in and commenced to putting the ordeal in motion. As the anesthesiologist proceeded to insert the needle into Tasha's arm, he relayed everything he was doing, but she kept her eyes closed. She hadn't even known the doctor walked into the room until she heard his voice.

"Lisa, I'm Dr. Blair and I'll be the one performing the procedure today," he said as the other nurse that was helping set up aided him in putting on his gloves, a gown, and his mask.

As Tasha began to feel drowsy, she heard footsteps coming towards her. When she opened her eyes, she screamed. It was the man from her dream! The faceless, but pitch black eye man she thought she'd never see again – especially in the flesh. Immediately, she began kicking, knocking the table of instruments to the floor. The anesthetic was quickly bringing her motions to a halt. Everything in Tasha wanted to get out of that room. Suddenly, she jumped off the table and tried to stand to her feet. She could hear the nurses and doctor yell out for her to calm down, but Tasha didn't want to. She knew whatever it took; she had to get out of there – and fast. Bobbing and weaving as if she had just gone two rounds with Tyson, it was almost impossible for her to stay on her feet. She fell, but continued to get back up. She stood up against a back wall holding something she had grabbed off of the floor. Suddenly, she felt something very strong grab her until her world went black and she felt no more.

*   *   *   *   *

"Lisa. Lisa. Open up your eyes."

Slowly, Tasha tried to open her eyes but they felt as if they were glued shut.

"Lisa Jackson. Open up your eyes," she continued to hear someone standing over top of her say.

"Where am I?" Tasha managed to ask through her groggy state.

"You're in a doctor's office," the voice answered.

As Tasha managed to get her eyes open and focused, she was in a room with four other women. She could hear at least one of them snoring and the sound of a television in the background. She knew it was the recovery room.

"What happened?"

"You came in to terminate a pregnancy," the nurse began.

Suddenly Tasha tried to jump up again, but found something restraining her. Her arms had been tied to the bed.

"Calm down, Lisa. Calm down," the nurse said as she gently caressed Tasha's arm.

Instantly she began to cry. She did not know what had happened, but she knew it wasn't good.

"Lisa. We have your Aunt Vivian here."

Tasha began crying even harder. How did they know to call her Aunt Viv, she thought? When she turned her head, Lisa was standing there. She walked over and began rubbing Tasha's head. "Calm down, honey. I'm here. I'm here." Thank goodness Lisa looked older than what she actually was, or else, there would have been no telling what could have happened to Tasha.

"Thankfully our security officer noticed an unfamiliar car parked out front. It was your aunt," the nurse said. "Once you collect yourself, we'll discharge you."

When the nurse left the room, Lisa leaned down and kissed Tasha's forehead. That was all she really could do for her.

Fifteen minutes later, Tasha was in the bathroom getting dressed. Lisa had signed all of the papers needed for discharge, and both girls were preparing to exit the building. Not until Tasha got to the car, did she realize she could walk without any help.

109

"Please tell me what happened in there?" Tasha asked as Lisa drove home.

"I'll tell you this much – you almost went to jail for cutting up some people; and you better think of a way to tell your folks they're gonna be grandparents."

CHAPTER 22

A week had passed before Tasha was back to her normal self. Her mind had continually gone over the clinic incident dozens of times. And still, she had no idea what to do next. Going back to work was probably the best thing for her – at least it kept her occupied – especially her mind.

The days were long but Tasha didn't have a problem with that. As long as she stayed out of the house and out of her parents' reach, she still had time to think of how she would break the news to them. Her body was continuing to grow – especially her belly. She had been very careful of what she ate and when she ate it. She knew since she worked evenings, the only real time for her to eat would be at night. And anyone who's ever dealt with a weight issue knows better than to eat and go to sleep. She did everything she could to modify her food intake. She ate salads constantly and drank plenty of water. Her other favorite meal was grilled chicken. That way, she would still get a meat to keep up her energy. Whatever she had to do, she did. Thankfully, she worked at a plus sized clothing store, so buying clothes to fit her changing figure was not a problem.

As the summer progressed, Tasha's job kept her busy. Although she did everything in her power to stay away from her parents, she still managed to make it to service every week as she had promised them.

One mid-July Sunday afternoon, as the service was closing, the Pastor ended the benediction with, "Turn and hug your neighbor." As the members of the congregation hugged and praised the Lord to each other, Sis. Margaret came from across the church and began to hug Tasha. By this time, Tasha had learned how to maneuver her body so no one could feel her protruding belly; like how they teach a woman to hug a man without rubbing up against him. The hug initially started off friendly, until Sis. Margaret began speaking in tongues. "Oh no, not now," Tasha thought as she lightly tried to pull away but the evangelist held her too tight. Sis. Margaret was known for giving out "words from the Lord." Some people would say she was propha-lying, because she was never on point of what was happening in the person's life; but she was convinced God had indeed spoken to her about them. Tasha knew whatever Sis. Margaret was about to do wasn't going to be good.

"I say, I say unto you...," is what Sis. Margaret continued to say as she spoke in tongues between her saying and her pacing.

Tasha didn't know what to do. Her first instinct was to run, but her parents had taught her to respect elders and especially so called ministers of God.

"A mighty woman of God. Mighty woman of God shall come forth. Mighty. Mighty. Mighty. A mighty woman of God shall come forth."

Tasha was horrified this was happening and somewhat relieved because the church was almost completely cleared out. Only her mother and the musicians having a meeting remained to see the entire ordeal. Tasha wasn't sure what Sis. Margaret was taking about. She was probably talking out of her head as she did so many other times. All she could do was stand there until the evangelist was finished.

When Sis. Margaret began walking away, bent over and still speaking in tongues, Tasha ran into the bathroom. She needed a few minutes to get herself together. What in the world was Sis. Margaret thinking? Why would she do that? What had I done to her that she would try to play me like that? Tasha thought as she gazed at herself in the mirror.

When Tasha emerged from the bathroom, her father was standing in the side exit talking with the Pastor. She hoped they weren't talking about what had just happened. Al, the drummer, made the loony sign on the side of his head as Sis. Margaret left through the front door of the church. "She crazy," Tom, the organist said as he and Al laughed out loud. "You ready, sweetheart?" Jared said as he and the pastor hugged and said their goodbyes. Tasha didn't answer. She just walked towards her father, and outside where her mother had been talking with the pastor's wife.

When the three of them got into the car, Tasha could tell her mother was obviously upset. Priscilla's face hadn't changed much, but Tasha knew her mother. Tasha wouldn't say anything about it and she hoped neither of them would either, but she knew that was near impossible.

"I can't believe she did that," Cilla said as they drove home.

Tasha didn't respond but Jared answered with, "You know how she is."

"I don't care how she is. She should be sat down for doing that. She is completely outta order and everyone knows it – over there propha-lying to people!"

"Well, you're not the Pastor, so until *he* sits her down, you have no say so in the matter. Just let God handle..."

Cilla cut him off before he could finish. "Now you know that was outta order. The word says we should do everything in decency and in order."

"I know what the word says. And it also says, judge not lest ye be judged," Jared said.

Tasha said nothing. She just sat in the back seat staring out of the window. It was just like her father to see the good in everyone. She kept quiet as her parents went back and forth on the topic. When Jared pulled the car into the driveway the three of them sat there for a moment.

"Honey, are you okay," her father asked looking at her through the rear view mirror.

Tasha just put a fake grin on her face "Yeah Daddy, I'm fine. Sis. Margaret don't mean no harm."

"Huh," Cilla said as she got out of the car and stormed into the house.

*   *   *   *   *

The days continued to fly by. Cilla always told Tasha once the Fourth of July came, it was time to prepare for the next year of school, and she was right. The fall clothing line began arriving at the store. When Tasha opened the first box, her heart skipped a beat because she knew she would not be going back to school – not if she didn't handle her problem, and fast.

113

The store was beginning to receive a steadier clientele. The kids were preparing to return to school which meant clothes shopping. Tasha noticed how so many more teenage girls were wearing larger sizes. She had been hearing about the increase in obesity among teenagers, but she had no idea the problem was so great until they came into the store. There were fifteen and sixteen year olds wearing size 30W. Tasha felt her size 16 was too much for her frame, and she was almost twenty years old.

As the pace of the store picked up, it gave Tasha the escape she needed – busyness. She never did drugs or drank, so her only escape was to stay busy. Most of the time she read anything she could get her hands on, from old textbooks to thousand page novels. *"Roots"* was her favorite book of all times, but her favorite author was Toni Morrison; probably because she wrote like Tasha's grandmother talked – back and forth.

One Saturday afternoon as the store was bustling with customers, Tasha noticed a poorly dressed middle-aged white woman with dirty blonde hair and a gut halfway to her knees. With her was an oversized teenager who looked just like her – probably her daughter. At first, they seemed to just be regular customers, until the older woman came to ask that one of the dressing rooms be opened, and Tasha noticed several bags that appeared to be empty. It was customary for the sales associates to secretly count the number of items a customer had before going into the dressing room, so that's what Tasha did. Ten minutes later, when the dressing room door opened and both women emerged; Tasha's eyes only noticed half of the original six items. Already busy at the cash register, she motioned for another associate to keep an eye on them. As the young white female associate closely watched the two women, she also noticed the older woman enter the dressing room twice but only reappearing with half of the items. Tasha and the young associate continued to keep eye contact until Tasha was finished at the register, and was able to approach the woman and her teenage daughter.

As Tasha followed the woman and her daughter to the exit, she stopped them just as they were about to walk out.

"Excuse me, Ma'am," Tasha called out.

The two acted as if they didn't hear Tasha's call until she shouted again – "Ma'am!"

114

"Yeah?" the older woman said as the teenager stood there quiet and obviously nervous.

"Ma'am, may I check your bags," Tasha said trying to be discrete.

"What for?" the woman questioned.

"If you would just follow me to the back, I could check your bags and let you leave."

"What the hell do you need to check my bags for," the woman yelled.

Heads began to turn as all attention was now on the commotion. Just then, Julie, the young white associate who had been helping Tasha scope the two out, walked up.

"Tasha, do you need some help?" Julie asked.

"Thank goodness for some real assistance," the older white woman smirked, turning her face up.

Tasha stood back to see what Julie could do even though she was only an associate, and Tasha was the assistant manager.

"Ma'am, there's no need to yell. Ms. Daniels here has a suspicion there could be some stolen items in those bags."

"Mom, let's just go," the teenager said slightly pulling on her mother's arm.

"Don't no dumb Nigger scare me," the woman lashed out.

Both Tasha and Julie's heads drew back; along with several other shoppers who had heard the comment. At that moment, two young white security guards walked through the entrance.

"Is there a problem here?" one of the guards asked.

Julie didn't say anything, she just looked at Tasha.

"Julie, can you finish with the remaining customers, while I handle this"?

Some of the customers had begun to leave once the woman began raising her voice. The other customers remaining continued paying for their things, as two other associates now operated the cash registers.

"Don't take no orders from no Nigger," the woman demanded, as Julie began to walk away. "She's only a cashier. You're the boss!"

"Ma'am, we would like to talk with the manager," one of the guards said, motioning for Julie to come back over.

"I am the manager," Tasha said trying to keep her composure but obviously offended.

Tasha was upset. She had never been called a Nigger – at least not to her face. If Julie hadn't spoken up, they probably would not have believed she was who she said she was. After calling the police, making out a report, and seeing the woman and her daughter handcuffed, Tasha wanted to slap them in the face, but it would have been pointless. Even as the police questioned Julie on what exactly had happened, the woman called her a "Nigger lover" from across the room. Tasha could not believe racism was still so alive in the 21st Century. But what else should have been expected? After all, they were still in the deep south.

*   *   *   *   *

When Tasha returned home that night, she was exhausted. Besides the shoplifting incident, she had worked ten hours due to the manager calling out sick. There were five messages on her bedroom door – two from Lee, one from Nicole, one from Lisa, and one from a guy who didn't leave his name. Tasha wondered who the guy could be but she was too tired to worry about it then. Although it was just a little after eleven and she knew Lee and Lisa were waiting for her call, her only thought was getting in her bed and singing herself some lullabies. "I'll call 'em back tomorrow," she thought to herself as she slid into her nightclothes, turned the air conditioner to medium, and slipped into dreamland.

The next morning Tasha could hear the birds chirping and the music blasting. It was a ritual of her mother's to play gospel music extra loud on Sunday mornings. As a deep baritone voice crooned she knew it could only be one person – Reverend James Cleveland. Cilla was the ultimate Cleveland fan. His raspy voice and powerful lyrics set Cilla in the perfect mode for praise and worship. Tasha could also hear her mother singing along with the lyrics to "I Don't Feel No Ways Tired," which was her favorite song. Anytime the devil would attack, Cilla would always put that song on repeat. That was her way of telling the enemy she was going to be on the Lord's side 'til the day she died. Tasha figured

116

her father was probably in the den reading a few chapters as he did every morning – no matter which day it was.

Tasha knew sooner or later her mother would be knocking on her to door to wake her for Sunday service, but this week Tasha was going to have to decline gracefully. There would be no way she could get up after the day she had had.

Tasha heard a knock at her door – precisely as anticipated. She quickly covered herself with a sheet before answering, "It's open."

Cilla walked in greeting her daughter with a cheerful, "This is the day the Lord has made, let us rejoice and be glad in it!"

"Morning," Tasha said as she buried one side of her face into the pillow.

"You going to church this morning?"

"I don't think so. I am exhausted from last night."

"What happened last night?" her mother asked.

"A shoplifter." Tasha didn't want to get too much into details, so she left it at that.

"Sin, sin, sin," Cilla said as she shook her head.

Tasha didn't respond to her mother's comment. Tasha hadn't even noticed that she had dozed off until she could feel someone pulling the covers off her. When she snatched them back, she could see the strange look on her mother's face.

"Sorry, Ma. I must have drifted off."

Cilla just laughed. "Go 'head and get some rest. I'll see ya later," she said as she left the room closing the door behind her.

*   *   *   *   *

That was some much needed rest Tasha thought when she opened her eyes. During her sleep, the telephone had rung a few times but she was too tired to get up and get it. Her first instinct was to put on her neon green knee length sun dress. She had not worn it since coming home in May. It was probably too small by now, she thought as she grabbed it from the closet, held it up to her body, and modeled it in the mirror. Even if it did fit, it would hug her body so tight that her secret would be out for sure. Instead, she opted for her ankle length jean skirt, neon green sleeveless straight shirt that she had brought two sizes too big, and her neon green and

117

white Keds. Tasha was never one for lots of colors until Lee began delving into her wardrobe. Lee let Tasha know that because of her complexion and mystique features, she could try an array of colors without being too gaudy. After admiring her attire from head to toe, she realized her friend was right – once again.

That afternoon, Tasha decided to visit her grandmother. Her days had been so busy that she never had time to spend with anyone. First, she called Lee back. They spoke for about an hour before Tasha called Lisa back. Both girls had the same question for Tasha – "Did you tell your parents yet?" Of course the answer was "no". It was still going to be a few days before she would get up the courage to expose her secret to the world. At least Nicole didn't bother her with her condition; mainly because she knew nothing about it. She just wanted to see if Tasha was available to go out with a few of the girls from high school. By the time Tasha called back, it was the next day which means she had missed the mini reunion and all the fun – if there were any. But, that was okay with Tasha because she didn't feel much like being around people. She still hadn't figured out who the guy was that left the message. She concluded whoever it was, if he wanted her that bad, he would have left a name or would call back.

When Tasha entered her grandmother's house, her grandmother was sitting at the kitchen table reading her bible and humming a spiritual. Although it was early August, the air conditioner was off and she had a quilt across her legs as if she were cold. Only an oscillating fan on low blew cool clean air throughout the house. It was so good to see Nana. Her birth name was Marlene, but all of her grandchildren called her Nana, simply because that's what southern folks did. Tasha chuckled when she bent down to hug and kiss her grandmother, because of her attire. She wore an old fashioned night gown. It was long sleeved and floral, and quit at the knee. Her knee-highs met where the hemline of the gown ended. It was the perfect picture of a house mother. Marlene was a short petite woman, only about 4feet 11 inches tall, and weighed presumably 110 pounds soaking wet. Her peaceful spirit showed on her countenance, as a welcoming smile was always etched across her face. Although her hair was a beautiful snowy white, she always wore a turban because she believed holy women should keep their heads covered. At age seventy-four, wisdom and grace were her signature characteristics, while honesty and humility were her star qualities. No doubt about it, she was certainly a virtuous woman. Her favorite saying was, "Ain't that the truth." Each time someone agreed with what Marlene said, she would respond with, "Now ain't that the truth."

"Nana, what's new?" Tasha asked her grandmother as she took a seat besides her.

"Oh, nothin' much."

"Did you go to service this morning?"

"Of course, baby. Nana's favorite place is the Lord's house," Marlene declared.

While Tasha sat and listened to her grandmother quote verbatim the preacher's message, she wondered about the woman sitting across from her. What had her life been like? Had she ever been an embarrassment to her family, as Tasha was to hers? Tasha wanted so badly to tell her Nana all of her secrets. She knew if anyone was loving and sympathetic, Nana would be.

Tasha interrupted her grandmother. "Nana? Can I ask you something?"

"Of course, baby."

"I have something on my chest I need to get off, but I don't know how to tell it."

"Just say it baby," her grandmother crooned in her smooth southern accent.

"It's not that easy, Nana."

Nana paused for a minute to choose her words carefully. "Sometimes having to reveal a secret is not easy, especially when you will certainly be chastened for it." She took a sip of a glass of water that had been sitting on the table. "I know people make mistakes, but I also know it's up to them to either handle them maturely or run like cowards and cover their sin. Either way, the music has to be faced."

Tasha's eyes widened. Was her grandmother's discernment kicking in? Did she know that much about Tasha that she knew her secret would bring on those types of consequences?

"Nana, do you know my secret?"

Marlene laughed out loud. "Sweetheart, Nana has been on this earth long enough to know lots of secrets. And one thing I am very sure about is that you are in the family way."

119

Tasha wanted to cry but she couldn't. She was too shocked at her grandmother's observation, although very true.

"Because I haven't gotten a call from your mother, I take it you haven't told her or your father as yet?" Marlene said with one eyebrow slightly raised.

"No, ma'am," Tasha confessed with her head bowed in shame.

The older woman grabbed the hand of the younger one. "Tasha, I know you're a good girl. You have always been, so I know for something like this to happen, it was a sheer accident. Am I right?"

"Yes."

"Well, now that it has happened, you have to be a woman about it. You have to tell your folks before they find out."

Tasha lifted her head swiftly. "Nana..."

She didn't get a chance to finish her words before her grandmother cut her off. "No. I'm not going to tell on you. You're a grown woman and that's your business. But I will tell you this. From the shape of your nose and hips, I know you're at least seven or more months, so you better decide when you're going to let your folks know."

"I've been trying to find a way to tell them, but..." Tasha began to sob.

"Hush now," Nana said as she patted her granddaughter's hand, "everything will be okay."

"They're going to kick me out."

"I doubt that. They will be hurt, but I don't think they will put you out."

Tasha continued to sob.

"If it be so, you have to deal with it. Just remember, I always have room here."

Tasha knew at that very moment her life was about to change – even the more.

CHAPTER 23

With five days before school was to start, Tasha had yet to pack her clothes. Cilla had questioned her about being ready to return the next weekend but Tasha just gave her an "I'll be ready by then" remark. It had been almost two weeks since Tasha and her grandmother had talked and she had still not revealed her secret to her parents. It was getting to the point that Tasha's life revolved around lies and seclusion. As long as she was alone, she was fine. The moment someone stepped into her presence, she balled up like a turtle protecting itself from an enemy.

Lee had called her to ask her if she would be returning on the twenty-first, and Tasha gave her a "for sure" answer that she would be there – with or without child in womb.

As usual, Tasha began packing her things that Monday morning after her parents had left for work. She knew the routine of packing summer clothes and winter clothes in separate suitcases. The fact that she had brought a whole new wardrobe to fit her flourishing figure left little room for "maybe outfits." Tasha figured if she could take two days to pack, that meant she could leave two days earlier and just stay with Lee in Philadelphia. That way, she would already be out of the house before she sprung the news on Cilla and Jared. That was a perfect plan, she thought as she sat on her bedroom floor rolling up clothes and neatly packing them into several different suitcases. Her agenda was set and she knew exactly what to do.

By Wednesday, she was packed and ready to roll. She had already arranged to stay with Lee. Then the two of them could drive into Baltimore together. It was perfect. Her last day of work was that night, so she had all Thursday morning to load her car and leave, before she was even missed.

Thursday morning came like any other day. The sun was shining, the birds were chirping, and the bacon was frying. When Tasha got up to pee it was a little after 7:30. She could hear her parents down in the kitchen discussing a few house bills. She could also hear Diane Sawyer's voice, which meant the television was tuned to "Good Morning America". She knew her parents were on their way out, so she told herself, "*Just give them thirty minutes and the house will be all mine's.*" When she returned to her room, she hit the mute button on her remote control. Tasha always slept with the television on and the volume either on low or on mute. It was one of those pet peeves of her's – to have some form of noise, whether it was TV or radio. She flipped through the channels until she came to the "Good Morning America" show her parents had been watching. Diane discussed the rise in HIV among teenagers and young adults. The rates were astronomical, Tasha thought, as she stared at the clock waiting for it to read 8:10. The study showed the highest rates of infection were among black women between the ages of 15-45. Although the information was important, she didn't pay much attention because she had only been with one man and she figured he was clean. The study spread across the country, with interviews from teens that were infected. "Uh, uh, uh," she said as she watched a young white girl from a middle class background go coffin shopping with her parents. As the interviews continued, she could hear the front door open and close, an engine start, and a car pull out from the garage. "Finally, they're gone," she said as she jumped up and headed to her closet to pick out an outfit for the day. She knew it would have to be something comfortable because she knew she would be driving for almost twenty hours. She knew she had had enough sleep to drive at least twelve hours straight that day, stop at a motel for the night, and then hit the road first thing in the morning.

The house sounded still and quiet from upstairs. She had picked out white Capri pants and a white oversized sleeveless blouse that fit her breasts then flared outward. It was stylish yet comfortable. She gently lay the clothes on the bed not to wrinkle them, turned the radio on to the station that played oldies, and headed for the bathroom humming the song playing – "*Ain't Too Proud to Beg*". Tasha moved freely through the hallway as she waited for the bathtub to fill with water. Once she returned to the bathroom and disrobed, she caught a glimpse of herself in the elongated mirror hanging on the back of the door. She was amazed at the shape her body had evolved into. That was the first time in months she had seen her body fully naked. Her skin was smooth and creamy – like vanilla pudding. It had both a glow and an essence that exemplified a woman of integrity and intrigue. Both breasts were full and plump. Her nipples were as hard as bullets waiting to be fired off. They stood at attention when a light breeze blew through the bathroom window. The roundness of her belly was engaging. As she massaged and caressed the child that grew inside, she felt a kick. Actually, she saw it. When Tasha looked in the mirror, she saw and felt something foreign outlining her abdomen. An arm or maybe a foot poked out through the skin as if it were trying to escape. It was both an amazing and scary sight. Continuing to stroke her body, she ran her hands across her hips. They had bloomed and spread into those of an African queen. At that moment, she knew exactly what the saying "baby making hips" meant. Turning slightly to the left, she noticed her enlarged backside. It had curved even the more. Tight and firm, she grabbed and squeezed it as a slave master would do as he considered the buy. Wow, she thought, as she eased into the lukewarm water.

After getting dressed, she sat on her bed and began writing her parents a goodbye letter; she planned on being gone by the time they returned from work. Her father had packed her car up the night before and she was mentally going over anything she may have missed when the doorbell startled her. Immediately, she heard her mother call up the stairs, "Tasha, do you have five dollars I can borrow?" Tasha had no idea her mother had been home the entire time she was prancing around. She figured she had left when the house got quiet, but then remembered she only heard one car start up and pull off. "Yeah Mama, it's in my wallet." Instantly it dawned on Tasha that her mother had told her the new washer and dryer would be delivered today. Darn! Now Tasha knew she had to say goodbye to her mother the proper way. Tasha decided not to go downstairs until she heard the door close, which meant the delivery men were gone. Adjusting her hair and gathering her thoughts, she emerged down the stairs. Her mother was sitting on the sofa with a grim look etched across her face.

"Hey Mama," Tasha gleefully said as she gracefully bounced down the steps.

"What is this?" Cilla angrily asked holding up a crinkled sheet of paper.

Tasha didn't recognize the paper so she answered, "I don't know."

"It fell out of your wallet when I was getting the money."

Tasha's heart began to race. *Please don't let it be what I think it is*, she said under her breath.

"This paper says you're pregnant!"

Tasha didn't say anything. She just stood there with her head bowed in disgrace.

"Please tell me it's not true," her mother pleaded.

Still no answer.

"It can't be true. You don't even look as far along as this paper says."

Again, not a peep came from Tasha.

"Say something!"

She couldn't. She just covered her face and loudly cried.

"How could you do something like this?" Cilla screamed out, and then suddenly jumped up and slapped her daughter across the face before she even realized her hand was raised!

Again, Tasha didn't answer. She fell to her knees as her mother stood over her yelling, "God help me!"

From the position of Tasha on the floor, her mother could clearly see the shape of her daughter's circular belly. She had hoped all this was a dream, but when Tasha's shirt was pulled to the side as she slid on the carpet, she knew it was no dream. Cilla didn't know what else to say. When she realized what was happening, she took a few steps back and sat on the sofa in silence. Tasha was still stretched out on the floor with her hands over her face sobbing.

"Get up!"

Tasha didn't move, but her crying had calmed to a whimper.

"Get off the floor," her mother repeated.

Tasha began picking herself from the floor and looking for a chair. When she sat down and grabbed a few tissues from the coffee table, her mother began taking deep breaths.

"According to this, you're about eight months. Is that right?" Cilla asked holding up the paper.

"I think so."

"What do you mean you think so? Haven't you been to a doctor?"

Tasha just put her head down.

Cilla let out a sigh. "You haven't been to a doctor," she began to yell, but quickly realized her tone.

"I just thought..."

"Thought? Obviously you didn't," Cilla interrupted.

The room got quiet. Neither Tasha nor Cilla said anything. The mother sat there looking up to heaven while the daughter lowered her head. Distress had formed a hot thick cloud around the coolness the air conditioner provided. Moments later, the silence that controlled the room was arrested by Cilla demanding Tasha to come with her. No questions were asked. Tasha just got up and followed her mother as she grabbed her car keys and headed for the garage.

*   *   *   *   *

"May I help you?" a woman behind the glass window said. Cilla and Tasha had arrived at the doctor's office in record time. It was amazing the police didn't pull them over; according to the speed Cilla was driving.

"I would like to see Dr. Mason – if he's here."

"Do you have an appointment?" the receptionist asked.

"No. This is an emergency."

"What seems to be the problem?"

"She's having some female problems," Cilla said pointing to Tasha, but never turning around to look in her direction.

"Actually, Dr. Mason's schedule is full for the rest of the afternoon. Would you like to make an appointment for another day? Perhaps Friday?

"No. I need to see the doctor now," Cilla demanded.

The receptionist looked at Cilla, then at Tasha and back at Cilla. She could tell by Cilla's bloodshot eyes something was seriously wrong, and she wasn't leaving until she saw a doctor. "Wait one moment here, ma'am. I'll see if the doctor can squeeze you in."

When the receptionist returned with Dr. Mason, Cilla was still in the same stance. She looked as though she had not budged one inch – not even to breathe.

"How can I help you Miss...?" The doctor was trying to remember Cilla's name.

"Mrs. Daniels."

"Ah yes, Mrs. Daniels."

"My daughter here is having some female problems."

The doctor looked over Cilla's shoulder and saw Tasha standing there with a look of guilt and confusion on her face. "What seems to be the problem, young lady?" Dr. Mason asked.

"I'm pregnant." Tasha barely got the words out.

"You are?" the doctor asked as he, Cilla, and the receptionist all focused on her belly.

"Yes," Tasha said in a quiver. She could hear her mother's breathing escalated.

"She's about seven or eight months, and hasn't seen a doctor as yet," Cilla yelled.

"Okay," Dr. Mason responded and told a nurse walking by to get OB Room 4 ready.

Within fifteen minutes, Tasha, Cilla, and a nurse were entering the prepared room. A fear gripped Tasha, instantly remembering the last time she was in a doctor's office to handle her pregnant situation. While the nurse prompted her to get undressed and adjust herself on the table, the doctor walked in. After going through the customary questioning involved in pregnancy, he told Tasha he would have to examine her. As he parted her legs, she was tense. She wanted so badly to talk to her mother, but knew that was the last thing Cilla wanted. When the doctor slid his fingers inside her she let out a slight shriek. "Just breathe," he cautioned. Her mother and the doctor didn't know it, but that was Tasha's first GYN exam.

"So far everything seems normal, but since your abdomen isn't the normal size of a fetus at thirty or so weeks, I want to do an ultrasound to measure the fetus' position, weight, height, and vertebrae," Dr. Mason announced, as he tossed the used gloves in the garbage.

When he flicked on a huge machine that was sitting to the side, a computerized monitor lit up. As he squirted the cold gel on her belly and placed the stick in the midst of the gel, a sound of life instantly filled the room. The heartbeat was clear and strong. Without delay, Tasha looked at the screen. She could finally see what she was carrying; what she had tried to ignore but was unsuccessful. She saw her mistake manifested in the flesh. She could hear her mother crying from across the room. How she wanted to console her, but the tears were her fault. The doctor didn't stop – not even to ask questions. He just continued with the examination. He went over step by step the activity of the fetus; of how it was a bit small for its age, but didn't seem to have any complications. The encounter became too much for Cilla, which caused her to leave the room in tears. As the doctor completed his examination, he filled Tasha in on what he figured she didn't know or refused to admit to.

"According to your last menstrual period, the size and formation of the vertebrae, I would date the fetus to be approximately thirty-five weeks." He could tell by her face that she had tons of questions. "You are a bit underweight – as far as carrying a fetus, but you seem to be a normally healthy teenager. What I would suggest is that you enhance your protein intake. That way, the fetus will have a better chance of propelling to a normal weight for the remainder of the term." A tear rolled down the side of Tasha's face. "I know you're scared, and I know your mother is upset, but the truth of the matter is you're pregnant, and you now have to take care of yourself." Tasha nodded her head in agreement. Dr. Mason eased Tasha's heart and mind when he said, "she is just fine."

*   *   *   *   *

The silence during the ride home was excruciating. Cilla never said a word to her daughter – let alone even looked her way. When they got in the house, Cilla headed straight to her bedroom. Tasha didn't know what to do. She wanted to talk to Lee, but didn't want to bother her. Lisa also crossed her mind, but she was already back in school, and since it was only ten after twelve, Tasha knew for sure she wasn't available. All Tasha thought to do was go for a drive. When she returned home three hours later, her mother and father were sitting in the living room. She didn't know what her mother had told him thus far, so she just waited for either of them to say something before she opened her mouth.

"Is it true?" Jared asked.

"Yes."

He began rubbing his hand across his head.

"How could you, Tasha?"

The tears streaming down her face was her answer. Not another word came from her father's mouth. He simply got up, walked past Tasha as if she were not even standing there, and went into the den closing the door behind him.

"I think you better go stay at your grandmother's for the night. I already called her so she's expecting you," Cilla said as she walked away leaving her daughter standing in the middle of the living room floor.

When Tasha got to Marlene's house, Marlene greeted her with a big hug. As the two stood in the doorway, the teenager found refuge in the arms of her elder. That was exactly what she needed – mercy. Marlene bid her granddaughter to eat dinner, but Tasha declined – heading straight for the spare bedroom. "I love you darlin'," her grandmother said as Tasha disappeared behind a closing door. With the excitement of the day, everyone, even Tasha, had forgotten it was her twentieth birthday.

CHAPTER 24

Two weeks had passed and nothing had changed. Tasha's parents still refused to talk to her, she was still staying with her grandmother, and most of all, she was still pregnant. School had already begun which put Tasha in an even bigger funk. She had spoken to Lee quite a few times and told her how everything transpired; but the point of the matter was Tasha was in a bad situation, and no one could do anything about it. Her friend filled her in on what was going on at school. She had promised Tasha she wouldn't tell anyone Tasha was pregnant, even though so many had asked about her. She just told them Tasha decided to take a semester off and work and return in the spring. She needed a lie that was easy to remember and easily believable. John was the only person Lee actually wanted to tell the truth to. She knew how he felt about Tasha, even if Tasha didn't want to believe it herself. Through all the two hour, every other day conversations, and the dozens of e-mails each week, Lee's friendship was just enough to keep Tasha sane; that, and the daily talks with her grandmother. One thing, if any, Tasha was most grateful for, besides having somewhere to live, was the love and compassion her grandmother showed her. At a time like this, that was what she needed most.

The delivery date continued to creep up on Tasha. The closer the time got, the more she thought of what would happen. Will it be painful? Will I have complications? Will the baby be alright? She constantly beat herself up with question after question; worry after worry. She had never been this close to someone pregnant, so she didn't know what to expect. She asked Nana how it was with her own children, but her grandmother never told her horrifying stories, only those of love and joy. She wanted her granddaughter to know that no matter what people said – even her parents – this child was going to be a blessing.

Tasha had also managed to gain some weight; not much, but enough to ease the doctor's fears when she went for her weekly check-up. Dr. Mason had told her that she needed weekly care since she was within six weeks of her delivery date. Tasha obeyed and had been faithful with her appointments. Two weeks before her actual due date, she went for her regularly scheduled two o'clock appointment. As she was being examined, she could see the strange look on the doctor's face. Not sure of what the problem was, she waited to see if Dr. Mason would tell her what was wrong before she asked.

"From the size of your cervix, I would say that you're already two centimeters."

"What does that mean?" Tasha asked.

"Well, it could mean two things. One, we miscalculated your due date and you are actually forty weeks already. Or two, we calculated your due date correctly and you will just be going in early. Either way, you're already in labor."

Tasha just lay on the exam table with her mouth hanging open. She couldn't believe it. This was the moment she had dreaded most, and it was here.

"So what should I do?"

"There's really not much you can do except let the labor naturally progress. Sometimes when a woman goes into labor, it could be a false labor which means she begins having sporadic contractions. Every woman is different, but it generally means there are still a few more days before she is actually in active labor. On the other hand, some women will immediately go into active labor and it could be only a matter of hours before they're ready to deliver."

Following each syllable that formed in Dr. Mason's mouth, Tasha focused directly on his face. She could almost hear her grandmother talking – simply because earlier that morning, over breakfast, Marlene made a statement that she thought Tasha would go in early; especially with the way her stomach had begun to take shape. The more the doctor talked, the more she felt anxious. Inside she was emotionally unstable, but outside she was as cool as a fan.

"Like I said, every woman is different, so all we can do is wait to see if you're in the first or second group."

"I feel fine."

"That's normal," Dr. Mason added. "I wouldn't really concern myself until your embryonic sac breaks. Until then, you're not in any danger of infection or anything like that."

"So are you telling me I should go home until my water breaks?" Tasha asked.

"That's exactly what I'm telling you."

There was nothing Tasha could do but wait. After what the doctor had told her, and what her grandmother had said earlier that morning, it almost seemed evident that she would go in early – when? – only God knew.

That night as Tasha talked to Lee through Instant Message, she felt the urge to pee. That was nothing new because she had become accustomed to peeing every other hour. As normal, she peed, but when she returned to her room and sat on the bed, she felt a sharp pain in her butt. She paid it no mind until she felt another one fifteen minutes later. Still talking to Lee, she instantly felt a gush of warm water run down her leg. "I know I didn't just pee myself," she thought as she stood to her feet and felt the last little bit trickle down to her sandals. Tasha typed in she thought she might be in labor so she would give her a call once she knew for sure what was going on. Across the screen were the letters OMG, OMG; Lee was in as much shock as Tasha was. "Call me when you get a chance," was what her friend wrote just as Tasha was signing off.

Indeed Tasha was in labor. She managed to get herself to the hospital just as the intensity of the contractions became unbearable. When the obstetrician on shift examined Tasha, she was already ten centimeters. There was no time for anesthesia. There wasn't even time to call Marlene or Aunt Viv – the two she had on her list for when she went in labor. It was only time to push, and that's exactly what the nurses screamed as they held her legs in the air.

*   *   *   *   *

The next morning, Tasha was still exhausted. Looking down at her new daughter, she couldn't believe her eyes; the baby was the spitting image of both Jared and Curtis. It was amazing. She wanted to cry and laugh and scream all at the same time. Instead, she kissed the child's forehead. From the time she had felt her first pain, to the time she delivered, it had only been a matter of an hour or so. She hadn't even had time to panic. It was just after 10 that Wednesday morning when a male nurse came in to take Tasha's vital signs, as she was finishing up feeding the baby and had laid her in the hospital bassinet. "Good morning, good morning," the nurse cheerfully sang as he attended to his routine. When the nurse exited the room, Tasha looked back over at the baby. Moments later, she heard another voice say "Good Morning." When she turned thinking it was the nurse returning to run more tests, she was shocked to see her father standing there.

"Good morning," Tasha replied as a knot began to form in her throat.

"May I come in?"

"Yes, please."

As he walked closer to the bed, the baby began to whimper. Tasha wasn't sure of what to do. She wanted to attend to the baby but she couldn't take her eyes off of her father. It had been almost two months since they'd spoken.

"May I?" Jared asked, reaching for the child.

"Of course." Tasha's heart was beating so fast, she was scared it might pop out of her chest.

"She's beautiful," Jared said as he pulled up a chair near the bed and took a seat.

"What's her name?"

"Chanelle." Chanelle Miriam Daniels."

Jared quickly lifted his head, looked at his daughter, than dropped it again. "Miriam, huh?"

Miriam was Jared's mother. She had passed when he was only five years old, but he had remembered enough about her to tell Tasha many stories. That name was always special to him and oft times, while Tasha was growing up, he would ask her to name her first daughter after his mother. Deep within, he was ecstatic she had honored his wish, even after all that had happened.

The two sat there in silence. The nurse had come in and out two more times before Jared decided to leave. As he kissed the child and laid her in the bassinet, he began to leave the room with just a simple goodbye. Suddenly, he turned and walked over to Tasha. "I hope you can forgive me for turning my back on you," he said. Immediately, tears began to stream down Tasha's face.

"You were a gift given by the Lord and you have been more than your mother and I could have wished for. You have been my life, my inspiration, and my best friend at times. You kept me going when I was weak and you kept me hoping when I wanted to give up." Tasha's silent tears turned into a sob. "Thank you for making this the second happiest day of my life," he said looking over at the sleeping baby. "August 17, 1984 was my first." Without saying another word, Jared grabbed his daughter's hand, bent down, and kissed her cheek. "I love you, Daddy." Tasha said as her father strolled out of the room humming the tune *"God Has Been So Good to Me"*.

That night, after Tasha pondered the conversation between her and her father, and how their relationship would be as good as new; she received a phone call from Lisa saying Jared had been killed in a car accident earlier that afternoon.

CHAPTER 25

Over two hundred people turned out to pay their respects. Jared was certainly a well loved and appreciated individual – according to what people said. Dozens of ministers, evangelists and Pastors; and a slew of family and friends dedicated songs, poems, scriptures, and whatever else they could think of on local radio stations. In his will, he had requested that Tasha read Psalm 91 during the eulogy. That was the hardest part for Tasha to handle because she knew what that scripture meant to them – him and her together. She cried during the entire reading.

The morning of the funeral, Tasha showed up at her mother's house with the baby, but little was said between the two of them. Everyone thought it was because of Jared's death, but Tasha and Cilla knew it was much more. Lee flew down for the weekend so she could help Tasha with the baby; she was a life saver. With the funeral planning, cooking, and responding to visitors, Tasha was zonked. Then, with trying to tend to the baby, there was little time for her to catch her breath. Lee basically looked after Chanelle the entire weekend. She bathed, fed, changed, and put her to sleep. That gave Tasha the time to be fully devoted to making sure her father's funeral was organized – as much as her mother would allow. Cilla would tell her to go see about the baby, but she kept telling her the baby was fine – she just wanted to help. People who had not seen Tasha in more than six months all made the same statement – "I didn't know you were pregnant." She even overheard one Evangelist say, "That bastard baby was probably what killed him." She tried not to pay the comments any attention, but she couldn't help but to still feel ashamed.

After the guests were gone and Lee had taken Chanelle back to Marlene's house, only Cilla and Tasha remained. She noticed her mother had avoided her all day, but she tried not to take it to heart. It had been almost two months since they had actually spoken and Tasha couldn't take it anymore.

134

"Everything was beautiful," she said as her mother began clearing the dining room table."

"Uh huh."

"Daddy would have been proud," Tasha added.

"Yup." Cilla just continued to clean up as if no one were talking to her.

Helping her mother clean off the table, Tasha could hear Cilla's breathing increase. She knew it was a sign of her being agitated.

"I got it," Cilla asserted.

"I just wanna..."

"I got it!" Cilla hissed. "Why don't you go home and tend to your baby!"

"Daddy forgave me. Why can't you?"

Cilla didn't respond. She just picked up her cleaning pace.

"Chanelle hasn't done anything. She's innocent. Why can't you accept her?" Tasha demanded.

"She was conceived in sin, which makes her guilty!"

Tasha didn't say a word. Her heart was crushed but she just set the plates back down on the table and left.

When she got home, Lee was sitting on the sofa watching the Bernie Mac Show. From the look on Tasha's face, her friend could tell something was said that really hurt her feelings. She had learned by now not to probe right away, but give Tasha time to calm down. Tasha headed straight for her bedroom where she knew Chanelle was. She stood over the bassinette where her daughter was sound asleep – curled in a ball with her butt poked in the air. Tears began to form in Tasha's eyes; not regretful tears but joyful tears. For the first time, she was thankful Chanelle was there. When she left the room, leaving the door slightly ajar, she settled on the sofa next to her friend who was humorously enjoying the show. For several minutes neither girl said a word. They both just laughed at Bernie Mac's funny antics. When the credits began to roll, Tasha turned to Lee and smiled. "Thank You," she whispered. "For what?" Lee uttered as she reached over and embraced her friend.

CHAPTER 26

"Happy New Year!" is what Dick Clark screamed as Tasha watched TV. A new year had begun but nothing had really changed. It had been over three months since Tasha buried her father and the grief was still unbearable. She and Cilla had still not reconciled, and Chanelle was getting bigger. Tasha knew it was time to find a job now because she didn't feel it was right living off her grandmother – although Nana repeatedly said she didn't mind helping. Tasha knew she would have to move on with her life, but losing her father was the worst thing that had ever happened to her.

The job search went well. Ashley Stewart welcomed her back without a problem. She even managed to get the morning shift and every other weekend off. The hours were perfect because Marlene had volunteered to watch Chanelle until she got a little older, and Tasha could afford day care. Again, Tasha knew God was looking out for her. She had even begun attending a nearby church. It was small and quaint but accepting. At first, she was a bit skeptical of a Methodist church because she had grown up Apostolic, but when she heard the word being taught, she knew they had "the truth" as well.

As the months progressed, all was well. Spring sprung and then summer and then fall began to show its face once again. Tasha had celebrated Chanelle's first birthday by throwing her a small party, but at the same time was unable to freely celebrate thinking of the anniversary of her father's death. Tasha had been spending a lot of time with Nicole – helping her prepare for the wedding. It had been moved twice due to financial trouble, but when the day came, the wedding was beautiful. Nicole looked gorgeous in her white gown. Tasha and the bridesmaids wore Cranbury colored gowns for their Christmas Eve ceremony, while the groomsman wore ivory three piece suits with Cranbury accessories. Throughout the evening, the best man continually eyed Tasha from across the room. He was handsome – tall, dark, bald, built like a linebacker, with a smile that would give Denzel a run for his money. During the bride's and groom's first dance to Alicia Keys' *"If I Ain't Got You"*, he approached her as she came from the bathroom.

"I don't think we were formally introduced. I'm Brian," he said extending his hand.

"Nice to meet you, Brian. I'm Tasha," she replied as she accepted his hand.

"I have been wanting to approach you all during this week's rehearsals but didn't want to seem forceful."

Tasha just smiled. She was pleased with his manners and maturity.

"So, are you having a good time?" he inquired.

"Yes, I am. Everything came out beautifully – especially Nicole and Marcus."

"How long have you known Nicole?" Brian asked as he eyed Tasha.

"I went to Kingston with Nicole and Marcus."

The two stood there in silence grinning for a few moments. Brian was waiting for Tasha to give more information about herself but she didn't seem to be so willing to share. Suddenly, an announcement for the bridal party to join the couple on the floor for a dance interrupted their conversation. Soon after, the maid of honor spotted them and waved for Brian to come to her.

"I'll see you on the floor," Brian said as he walked away but still looking back.

That night Brian and Tasha danced a few times, took pictures with the bridal party, and were labeled as being the next to marry when they both caught what was thrown – the bride's flowers and the groom's garter belt.

*   *   *   *   *

Spring came in like a flood. That April was the most rainfall Dunbar had seen in over five years. Countless homes and businesses had been destroyed. Several neighborhoods in Polk and surrounding cities succumbed to millions of dollars worth of damage. Tasha managed to keep dry – she and Brian. They had been spending a lot of time together. Lee heard so much about Brian, but had yet to meet him face to face until he and Tasha drove up to Baltimore for her graduation. Tasha's grandmother offered to keep Chanelle for the four days they would be gone, but Tasha declined knowing Lee would be delighted to see her goddaughter. Plus, Marlene was soon to be seventy-five years old and beginning to move a bit slower. Tasha didn't want to leave that type of burden on her grandmother. When Tasha first brought Brian home, she could tell her grandmother was thinking something without opening her mouth. After a few times of him visiting, Marlene asked Tasha a question that puzzled her.

"You like this guy?"

"Yeah, Nana. Why?"

Tasha knew from the way her grandmother posed the question she saw something about him that wasn't right.

"Just asking. He seems nice but...," Marlene paused.

"But what?"

"Just... be careful sweetie. Be careful."

That statement remained in the back of Tasha's mind each time they were together, but he had yet to show her he wasn't right. He was always a perfect gentleman, respecting her wishes of not to have sex although they had slipped up once and after that, had come close quite a few more times. He was great with Chanelle; she had even begun calling him Daddy. And he always spoke of the future; referring to him, Tasha and Chanelle as a family. Not to add, he was well educated and very well employed.

When they arrived in Baltimore that Friday afternoon, the look and smell of the city brought back streams of memories for Tasha. Her immediate thought went to Curtis, but she didn't allow it to take control of her mood. When the metallic colored Acura sitting on 22's pulled up in front of Baker Hall, all heads turned. The women were looking Brian's way and the men Tasha's. One girl recognized Tasha and spoke. "Good to see you," Tasha said as she entered the dorm in search of her best friend. She could hear Lee laughing from down the hall.

"Ms. Dickinson, we have a problem out here," Tasha said disguising her voice.

"What is it now?" Lee said as she stormed into the hallway.

Without warning, Tasha jumped out from behind a door frightening her friend half to death. The two embraced as if they hadn't seen each other in years.

138

"I should knock your ass out for scaring me like that," Lee joked.

The two stood there wearing all smiles.

"Where's my girl and that Mandingo of yours?"

"I left 'em in the car," Tasha said eyeing her friend. As usual, she looked amazing. She had gained a few pounds but she wore them well. Her white Capri's, with a pink fringed sleeveless D & G turtleneck complemented her hour-glass shape. Her light pink matching sandals outlined in gems gave the outfit even more flare. Tasha noticed Lee's usual micro-mini braids were curled instead of wrapped giving her golden skin a fresh vibrant look. Her hazel eyes shimmered with the shoes and the diamond pendant she wore around her neck.

"You can't leave a man unattended out here with these vultures swarming," Lee said as they headed for the car.

"I love your hair," Tasha said.

"I know." They both laughed as they made their way outside into the bullying sun. Brian was standing up against the car with a half dozen women surrounding him – each taking turns playing with Chanelle.

"See what I mean," Lee said pointing to the flirting women.

Even before Tasha could speak, Lee jumped in..., "So this is Brian?" From that point, Tasha had nothing else to say. She knew her friend would take over the conversation so she just stood back and let her go for what she knew.

That night at dinner, they got acquainted and reacquainted. Michael met them at the restaurant. He was in his second year of Law School at Howard -- just as he had planned. He and Lee had managed to fight through the drudgery of young couples and make it work. Tasha was so proud, even of Lee, for staying an extra year and taking summer courses which allowed her to graduate with a Master's Degree in Education.

The remainder of the weekend was glorious. The graduation ceremony was pleasant – hot, but not too long. Tasha got a chance to spend some time with Lee and Mike, and reminisced about old times. They got a chance to meet Brian. And, to top it off, Mike proposed to Lee which surprised everyone. That time with friends was exactly what Tasha needed. As she, Brian and Chanelle drove home that Monday morning, leaving more memories behind;

Tasha quietly thanked the Lord for yet more blessings – love and serenity being at the top of the list.

CHAPTER 27

The day before Chanelle's second birthday Brian was to meet Tasha for lunch. They were going to discuss the party they had planned for the baby at Chuck-E-Cheese, and their upcoming wedding. She noticed he had been a bit secretive lately, but paid it no mind after he proposed a month earlier. She figured he had a lot on his mind since he was handling the bulk of the wedding's financial burden. "I don't believe in long engagements," is what he told her so they set a date for December 6th.

Tasha waited for an hour, but Brian never showed up. She called his job once and his cell phone twice before thinking something must be wrong. When she pulled up in front of his house, she noticed an unfamiliar car in his driveway, which was not his. She sat there for a moment to scope out the rest of the street when she spotted his car parked at the end of the block. She used the key he had given her and went through the back door. She could hear a man humming and a shower running. Slowly, she crept up the stairs towards the bedroom. She noticed his suit sprawled across the bed and another set of clothes on the floor that apparently didn't belong to her man. "This can't be happening," she thought as she stared at the foreign clothes. Her immediate thought was to burst into the bathroom and catch them, but she held her composure. She wanted to wait for Brian and the mystery woman to emerge from the bathroom so she could encounter them face to face. When she heard the shower stop, she took a stance in the middle of the bedroom floor. No matter what, she was going to confront them. As the bathroom door creaked open she could hear loud slobbery kissing – it turned her stomach upside down. Her heart raced a hundred miles a minute. Suddenly, appearing in front of her were Brian and another man, both standing in the nude. Her mouth dropped open, and she felt faint, but refused to let herself hit the floor.

"What the hell!"

"Baby, Baby. Let me explain," Brian pleaded while trying to grab her hand.

Tasha pushed him away until she made her way down the stairs and out of the house. He ran behind her, still nude, but she kept moving – getting in her car and driving away without ever looking back.

*   *   *   *   *

Tasha was heartbroken. It felt like she had experienced another death. Almost a week passed and she had still not left the house, not even to go to work. She had not answered the telephone or returned anyone's messages – especially the more than fifty Brian had left. The only person she talked to was her grandmother. Being the humble woman, Marlene never once said, "I told you so." She only showed love and support. "Call and talk to your friend," Marlene suggested. The next day Tasha called Lee.

"Where you been, girl? I had been trying to get a hold of you for like a week now."

"I know. I have been going through some shit."

"Oh my God. What the hell den happened that got you cussin'?"

"That faggot!"

"What faggot? Lee inquired.

"Brian! He's a faggot!"

"What you talkin' 'bout T?"

"I caught Brian with... with a dude."

"What!"

The conversation got quiet. While telling her friend what happened she could feel the anger building back up. Lee didn't speak. She just listened. When Tasha began rambling, her friend finally interrupted.

"T, I gotta tell you something.

Tasha got quiet as her friend said, "I knew about Brian."

"What'chu mean you knew about Brian?"

"I knew he was funny."

"What?" Tasha yelled through the telephone.

"When y'all came for my graduation I saw a dude eye him from across the restaurant. Me and Mike saw it."

142

Tasha thought back to that night. She tried to picture the faces of every man in the restaurant but it had been too long and she couldn't remember. She did recall when Brian got up to go to the bathroom, and was gone for quite some time. When she went looking for him, he was coming from the men's bathroom. The more Lee talked, the more Tasha began piecing things together. Even that night, another man who was coming from the bathroom walked by Brian and Tasha, and said "faggot," but Tasha paid it no mind. She figured he was talking to someone else. Her mind also took her back to another night when she and Chanelle were going to Brian's house for dinner and a strange man was coming from the house. "Who was that?" she asked, but he answered with, "That's my cousin." Later that night, she found a pair of men's boxers obviously too small for his muscular frame stuffed under Brian's bed. The more she listened to her friend, the more regret she felt. The signs were so obvious now. Why didn't she see them before?

"He's probably one of those D-L bruthah's."

"That is sickening. I don't wanna talk about it no more."

"Okay. But can I ask you one last question?"

Tasha didn't answer. She just waited for her friend to ask.

"What you gonna do with the ring?"

Tasha looked down and realized she was still wearing it. "I'm gonna mail it to his ass."

"Don't do that!" Lee yelled.

"What?"

"Keep that shit, girl! That's the last thing you gonna get from his ass. Do something – anything – but don't give it back!"

"But I don't want it."

"Then sell it. I know he paid a whop for that rock, so sell it and go get yourself something nice."

When Tasha got off the phone, she went in her bedroom, checked on her sleeping daughter and got her clothes ready for work. As with all the other tragedies -- life had to continue.

Leaving for work the next morning she noticed a homeless man picking through trash cans. "Ma'am, could you spare some food? I'm really hungry," he asked as he approached her car.

"Wait one minute." She walked Chanelle back in the house, and grabbed some bagels off the counter. When she returned, the man was wiping the dirt from her car with a rag he had taken from

143

his back pocket. She handed him the bagels and he thanked her. "Jesus loves you," she said as he began walking away.

He paused and turned to look at her. "I know," he said as he held up the bagels and smiled.

"Wait," Tasha yelled. "Do you mind if I ask how you got like this?"

"Well ma'am, I lost my job and my wife died all at the same time and... and I didn't feel like I could live anymore."

"How long were ya'll married?" Tasha probed.

"Thirty-three years."

Tasha's heart went out to the man. He didn't smell like a drunk or look like a crack-head. She knew he was just heartbroken – as she was. She looked down at her finger, took the ring off, and handed it to the man. She didn't say another word. She simply put her daughter in the car and drove off.

CHAPTER 28

Another new year had come. Not much was going on in Tasha's life except for her daughter and her job. She was helping Lee plan for her's and Mike's May wedding. There was no way she could travel back and forth to Washington, D.C., where Lee and Mike were now living; so they communicated through dozens of e-mails. Lee managed to find her dress, the bridesmaids' dresses, and the groomsmen's tuxes from a small shop in Camden called "The Bride of Christ". It was right outside of Philadelphia, so when she came home to visit her mother for a weekend, she was able to choose the colors, get fitted and leave a deposit. Mike had graduated from law school with honors and was working for a prestigious firm in the Upper Marlboro area.

Lately, Tasha was watching her daughter get bigger while her grandmother got weaker. She and her mother had still not spoken after two years, but Tasha often thought of her. They occasionally saw each other at family gatherings, but Cilla never acknowledged her. It was a painful reminder of how Tasha had disappointed her parents. One March afternoon the telephone rang. When Tasha answered, she knew from the voice it was her mother. Immediately she said "hold on" knowing Cilla wanted to speak with Marlene.

"Wait," Cilla said. "I'm calling for you."

Tasha was taken aback. "Yes?"

"How are you?"

Tasha swallowed hard. "I'm fine. How are you?"

"I'm fine," Pat responded.

They both got quiet. Suddenly, both women began to speak at the same time. Tasha quieted down and let her mother talk.

"A funny thing happened to me while I was out shopping this morning. I saw the cutest dress for a little girl. I just had to get it."

Tasha wasn't sure what her mother was saying so she just let her talk.

"The baby wears a size 3T, right?"

"Yes," Tasha responded, curious as to why her mother was asking these questions.

"I have to take Mama to the doctor's this afternoon, so when I come pick her up, I'll drop the dress off."

Before Tasha could thank her mother the telephone went dead. Hours later, Tasha woke up from a nap. When she went in the kitchen to fix an early dinner for Chanelle and Nana, she saw the prettiest light pink and white satin dress lying on the dining room table. From that time on, whenever Cilla would call for Marlene and Tasha answered, they always exchanged "hellos".

Two weeks before Lee's wedding, Tasha realized it was almost Mother's Day. When she made reservations for her and Nana at Ned' rag Evilo, she thought of Cilla. She would love to invite her but didn't want to push it. Her grandmother came in just as she was hanging up the telephone. She asked her about a picture of Chanelle she couldn't find. Marlene's answer shocked Tasha.

"I gave it to your mother."

"Why?"

"'Cause she asked for it," Marlene said without any remorse.

"But why?" Tasha asked.

"'Cause that's her grandbaby. Regardless of the fact, Chanelle is her flesh and blood and it's been long enough that Cilla acted like she wasn't."

Tasha sat in silence as her grandmother continued.

"I have been tellin' your mama, and you, for over two years now to stop this foolishness."

Tasha bowed her head in shame.

"I ain't gonna be here forever, so ya'll betta act like ya'll got some sense and patch this stuff up. We family, and family stick together no matter what."

Tasha had never heard her grandmother talk that way, but she knew she was absolutely right.

That night Tasha got an idea. It was risky but she had nothing to lose. When Sunday came, it was a beautiful morning. The sun was shining, the birds were chirping and the bacon was frying. After getting she and Chanelle dressed, Tasha headed across town. When she pulled up, she noticed the house had been painted. It was fresh and clean. She noticed her mother's car still in the driveway. "Good, I made it before she left for church," she thought as she rang the doorbell. When Cilla opened the door, Tasha smiled. She wished her a Happy Mother's Day and handed her a card. Cilla smiled back and graciously accepted the envelope.

"Should I open this now?" Cilla asked.

"Yes, please."

As Cilla read, Tasha could see the tears forming in her mother's eyes. "Thank you," she said as Tasha reached in her purse and handed her mother a tissue.

"This is absolutely beautiful."

Both women stood there in silence – but only for a moment before Tasha began talking. "I have missed you so much."

Cilla's eyes filled with tears once again. "I have been through so much the last few years and I needed you to be there," Tasha said.

Cilla tried to interrupt her daughter but Tasha continued on.

"I know it was God that allowed me and Daddy to reconcile; and I know it's God's will that I'm here right now."

Cilla no longer wiped the tears running from her face; they were coming too fast.

"Mama, I ask that you forgive me for the pain and embarrassment I've caused."

Cilla fell into her daughter's chest. "Please forgive me," Cilla bellowed.

"I already have," Tasha whispered in her mother's ear as the two hugged tightly.

In the middle of their reunion, Tasha could hear Chanelle whining from her car seat. Cilla walked over to the car, took Chanelle out, and hugged her snugly; she was wearing the pink and white satin dress. While Cilla adored her granddaughter, Tasha pulled a huge wrapped gift from her trunk.

This is for you," she said handing it to her mother.

"Open it for me."

When Tasha pulled the wrapping off, Cilla almost fainted. She began shaking and hysterically crying while smiling at the same time.

Through the tears, Cilla asked, "Where did you get this from?"

147

"I had it custom made." It was a painted portrait of Chanelle sitting on Jared's lap. Finally, they were a family again.

CHAPTER 29

Life was good. The wedding was beautiful. When Tasha showed up in Philadelphia with Chanelle and Cilla, Lee was ecstatic. They walked and talked together as if no separation was ever between them. Cilla must have taken three rolls of film, just of Chanelle walking down the aisle. "She is the most precious flower girl ever," her grandmother hollered out. At the reception, Lee changed from diamond studded eggshell Prada pumps into a pair of white Reebok's. She and Mike were introduced with the song *"You're All I Need To Get By"* playing in the background – the Meth and Mary version. Lee and Mike were happy; they smiled until the fight broke out. Lee's Uncle Buster and Mike's gangsta' cousin Darrell got into an argument over the best era of music. All was fine until Uncle Buster called Darrell a heathen. That West Baltimore spirit rose up, and the rest was history. After the police came and hauled both of them away, along with six other men and women, the celebration continued as normal.

"They always gotta mess shit up," Lee yelled at her mother – referring to her uncle and cousins.

Tasha's toast as the maid of honor calmed the atmosphere. She thanked God for both Lee and Mike, and for how God had allowed them to be a part of her life; how they had encouraged her through the rough times; and how they "had her back" during the sticky situations. Most of all, she applauded them for beating the odds of being from the projects and single mother homes with disadvantages. There was not a dry eye in the place.

When Tasha returned home after seeing her friends off on their honeymoon, she had a message on her machine from her job. Natalie, the manager said she wanted to meet with Tasha at 8:30 Monday morning – before the store was to open. For some strange reason, Tasha had trouble sleeping that night. She had a feeling something was going to happen, but she wasn't sure what it could be. The next morning Tasha met Natalie as she had requested. Within ten minutes of the conversation, Tasha couldn't hear anything. She had blanked out after her manager said, "I'm gonna have to let you go." Confusion flooded Tasha's mind as to why she was being fired. Natalie gave her a story of money missing and not being accounted for. Tasha was both shocked and hurt that they would insinuate she had been stealing. She tried to make sense of the situation. It all became very clear when Natalie made the statement, "They had to get rid of somebody." Tasha knew exactly what she meant – blame it on the nigga! Tasha didn't even let the manager finish her sentence before she handed over her key and walked away.

What next? Tasha thought as she drove home. It seemed like every time something went right in her life, something quickly went wrong. It was getting to the point she didn't want anything good to happen. That way, nothing bad could follow. Heartache was becoming a pattern. "What did I do wrong?" she began to question God as she rode past her house and continued driving.

"What do you want from me?" she yelled out.

Immediately, her mind began to flood with her father's words, "Tribulations are a part of life – everyone's life. But what the devil meant for evil, God always meant for good."

The tears streamed down her face. The trials of life were becoming unbearable. The longer she drove, the more she prayed. Her father, being a military man, always told her prayer and time were the two most important things. "Prayer is not contingent on time but time is contingent on prayer," he would say. That's why she constantly watched the clock. She continued to hear the words of her father, "money can be replaced but time can't, so use it wisely." She continued to beg and plead with God. "If one more thing happens, I'm gonna lose it," she told herself.

Before she knew it, it was almost 4:00 and time to pick up Chanelle from day care. Tasha had finally convinced her grandmother that placing the baby in child care would be best. They both knew Marlene was getting slower and weaker but they didn't want to accept it. When Tasha got home, Cilla was at the house. Chanelle ran and jumped in her grandmother's arms. That caused a huge smile to grace Tasha's face. As Tasha cooked dinner, Cilla played with her granddaughter while Marlene watched the news.

"All this killin' is makin' me sick," the elderly woman shouted.

"The Lord is comin' back soon, and the devil knows it. That's why he's on a rampage," Pat explained.

"I hope I'm outta here before then."

"Don't say that, Nana," Tasha interjected, "you're gonna be here forever."

Marlene chuckled. "No honey. Nana is gettin tired."

"What we gonna do without you?"

"The same thing I did when my mama and grandmama passed – keep livin'."

Cilla quickly looked up at her mother. "Aw Mama, don't talk like that."

"Okay babies. Nana is gonna behave."

The women got quiet. Only the television, the playing child, and Marlene humming "*Jesus is mine,*" could be heard – and clearly understood.

Cilla had a great idea. "Let's get a generation portrait taken."

A family portrait was a good idea. Each woman looked beautiful – representing their respective ages and stages in life. When the photographer took the pictures, he continued to comment on what a wonderful idea this was; to have four generations of women from one family – all healthy and graceful.

"The pictures will be framed and ready in three days," the cashier said as the women left the studio. Out to lunch that afternoon, Marlene told Cilla and Tasha of the dream she had the night before; of how she was running in a race and after a few miles she became tired. As she stopped to get a drink of water she saw her children run pass. Next, she saw her grandchildren run past – strong and healthy. When she sat on the curb, she saw Chanelle run past.

"Wow, I thought. The baby is running too," Marlene said.

Cilla and Tasha just listened.

"When I woke up, a spirit of peace rested on me. It was absolutely marvelous," she declared.

As the women drove home, Cilla and Tasha talked about job leads while Marlene sat with a smile.

The morning the studio called to alert them the pictures were ready for pick up; Tasha went into Nana's room to check on her. It

151

was quiet and dark – as it had been the night before. Her bible was opened to Psalm 37 with verse 25 highlighted. While Marlene peacefully slept, she slipped into that spirit of peace she had talked about.

CHAPTER 30

A month after the funeral Tasha moved into an apartment. Her mother had asked her to come home, but she refused. She felt she needed to be on her own. On the other hand, she did accept a part time teller position at the bank. Marlene had left her some money which helped her pay the rent while she began to take a few night courses. Tasha knew finishing her education was the only way she would be able to support herself and Chanelle comfortably. For the time being, she had to buckle down and stay focused. Cilla was a major help; she watched the baby while Tasha went to school. Some weekends, Cilla even kept Chanelle so Tasha could work a few hours overtime for some extra money; or just to give her time to finish school work that was due.

Chanelle had just turned three. The older she got, the more she resembled Curtis. One night as Tasha was getting her ready for bed, she told Chanelle to put up her toys. Chanelle acted as if she didn't hear her mother, although Tasha knew she did. "Chanelle, I said put up your toys; time for bed." Again, Chanelle continued to play. When Tasha walked over to the child and grabbed her toy, Chanelle gave her a look. It startled Tasha because she knew that look. It was the same one Curtis gave her when she told him she was pregnant. That same look that said, "I'm not trying to hear what you have to say." Tasha felt her hand rising to hit the child but she quickly came to and instead threw the toy to the floor and walked away. She went in her bedroom to collect herself. As she sat in the chair she had taken from Marlene's room when she moved, she felt ashamed. Ashamed because she had never felt rage like that before – especially not towards her daughter. She replayed the look over and over again in her head. Why had she gotten so angry? As she pondered the question, she could hear tiny footsteps coming down the hall. She knew Chanelle was on her way to the bedroom. The little girl, in her Sponge-bob pajamas, walked over to her mother and crawled into her lap. Tasha closed her eyes and began rocking back and forth as she hummed the song, "This Little Light of Mine," causing the child to fall asleep within minutes. That night Tasha did something she hadn't done in years. She laid the baby in her bed, got down on her knees and began praying. It was almost 4:00 am when Tasha opened her eyes. She had obviously fallen asleep on the floor. When she got up, she crawled into the bed with her daughter, pulling her close.

*　　　*　　　*　　　*　　　*

Early November Tasha was studying for mid-terms. So far, she had been doing really well in both her biology and calculus classes. She switched her major from education to nursing when she had everything transferred from Coppin State to Jacksonville University, causing her to lose a few credits.

Leaving the library late one night, she noticed a gray van parked besides her car with the lights still on. The campus parking lot had been full which caused her to have to park around the side of the building. She paid the beat up old gray van no mind until she heard a man's voice say, "Hey, Red." She didn't respond. Again, the man tried to get her attention, "Red!" As she fumbled with her keys she could almost smell his breath from the van; it reeked of alcohol and marijuana. When the passenger's door to the van opened, a tall, thin, copper complexioned man with cornrows stepped out. He strutted over to Tasha trying to talk but she just kept saying, "Please leave me alone." "I just wanna talk, Red," the man said. He continued to make derogatory statements about her and towards her that made her all the more nervous. She could hear the laughter of another man coming from the van – laughter as if the man trying to rap and her fear were funny.

"Duce, leave that bitch alone, she don't want you," the mysterious voice said as he continued to laugh.

"Yes she does," the tall thin man said now standing right behind Tasha.

When she turned to walk in the opposite direction the man jumped in front of her.

"You want me, don't you," he insisted hunched in a tackling position.

154

"Please leave me alone," Tasha pleaded trying to make her way around the man.

The man stood up straight, said, "A'ight Red, I'll leave you alone," and took a quick glance around, right before he grabbed her by the throat and covered her mouth!

Tasha struggled and fought as the man dragged her to the ground. His weight had her pinned while his right hand concealed her screams and his left ripped off her blouse!

"Shut the fuck up, bitch," the man ordered as he fondled her breast.

"Duce, what the hell is you doin'?" the man in the van yelled out.

No answer. Tasha fought with everything in her but he overpowered her. She could feel him forcing his fingers inside her; two, three, or maybe four! When the man removed his hand from her mouth to rip her jeans off, Tasha cried out, "Help me! Somebody please help me!"

Her screams seemed to go unanswered until she heard four pops in the air.

"Nigga, come on," the man still in the van yelled out as he started the ignition. Immediately, the man jumped up off Tasha, hopped in the van, and sped away as three young teenagers came running down the street. One of the teenagers was firing a gun in the air – that was the popping noise Tasha heard. The other two boys ran over to help Tasha up. She was crying hysterically and wiping the blood from her nose. The guy had punched her a few times trying to shut her up. As the boy with the gun walked over to the rest of them, he was talking on a cell phone, "Yeah, she's on Rose Ave."

By the time he hung up the phone, other people who heard the commotion began to gather around. The campus security had somehow been alerted and were coming around the corner when someone running down the block said, "The police are on their way."

A few girls who had gathered tried to cover Tasha's exposed body as a man from the crowd took off his shirt and gave it to her.

When the police and ambulance arrived, the campus security was already trying to get the crowd under control. The EMT's checked her out and the police took a statement, but Tasha refused to go to the hospital. After telling the cops several times she didn't know the man, she wanted to leave. They were beginning to make her feel it was her fault this had happened to her. "I just wanna go home," she told the white officers.

"Miss, you have to..."

Tasha didn't let the officer finish. "I'll deal with this tomorrow; right now I wanna go home!"

One of the EMT's began talking to Tasha. "I know you don't wanna deal with this right now, but it's best if you let us take you to the hospital. That way they can perform a rape kit and find any evidence the attacker may have left behind."

"I didn't get raped!" Tasha yelled.

Both EMT's and the police looked at each other.

"Yes ma'am, but this was a sexual assault," one of the officers stated.

Tasha put her head down and began to cry.

"Miss, it's your decision, but I recommend you allow us to take you to the emergency room to make sure everything is okay."

Tasha didn't speak she just nodded her head "yes".

CHAPTER 31

A month later the physical scars had completely disappeared but the emotional ones were fresh. She continued to wonder what she had done so badly that was causing her life to be in shambles. Cilla had insisted Tasha bring the baby and move back in with her, but Tasha refused. She knew hiding and letting fear run her life would keep her bound. Lee begged Tasha to come stay with her and Mike, but she refused that offer as well. "I can't. I have work and school still," she told her. Lee was furious that Tasha was trying to be so strong – especially since she knew she wasn't.

Tasha managed to finish out the semester with B's. It wasn't her normal A's, but she gave herself some leeway just because of what happened the month before. Everyone was shocked she had even gone back to school – especially her.

During the Christmas vacation Tasha tried to use the time to relax. Sure she still had to work, but she wasn't busting her butt trying to work, study, and care for Chanelle. One evening after working some overtime, she went to pick Chanelle up from her mother's house. "This letter came here for you," Cilla said as they sat at the kitchen table drinking a cup of coffee.

Tasha looked at the return address – Osborne Health Services. The name didn't ring a bell and she figured it was probably another one of those black women health studies she had received before, asking women to participate in their research, so she slid it in her purse.

Later that night, as Chanelle was sound asleep, she dug through her purse looking for a receipt. When she noticed the letter, she opened it and began to read:

Dear Ms. Daniels:
Osborne Health Services is a non-profit organization
that provides testing, medical care, and treatment for
individuals who have been diagnosed with or may

157

have sexually transmitted diseases.

Our main clientele are those who seek AIDS and HIV testing and those who are already living with the disease. While we cannot disclose the party in which the testing was performed (due to our confidentiality code), **It has come to our attention that you may have been exposed to the HIV virus.**

Our client has provided a list of names of people with whom He or she have had personal sexual contact or people of whom their sexual partner(s) have had (knowledgeable) personal sexual contact with. Your name was on that list. **If you are unaware of your HIV status, it is highly recommended you get tested.**

According to your last known address, a list of clinics and medical centers in your area, that perform AIDS and HIV testing, has been provided as a reference guide. You may choose any of those or use your own personal doctor.

If you have any questions or concerns, feel free to contact my office at 301-555-5483.

Sincerely,

Janice Morris
AIDS and HIV Counselor

Tasha was numb. Was this for real or a joke? Her mind raced. She knew it could only be two people – Curtis or Brian. Even that puzzled her because she had only had sex with both of them once. How could it be that she could have possibly contracted HIV with only having sex twice in her life? That question quickly flew from her thoughts when she realized it was certainly possible – especially getting pregnant after only her first time.

This was too much to think about, let alone handle. As she lay in her bed that night, she tried to sleep but it was impossible. Her mind jumped from Curtis to Brian. She found out about both men, albeit too late. Curtis' whoremongering ways kept her on edge. He had been with more women than she could count, probably more than she knew. On the same note, Brian had delved into a lifestyle that was infamous with sin and the backlash of it. She

158

knew of the one man, but were there other men she didn't know of? Were there women too? Her mind couldn't handle the possibilities both men presented. Tasha knew what she had to do, and first thing in the morning that's exactly what she did.

After Tasha left the clinic, she decided to go for a walk. She knew that ten days for her results to come back would be impossible to wait for. As she strolled down Main Street she felt as if she were in a maze. Each face she saw was a familiar one – as if she had seen them before. When she reached the corner, she kept walking, almost getting hit by a car when she didn't yield to their green light. Her mind raced. Was she sick? Had God punished her for not living up to His standards? Most of all, was Chanelle sick? If Curtis had given it to her, and she had not seen a doctor during her pregnancy, then how would she have known if she was infected? What about Brian? It was certainly possible he could have given it to her. Sure they only had sex once, but it was unprotected. And with his taste for men, there was no telling what he could have exposed her to. The overwhelming feeling of vulnerability crept into Tasha's chest. When her thoughts came back into focus, she was in an unfamiliar place. She looked at the street sign but didn't particularly know where she was. Panic gripped her. The faces she passed suddenly went from friendly to frightening. *"I gotta get outta here,"* she told herself. She began to walk faster – to the next corner and then the next. By the time she reached one corner, she realized she had walked twenty blocks. Gripping the stop sign, Tasha felt faint.

"Miss, are you okay," an elderly white woman asked.

Tasha looked at her as if she were an alien – not answering.

"Miss?"

Suddenly, the taste of hot sewer filled her mouth. There was nothing she could do but release it. By this time two other women had come over to see about her. The sweat was dripping from her chin although it was a cool January morning.

"Let's get her inside," one of the women said, pointing to a diner across the street.

Tasha could barely stay on her feet. The women called for a few guys walking by to help get her inside. Once they sat her at one of the booths, a woman walked over identifying herself as a nurse.

"I think she's sick," one of the elderly woman said.

A waitress brought over a glass of water.

"Young lady, what's your name," the nurse called out. No response. "Your name? What's your name?" the nurse asked again.

"Chanelle! Where's Chanelle?" Tasha mumbled.

"Who's Chanelle?" the nurse asked while trying to hold her head up to drink the water.

"My baby! My poor baby!" Tasha cried out.

The customers in the restaurant were all focused on what was happening. A woman in her early twenties walked over.

"Her name is Tasha," she said.

"Do you know her?" the nurse questioned.

"Not really. She was in my cousin's wedding."

"Can you find out where she lives?"

"Yeah." The girl pulled out a cell phone and began dialing. "Nic, I'm in Nifty Fifties and your friend Tasha is in here; she's sick. You know where she lives?"

The girl got quiet. "580 Virginia Avenue," she yelled out.

As Tasha lay crying with her head in the nurse's chest, the crowd began to disperse. "Tasha, are you okay?" the nurse sympathetically asked.

She shook her head yes.

"Do you need to go to the hospital?"

"No ma'am," Tasha answered, wiping her face with a napkin she had picked up from the table.

"Do you need a ride home?"

"No ma'am. My car is ..." Tasha stopped speaking and began looking around.

"Come on, I'll drive you to your car."

When the woman went to handle her bill, Tasha went into the bathroom. She stood and stared at herself in the mirror. She wanted to cry again but refused to let the tears fall. A woman in one of the stalls came out and looked at her. After washing her hands, the woman grabbed Tasha's hand; "It's going to be alright."

Tasha smiled as the woman exited the bathroom. She wanted so much to believe that to be true. When she came from the bathroom, the nurse and a man was standing at the door.

160

"You ready?" When the three of them got into the car, the woman said, "By the way, I'm Barbara and this is my husband, Jim."

The three drove in silence – only speaking of the car's whereabouts.

Pulling up behind Tasha's perfectly parked Honda, the nurse turned to face her. "Will you be okay?"

She shook her head "yes".

Fumbling through her purse, Barbara handed Tasha a business card. It had her name, address and telephone number. "Call anytime."

"Thank you."

Suddenly, Jim turned to face Tasha as well. "Do you mind if I pray for you?"

Tasha was surprised at the man's offer, but how could she say no? After all, prayer was exactly what she needed.

As Jim prayed Tasha stared at him. Neither he nor Barbara knew she was staring because they both had their eyes closed and their heads bowed. Tasha looked at his straight dark hair with a deep part on the left side. His bushy eyebrows and large nose gave her the hint that he may be German although he didn't have an accent. She then focused her attention on Barbara. Her short, blonde, bobbed hair lay gently over her forehead and ears. Her eyebrows were even and thin – as if she had just had them arched. Her makeup was flawless, but the lipstick was smeared – probably from eating. She stared at their wedding bands as they held hands. The woman's was white gold with three diamonds perfectly displayed. His was just a traditional band with one diamond stone in the center. Tasha then looked around the car. A child's car seat sat perfectly still – unlike if a child was in it. Tasha was not staring because they were white; she stared because she wondered how God could make provision like that. He allowed people like them to be there when she was in trouble. When Jim ended the prayer, he grabbed Tasha's hand, "God said, don't worry, all is well." Her eyes got huge. She didn't say a word; she just closed her eyes, shook her head in agreement and exited the car.

CHAPTER 32

Tasha's life was out of hand and she knew it, but there was nothing she could do. She was able to relax a bit after the results of her HIV test came back negative, but that still didn't make the thought of being put in a situation like that any easier. She had taken Barbara's offer and called her a few times – she was a big help – for prayer. Lee was the biggest help, especially with her humor and her ability to make everything seem as if it's no big deal. Even with her many conversations, Tasha never told anyone about her brush with death, not even her best friend.

When spring sprung again, Tasha began to look for another job. The bank suited her well, but she wanted something with a little more flair. Plus, being around her mother so much was beginning to wear on her. While looking through the Help Wanted Ads, she saw an opening for a security guard at the Alltell Stadium. That certainly wasn't an occupational field she was interested in, but neither was being a teller. She had gained confidence and had a suspicious nature – after all she had gone through. Hesitant, she convinced herself to check it out. The pay was good and she could see concerts for free. The day after she applied, they called her in for an interview. "When can you start?" the manager asked within twenty minutes of the interview. Within a week, Tasha was at her first assignment. It was the *Worship Alive Concert Series Tour*. That was exactly what she needed! To be in the midst of praises was going to lift her spirits – and she knew it.

All was going well for Tasha. After only three months, they made her a supervisor. She thought it was because the manager liked her, but she also knew she was doing a good job – like Jared had instilled in her. Lee and Mike had also begged her to allow Chanelle to stay the summer with them, and she agreed.

Late August meant back to school. Tasha had already registered for her classes. With just 20 credits left, she knew she could finish her undergrad by next fall. The summer concert tours were beginning to slow down. Tasha had worked almost every day for the last two months. Thankfully, Chanelle was away or else she would not have been able to work those kinds of hours without putting the burden of her daughter on her mother. As Tasha was leaving work one night, the manager called her into the office.

"You know the "Man Power" convention is coming next week?" the manager asked.

"Sure."

"Would you like to work the convention?"

"I thought all the slots were taken?" Tasha questioned.

"They were, but Clarice told me yesterday she couldn't do it. I need another supervisor to take her place."

"Well, my daughter is supposed to come home next week from Maryland; and I was going to take her down to Disney for a day or two," Tasha said.

"It pays time and a half," the manager sang with both eyebrows raised.

Tasha paused. She thought for a quick second – time and a half – that would give her enough money for a car she had been saving up for.

"I'll ask my friend if she can keep the baby for another week, and I'll let you know tomorrow. Is that okay?"

"That's fine," the manager said.

When Tasha went to reach for the doorknob, she could hear her boss,

"Um, um, um." She knew he was looking her up and down – focusing on her butt. That made Tasha really uncomfortable.

"I like what you've done to your hair," he said in his insidious southern accent.

"Thank you," she said trying to make her way out of the office.

"Tasha?" he called.

"Yes Mr. Williams?"

As the man walked towards her she backed up.

"You're doing a fine job."

She tried not to make eye contact so she looked at the fish tank sitting in his window sill. He looked like a slightly larger version of George Jefferson, except his forehead was much bigger. She could smell the stench on his breath – like he had been chewing on poop.

"Thank you," Tasha said with her left hand tightly gripping the doorknob.

The man pulled a business card from his pocket, "call me anytime – day or night."

The seduction in his voice and the smell of his breath made Tasha sick to her stomach. The closer he got, the more she wanted to scream.

"You have a nice night," Tasha said as she slammed the door behind her not allowing him to say another word.

*   *   *   *   *

Lee was glad to keep Chanelle for another week. Maryland's schools didn't go back until the last week in August, which meant she still had ten days of vacation. Mike was happy too. He had taken off a week just so he could spend some time playing Uncle. They were great with her. "If only God would bless them with a child," was a daily prayer of Tasha's.

Tasha got her mother tickets for the convention, knowing some of her favorite tele-evangelists would be there. Tasha had never seen so many men praising God; they were revved up.

As the stadium began to clear out, Tasha caught a glimpse of a man that resembled Curtis' old roommate, David. *"No way could that be him,"* she thought as she helped usher the crowd to the exits. It had been over four years since she saw him, and he certainly wasn't into the church thing back then. The next morning she spotted the man again. She told herself, *"This time I'm going to get close enough to make sure."* As she eased her way over to section F, she heard someone call her name. The voice was foreign. Again, her name was called. She turned to look but none of the faces were familiar. Instantly, a man from behind gently grabbed her arm. When she turned to see who it was, she was standing face to face with John. Her eyes widened as if it were Jesus, himself, standing there.

"LaTasha?"

"Oh, my goodness! Is that you, John?"

"It's me," he joked.

164

They stood face to face; unsure of whether to hug or just shake hands.

"It's really great to see you," he said leaning in.

"Likewise," she said as she lifted her arms to embrace him.

She almost didn't want to let go. He felt better than he had four years ago when he hugged her by surprise and he certainly looked better. Her mind raced. She wondered what he had been doing over the past few years. Was he married? Did he have children? She noticed a ring when they pulled away but it looked more like a class ring than a wedding band.

"How have you been?" he tried to scream over the arena full of cheering men.

"I'm doing okay," she replied.

They could barely hear each other. The crowd was too loud. They both began to laugh realizing it would be pointless to try and compete with the boisterous men. He held up one finger as he reached down in the nearby seat and grabbed a notepad and pen. He jotted something down, tore off the piece of paper, and handed it to her. "Best Western on Main Street. That's where I'm staying until Friday," was the note. Tasha shook her head in agreement. As she walked away she wanted desperately to look back. *"Was he watching her leave?"* she thought. "Probably not." She just kept on walking.

*   *   *   *   *

Later that night as she lay in her bed she twirled the piece of paper John had given her. She had already called and told Lee. Ringing in her ear were Lee's words, *"He was in love with you, girl!"* Was that true? *"Was he really attracted to me?"* she thought as she stared at the telephone. It was way too late to call. She knew Friday was only two days away and if she wanted to catch him, she'd better act quickly.

Thursday was the final day of the convention. Jakes was the last speaker and his message was, "Halt that Runaway Train." He came from the book of Kings. He talked about how Elijah was the most powerful prophet in the land at that time, but one word sent him on the run. The place was quiet for the first twenty minutes – almost surreal. Once he began to talk of how Elijah had to come to

165

himself in order to recognize his own power and influence, the place went up. Half of the men were screaming and the other half were crying. By the end of the night, the men truly had been loosed, and were set to go home to face whatever they had been running from.

As the crowd exited, Tasha stood close by the main door. She wanted to see if she could spot John and have him meet her later for coffee. Once the crowd began to thin out she figured he had probably exited through another door. It was customary for her to stay at least thirty minutes after the last door had been locked – to check the status of the building. When she got in her car, she took note of the time – 11:44pm. She wanted to call John before it was too late but didn't want to be disrespectful by calling so late.

Early the next morning, Tasha knew she didn't have to report to work until 4:00, so she dialed the number John had given her. A man, bright and chipper, answered the telephone.

"Good morning, this is John."

"Good morning John, this is Tasha"

"It's great to hear from you Tasha, how have you been?"

"Very well. Thank you."

Both paused from speaking. The silence had gone on ten seconds too long before John said, "Have you had breakfast yet?"

"Actually, I was just about to ask you that."

They both laughed.

"How would you like to meet at the Bob Big Boys, across from your hotel?"

"Sure, that would be great," John answered. "Let's say 10:00."

"Perfect! I'll meet you there."

When they hung up the telephone, Tasha felt herself getting excited. She didn't know why, but she was. She didn't want to allow her mind to get carried away with thoughts, so she turned the radio up loud and sang along as she got dressed.

Walking into the restaurant she could feel the butterflies flapping in her stomach. Why was she so nervous, she kept asking herself? It was only a simple breakfast with an old friend.

She spotted John sitting at a table not too far from the back. He looked great. He had certainly matured – physically. His caramel skin complexion was clean and clear. His close faded haircut made him look distinguished while his goatee gave him a look of maturity. He had certainly been working out. Tasha could tell that by the way his clothes fit, and he had obviously gotten some contacts because he no longer wore glasses.

As she walked over to the table he stood to pull out her chair. "Still a gentleman, I see," she commented.

"I can't help it. That's how I was raised," he said flashing a pearly white smile.

While the two of them sat and talked, they barely ate. The waitress had come over several times asking if they needed anything, but they continued to tell her, "No thanks, we're just fine." They talked about what had been happening in both of their lives over the past four years. John told her that he had graduated with honors and was offered a position at Texaco in Greensboro, N.C. He was happy about that because it meant he didn't have to move too far away from his hometown in Raleigh-Durham. The company also paid for him to return to school; and he was finishing up his last year and would receive his MBA. He told her he was not married but had dated someone for a year.

"As soon as I was gonna propose, she popped up pregnant."

Tasha tried to keep her mouth from dropping open. "So you have a child?" she inquired.

"That's the thing, she and I had never been together, so the child couldn't have been mine."

Tasha's eyes wanted to pop from her head.

"That devastated me. Although I loved her, I couldn't live with the fact that she had betrayed me that way; especially since I was saving myself for her."

Tasha felt the pain in his words.

"Enough about me. What have you been up to?"

Before Tasha began to talk, she took a deep breath. As she recapped her life from the past few years he listened intently. When she brought up Chanelle's name he interjected, "Yeah, I heard about that." In a way she felt ashamed but she loved her child. No matter what anyone said or thought.

As she continued to talk, he interrupted her. "Please forgive me if I'm outta line, but is what's-his-name in her life?"

Tasha chuckled. "Sad to say, but no."

John shook his head. "Do you have a picture of her I can see?" he asked.

When Tasha pulled out her wallet and handed the picture to John, his eyes lit up.

"Oh, my God! She is absolutely gorgeous! Just like her mother."

Tasha was flattered. "Stop it," she swayed her hand his way, "but thank you."

As the two continued to talk, both Tasha and John noticed the waitress staring at them.

"Why does she keep looking this way?" Tasha asked.

"Probably because we've been here so long."

When John looked down at his watch he said, "Oh my Lord, look at the time. It's almost 1:30 and my plane leaves at 3:00."

They both began to scurry for their things. When Tasha pulled out some money John gave her a strange look.

"What are you doing?" he asked.

"I'm paying for the meal," she said innocently.

"Honey please, put your money away."

Tasha wanted to say something, but she could tell from the look on his face that her money was not needed.

As the two left the restaurant, Tasha asked, "Do you have a ride to the airport?"

"I'm gonna catch a cab."

"No you're not. I'll take you."

"I can't let you do that. I'll just catch a cab."

Tasha didn't say another word, she just looked at him – the same way he looked at her in the restaurant when she pulled her money out. He got the hint.

"Okay. Just let me run over to the hotel and grab my bag."

While driving they talked casually – about the weather, the city and sports teams. Never once did they bring up anything personal. Arriving at the airport, John got out to get everything squared away. When he returned to the car, he began to say his goodbyes.

"Do you mind if I wait with you? I don't have to be to work until 4:00."

"Sure, that would be great," he said excitingly.

They had only been sitting there for fifteen minutes before his gate was called for boarding.

"Well, I guess this is goodbye – again," she said.

John handed her one of his business cards. He had even written his address, home phone number and cell number on the back. "Call me sometimes."

Tasha smiled. When the announcer made the final call for his flight, John hugged Tasha while whispering in her ear, "It was really good seeing you again." When they separated, she smiled and continued smiling as he disappeared behind the closing airplane doors.

CHAPTER 33

Mid-October had come and Tasha was back to the hustle and bustle of life. She was once again preparing for midterms, working full time at the arena, and chasing after Chanelle. The baby had just had her fourth birthday and she was now coming into her own. Her personality was fiery! She had charisma and could charm anyone. She far exceeded the normal development of a child her age. On Friday morning, Tasha took her to get a checkup, and Chanelle began talking to the doctor about why Jesus was killed. He sat in amazement as she spoke.

"How in the world does she know all of this?" the doctor asked Tasha when a nurse took Chanelle away to weigh her.

"My mother and I read to her – a lot."

"What else does she know?"

"Plenty! She knows all of her numbers – from 1 to 40, all of her letters, all of the shapes, and all of the colors. She's even starting to read. *I Can Read with my Eyes Closed* by Dr. Seuss is her favorite."

"Wow," the doctor remarked.

"When she comes back, ask her what her favorite color is."

As Tasha and the doctor continued to talk, Chanelle came running in the room, the black heavy-set nurse trying to keep up with her pace. "My, my, this girl is something," the nurse said. While the doctor continued with his examination, he began asking Chanelle some questions.

"I like the "ABC" song, can you sing it for me?"

With her squeaky four year old voice she began to sing, "A, b, c, ..."

He asked her a few more questions about numbers and shapes. When he got to the colors, he asked her about them. She gave him the answers he was looking for – red, blue, and orange. He glanced over at Tasha then back at Chanelle and asked, "Do you have a favorite color?"

She thought for a moment – as if that answer depended on her survival. "Yes," she answered.

"What is it? Pink, blue?"

She took another minute to think – "chartreuse," she blurted out.

His mouth dropped open. Tasha just sat over in the corner with a smile on her face – proud as a mother could be.

As Chanelle and Tasha were leaving the doctor's office, she spotted Brian coming from the coffee shop across the street. Obviously Chanelle had spotted him too because she started yelling, "Daddy, daddy."

Tasha tried her best to put Chanelle in the car before he saw them, but it was too late. When he crossed the street, they exchanged hellos.

"Daddy, Daddy," Chanelle kept yelling. Tasha just continued to call her name as if to shut her up. The child was reaching out to Brian.

"May I?" he asked reaching back for Chanelle.

Tasha let out a deep breath before shaking her head "Yes." When he opened the car door, the child leaped into his arms. They hugged as if they were experiencing a bonafide family reunion. While the man and child laughed and played for a few minutes, Tasha was becoming irritated and frustrated. She knew Chanelle needed a father and was extremely fond of Brian, but she couldn't get over the fact that he had done some horrible things. When Tasha couldn't take it any longer she took the role of the wicked witch of the west and broke up the reunion.

"Okay Chanelle, we have to go."

The four year old began to cry. Brian did his best to calm the child. "I promise to come and see you tomorrow," he said kissing the child on the forehead and putting her in the car.

Tasha's eyes were as big as baseballs. The comment made her even angrier.

"You promise, Daddy?" the child whimpered.

"I promise," he responded looking towards Tasha.

She didn't respond. She just got in the car and drove away.

Brian kept his word; he showed up the next morning. When Tasha answered the door she was surprised.

"How did you know where I lived?"

Brian paused for a moment – almost not wanting to answer.

Tasha began to shut the door in his face when he said, "Yahoo searches."

By this time she was steaming. "What the …!"

"I'm sorry but I knew you wouldn't have given it to me," he said with pity in his eyes.

As Tasha began to shut the door again, Chanelle came running from her bedroom.

"Daddy, daddy!"

Tasha knew she couldn't disappoint her daughter, so she opened the door wider so Brian could come in.

CHAPTER 34

Talking to John was a breath of fresh air. He always lifted her spirits. Originally, they began communicating through emails – at least twice a week. Then, it became four times a week. John asked her if it was okay to call sometimes. Of course she said "yes," so they agreed to talk every Saturday morning. That lasted maybe three weeks before the calls moved to Tuesday nights then Tuesday and Thursday nights. Within three months they were talking daily.

Brian was still trying to make his way back into Tasha and Chanelle's life. He would pop up unannounced, call at least twice a day, and leave gifts for both Tasha and Chanelle at the door. Valentine Day morning as Tasha was leaving for work, she noticed her car covered with dozens of long stemmed white and red roses. In a way she was flattered, but also upset. When she got home from work that evening, there were another two dozen red, white, and yellow long stemmed roses lying at her front door. There was also a card that read, *"I'm still in love with you."* That touched Tasha's heart – although she didn't want it to.

As she cooked dinner, she began to think about how she had once loved Brian. *"He was good to me,"* she told herself. But she couldn't negate the fact that he had been unfaithful. Her mind went back and forth. *"He said he was sorry and that he would never hurt me like that again,"* she reasoned. The wrestling of her mind and her heart was too much for her to handle.

A week later Brian showed up at her door. It was early – around 6:15 am. When she opened the door, she immediately said, "What's wrong?"

His face told her something had happened. He fell against her chest and began to cry. "My mama died!"

Tasha didn't know what to do. Her heart went out to him. She knew exactly how he felt and couldn't send him away. She had to be there for him – and she was.

The next couple of days she helped Brian do everything – choose a casket, order flowers, make arrangements for family and friends to come; and most of all, cope.

She allowed him to stay with her and Chanelle for a week – just so he wouldn't be alone. She knew Chanelle's presence would help. The arrangement was he had to sleep in the baby's room, and Tasha would put the baby with her – they both agreed.

One morning Tasha told Brian she was going to take the baby to school and run to the supermarket, and she would be back. She had taken a few days off from work to spend with him. When she returned all seemed well until Brian made a comment. "Don't have no dudes calling here!"

She was taken aback because she had no idea what he was talking about. She brushed it off, not giving it another thought. The next day she signed online to check her email. She heard the words, "You've Got Mail," but before she could click on the mailbox to see who the mail was from, she heard Chanelle calling for her from the bathroom. While she was gone, Brian walked over and clicked the mailbox. When he spotted the screen name "John Samuels" and the title that read, "I miss you," he hit delete. Four times he hit delete – each time he saw the name. He then walked into the bathroom as if he had done nothing asking, "Is everything alright with my two favorite girls?"

When Tasha returned to the computer and clicked the mailbox, only junk mail was there.

When she hadn't heard from John in over two weeks, she waited until Brian took Chanelle out to the park, then called John. When she got his answering machine she left a message, "Hey there John, this is Tasha. I haven't heard from you in a while and wanted to see if all was well. Give me a call when you get this message." He never returned her call.

*   *   *   *   *

After Tasha finished her paper, she went into the room to get ready for bed. Her mind raced. It had become normal for Tasha's thoughts to run on their own. Her life had seen so many changes that stability was the furthest thing from her brain. Prayer seemed to be the only thing that brought peace. And once again, she fell asleep praying.

In the middle of the night she felt someone kissing her neck. When she opened her eyes, Brian was standing over top of her.

"What are you doing?" she said pushing him away.

"I need you baby," he pleaded, lifting up her nightgown.

"Are you crazy? Chanelle is right here," she shouted looking down, but Chanelle was gone. "Where is Chanelle?"

"She's in her bed."

His hand gliding up her thigh gave Tasha a sick feeling. When she opened her mouth to tell him to get out, something strange happened; something she wasn't expecting. Instead of her lips moving, her hands did the talking – right upside his head. It's like she had gone out of control.

Tasha went into a swinging frenzy, only stopping when she heard the whimpers of a wounded animal.

Tasha didn't believe in violence. In fact, she had never even been in a fight. But this was a matter of life and death. She knew Satan wanted her dead and she knew that if she didn't fight for her life, then she would lose it – both physically and spiritually.

When Tasha came from the bedroom, into the living room, Brian was sitting on the sofa drinking a glass of water. She stood there, staring at him, trying to figure out who and what this man was. *"How had she gotten so low to allow someone who slyly meant her no good that deep into her life,"* she thought. She felt like there was a tug pulling on her soul. A tug that would pull her to a place she knew she would never be able to escape. This was her chance. This was her final escape – and she knew it.

"When I wake up, I want you gone," she said as she went into Chanelle's room and closed the door behind her.

When she heard her alarm clock sounding from the next room, she knew it was 6:30 a.m. Walking into the living room, she knew everything was back to normal – Brian was gone.

CHAPTER 35

It had been three months since Brian left. It was a strange situation, but Tasha knew it had to be done. She realized he was not the man for her. She knew that the first time they had dealings, but she thought it would be different the second time around – boy, was she wrong.

To top things off, a telephone call from Curtis didn't help any. In fact, it brought more fear and frustration. After almost five years of absenteeism, the man who broke her heart and left her pregnant popped up. What in the world was going on? Lee felt God was trying to tell her something.

"Well, whatever it is, he can just speak it and stop playing all these games," Tasha lashed out.

Her mind raced for the remainder of the day. Although she hadn't had a long talk with him, Curtis' voice sparked curiosity in Tasha. She had so many questions for him, the number one being, "Why show up now?"

"*Life was so unfair*," she reflected. By the time she rearranged the apartment, that too was just another unstable turn in her life. While she lay in her bed that Saturday night, floods of emotions attacked her – fear, doubt, hate, rage, loneliness, bitterness, and most of all, uncertainty. She had never felt so vulnerable in all her life. Out of nowhere, she began humming the song, "Great Is Your Mercy". The words to the song were coming so strong and so fast that she jumped up and began searching for the CD. When she spotted the orange colored cover with Donnie McClurkin's photo, she immediately began playing the song – straight to track 10 – hitting the repeat button. "Hope," is what she heard as Donnie and the others sang. Her heartache, rage, disappointment, and hate quickly turned to love, joy, and admiration. She knew that feeling; it had never left. Her heart was still after God. As she walked around the apartment, she began to worship; worship as she had never before. She worshipped until she fell prostrate on her living room floor. She could feel freedom entering back into her soul.

The trials and tribulations of life had beat her down so that she was hopeless, but all of that was about to change. Despite all she had been through, she knew without a shadow of a doubt that God had been good!

CHAPTER 36

Tasha started her new life off by joining a new church. The bible classes and Sunday school were excellent, and Chanelle loved going to the children's church. Work was work; it had been slow but steady so she was able to pay her bills, but the summer schedule was soon approaching and she knew what that meant – hectic. She had even saved up enough money to buy that used car she had been eyeing. School had gone really well this last semester. She ended with two A's which brought her GPA back up to 3.6. "*It feels so good to be free*," she told herself driving home that Sunday afternoon.

*   *   *   *   *

The telephone rang just as Tasha was leaving out for work one morning. When she answered she could tell by the woman's voice that it was Lee.

"I'm pregnant!"

Tasha began to scream along with her already screaming friend. "Are you serious?"

"Yes, I just came from the doctors and they said I am six weeks!"

"That is absolutely wonderful! Does Mike know yet?"

"Nope. He's already at work. Plus, I want to surprise him so I'm gonna save the news for dinner – I made reservations for Philips."

"Lee, girl, I am so, so happy for you."

Tasha could tell by Lee's voice that she had begun crying. "I never thought this would happen for me."

"I know but look how good God is!"

Silence filled the airways.

"I called you first because I wanted to thank you."

"Thank me? For what?" Tasha questioned.

"For always being here for me."

"What? I should be thanking you."

"No, I'm serious. All of the times I needed you, you were there. When I needed someone to talk to about my family situations, you listened. When no one believed in me and Mike, you did. You just don't know how much that meant and means to me – to us," Lee said, still crying.

"Girl, you have nothing to thank me for. Matter of fact, I thank God for you every day. I would have lost my mind by now if you hadn't been here for me."

By this time Tasha was crying too.

"I have prayed that this would happen for you and it did. God answers prayers!"

Both women were crying profusely, and without saying another word, they understood what was being said.

CHAPTER 37

Peace was good. It had been such a long time since Tasha had experienced total peace that she was taking no chances to jeopardize it. She continued to attend church every Sunday and tried to make it at least twice during the week. She read her bible constantly – early morning, lunch breaks and basically whenever she had a free moment.

She often thought about the men who had passed through her life. She wondered how Brian was doing. Hopefully he had gotten some deliverance from his spirit of perversion; and John, had he found another girlfriend? Was he happily settling down and possibly preparing for marriage? Curtis was her main thought. She wanted so badly to know why he had called a few weeks prior. Maybe he was calling her to say he was the one dying of AIDS? Or maybe he was feeling guilty for leaving her pregnant and it was eating him up? She wondered if he would call back. Lately, she had been missing her father. It had been four years since he died, but it felt like only yesterday. *"He and Chanelle would be a team to be reckoned with,"* she thought as she drove to work.

She reminisced about her life growing up. Jared and Cilla were good parents. They loved her unconditionally, and she knew that. She continued to think of how she did everything in her power to please them. Immediately, she began to feel sad. The disappointment of getting pregnant engulfed her thoughts. *"But, Chanelle was a gift!"* she quickly said before the thought could be entertained any more. Even her speaking it out loud didn't change her feelings – she knew she had been a disappointment.

Catching a glimpse of herself in the rearview mirror, she noticed the faded freckles on her face and her straight reddish-brown hair. *"Who am I?"* she thought. She had always been curious about her heritage. She knew Jared was half white but he never spoke of it. Cilla had told her a few stories when she was younger, but it was never openly talked about. Once when Tasha was about eight years old, she was helping Jared wash clothes. As she put them away into the drawers, she noticed a picture of a thin petite white woman holding a little boy with a tall, lean black man standing behind her. The baby couldn't have been more than two years old, and the woman looked no older than twenty. The man looked like he was in his early twenties and had a thin moustache. Because the picture was black and white, Tasha couldn't tell the color of the woman's hair or eyes. They must have obviously been grey because of Jared eyes, and her hair could have possibly been red because of Tasha's. Instantly it struck Tasha. The couple she saw in the picture so many years ago was probably her grandparents – Jared's parents. She immediately wanted to know more. When she got to work, she called her mother. She asked about the picture. When Cilla told her she had saved it, Tasha told her she would be there right after work.

*   *   *   *   *

It was about time Tasha found out the truth. She and Cilla sat and talked for over two hours. Tasha's mother showed her pictures Jared had saved. His adoptive parents had given them to him when he left for the service. When he was eighteen, he found out the real story of his parents. His birth mother and father was a mixed couple back in the fifties when that was unheard of. Her family had forced her to give the child up for adoption. They even had his father arrested for rape, but Miriam, his mother, refused to press charges against George, his father. She was sent away and he was ordered by the courts to never come within 100 feet of her or her family again.

The family that adopted Jared had been an older couple from Suffolk, Virginia. He always knew he had been adopted because he was much lighter than all of the other children, but they showed him plenty of love – it was the other townspeople that were biased against him. After Jared and Cilla were married, he would tell her of how the kids would call him "little Jew boy". He was always confused about that because why would they call him a Jew? The adoptive family raised him Catholic; but when he got into the service, he found out his birth last name was Stein, and that his birth mother was, in fact, Jewish. He was shocked because he had always known it as Daniels. Cilla continued to tell Tasha some of

181

the things he dealt with, and of the discrimination he experienced from the whites as well as the blacks. He said he never felt comfortable in his skin. Once he met Cilla, that's when he felt like his life began. He never looked back.

Everything made sense to Tasha now. Her questions of his parents had always been eluded and now she knew why. Her questions of hair and eye color were now understood. Contentment was now hers.

CHAPTER 38

Tasha had the fifth of July off from work so she decided to take the fourth off too. The holiday paid double time but she didn't worry too much about the money, especially since Lee and Mike were coming down for the weekend. Their plan was to go down to Disney. That Friday night, as she waited for them to arrive from Maryland, her telephone rang. When she answered, she heard a man's voice she didn't immediately recognize.

"May I speak with Tasha?"

"This is she."

"Hey girl, what's up?"

Immediately she knew who it was. It was Curtis.

"What's up?"

"Nothing much. How you doin'?"

Tasha wanted so badly to hang up the telephone, but she didn't want the fear gripping her heart to seem obvious.

"How did you get my number?" she asked.

"Yahoo searches."

She sucked her teeth. "That damn Yahoo," she thought.

A moment of pause was too much for Tasha so she blurted out, "How can I help you?"

"I wanted to see how things were going wit' you."

Tasha became confused. *"Why on earth would he care?"* she asked herself. She dare not tell him the hell she'd been through over the last few years – all because of him – so she played it off and said, "Wonderful! Everything is going wonderful for me!"

"Wow! That's good to hear."

Another pause made things awkward.

"So, I hear you had a shorty."

If he had been standing in front of her Tasha would have punched his lights out. What did he mean he heard she had a shorty? He knew he had gotten her pregnant. By this time, she knew he was up to something.

"Yes, I have a child," she said, trying not to reveal the anger she felt.

"Boy or girl?"

"Girl."

"What's her name?"

Tasha knew exactly what he was getting at.

"Her name is Chanelle. Chanelle *Daniels*." She made sure she stressed the last name because she knew that's what he wanted to know.

When Curtis began to talk, Tasha interrupted him. "Look, I'm really not sure why you called or what you want. And yes, Chanelle is yours. She is a happy, healthy little girl who wants for nothing."

He tried to interrupt her, but she continued to talk. "She's beautiful and extremely smart."

When she paused from her hurls of comments, he asked a question she didn't expect. "Can you send me a picture of her?"

"What?"

"A picture? Can I get a picture of her?" he asked.

Tasha didn't know what to say. She froze just like water in the arctic.

"You think about it," he said before she got a chance to answer. He gave her his mailing address and his email address. "Just in case you don't want to mail it, you can email it."

He still had that cockiness about him, she thought as she took down the information.

Another pause silenced the atmosphere before Curtis began to speak again.

"Did you get a letter in the mail?" he began.

"A letter?"

"Yeah, a letter from a clinic?"

Tasha's eyes widened. He must be the sick one. That's what he's calling about, she thought to herself. He's trying to right his wrongs before he dies!

"Yes. I got a letter and I'm fine," she declared.

"Good. Me too."

Tasha became confused. "What do you mean you too?"

"After I got the letter I went and had a HIV test and it came back negative."

When he said that, Brian immediately popped into her mind. *Then he must be the sick one. That's why the devil sent him.* Unawareness clouded Tasha's mind. "If Brian is the sick one, then why did Curtis get a letter," she thought? Her question was soon answered.

"I heard Lola got that shit."

"What?"

"Yeah. She was walking around with that shit while we were in school."

"How you know?"

"'Cause I called the telephone number from the letter and the clinic is in Baton Rouge – where she was from."

"Oh, my God. Are you for real?"

"Yeah. I know I was doin' dirt, but I usually strapped up."

Tasha snickered because she wondered with whom, because he certainly didn't wear a condom with her. She just stood there shaking her head. Call waiting broke her from the trance.

"Look, I gotta go."

"No sweat."

"Bye," she said trying to hurry him off the telephone.

"Like I said, I sure would like to see her," he added before Tasha clicked over and answered her other call.

When she clicked over it was Lee, "We're at the airport."

Tasha got excited. "I'm on my way," she said as she hung up and rushed out.

Her friends had showed up just in time. She knew it was going to be a long weekend and they had plenty to talk about.

CHAPTER 39

Late July, during prayer, John was heavy on Tasha's heart. Cilla had always told her that if God lays someone on your heart, then you ought to pray for them. That could be His way of letting you know they're going through something. Therefore, she specifically focused her prayer on John.

That night, as she cooked dinner, John still lay heavy on her heart so she decided to take a chance and call him. When he answered on the second ring, her heart began to race.

"May I speak with John, please," she asked in a timid voice.

"This is he."

"Hey there John, this is Tasha."

"Hey Tasha, how are ya?" he asked with a bit of excitement in his tone.

When they both paused, John began to speak, "What's new?"

"Nothing much. You were on my mind and I figured I would give you a call."

"Oh yeah?" he said, both pleased and curious.

They both began to indulge themselves in small chit-chat just to break the ice. It had been months since they spoke and Tasha didn't want to just rush in and begin to interrogate him.

"Is everything okay with you?"

Before he answered, he let out a sigh. "Well, yeah, pretty much."

Tasha knew from his response something was wrong but she didn't want to be too pushy. She waited a few seconds to see if he would relinquish the information.

"Are you sure?"

Again, he let out a sigh. "My sister's been having some health issues lately," he began.

Tasha sat and listened intently.

"The doctors say she has a form of leukemia and may need a bone marrow transplant."

Tasha could hardly breathe.

"Have ya'll begun testing yet to try and find a match?"

"The doctors say it's too early for that. But, she's been getting worse over the past few weeks and we can't bear to see her like this."

"How is your mama taking it?"

John swallowed hard before he began to speak. "She's a mess. We have just been praying and fasting."

"John, I'm so sorry. I had no idea. I knew something had to be wrong for you to stop calling."

"Yeah, it's been very trying, but that's not why I stopped calling. Actually, I really needed your friendship."

Tasha could feel her forehead wrinkling in question. "It wasn't?"

"No. I stopped calling because some dude told me you two were engaged and that ya'll were living together."

Tasha dropped her head. She knew exactly who that dude was.

"I even emailed you several times but you never replied. I figured it was true, so I left it BE."

"But I called and left a message on your machine, and you never called back."

"Yes I did, but that dude answered the telephone and cussed me out. After about the third time I called when he answered, I didn't try again."

Tasha could feel rage boiling in her chest. "What about the emails? I never received any."

"I don't know why. I sent several."

Immediately, she knew Brian had most likely deleted them. She was furious.

Both Tasha and John grew silent. She knew in order to make John understand she would have to explain. As she did, he never spoke. She wanted so badly to see his face – to see if he was believing her or not. She would just have to hope he did. After explaining, she exhaled.

"So, that man is out of your life?

"Yes."

"For good?"

"Yes," she said excitedly.

John exhaled. "So that means we can continue in our friendship?"

"I hope so," Tasha said laughing giddily.

She could now hear a little more pep in his voice, but the worry still remained – his sister.

"Now that that's said and done, what are ya'll gonna do about your sister?"

"Continue to fast and pray," John answered.

"Well, I will fast and pray from here."

"Thank you," was all John could say.

A few days later, the calling and emailing began again – as if it had never stopped.

*   *   *   *   *

Three weeks later John called. "We're going in for surgery tomorrow morning."

From their recent conversations, he had told her that the doctors had begun testing the family for a possible marrow match, and his matched perfectly. Of course he was willing to help – that was his sister.

"You know everything is gonna be alright, don't you?"

"Yes."

Tasha could hear the hesitation in his voice.

"Let me rephrase that. When will you be strong enough to come visit me?"

They both laughed.

"Everything will be just fine," he proclaimed.

"Yeah! That's what I wanna hear."

They talked for another hour; just about life and God and His word. They prayed and laughed. It was exactly what they both needed – especially John.

Right before they hung up the telephone, John got quiet before saying, "You are truly an angel sent from God."

Tasha didn't respond. She just allowed him to talk.

"Two years ago I asked God to send me what I need. He told me He would send someone with a kindred spirit."

Tasha began to smile, but John didn't know that.

"I really thank God for sending you."

188

After John finished talking, Tasha began: "I thank God for you too. Just remember, I'm here for you."

As they were hanging up, John screamed Tasha's name. Before the phone hit the receiver, she hollered back, "I'm here."

"Give me a month and I'll be there."

It only took Tasha a moment to know what John was talking about. They both began to laugh as they ended the call.

CHAPTER 40

Tasha waited anxiously at the United Airways terminal. It had been six weeks and John had kept his word – he was on his way for a visit. Although it was mid-September, it was still extremely hot. Tasha was a bit hesitant when John asked to come this particular weekend because it was Chanelle's birthday, and she didn't want to throw him in the mix. She was not willing to take the chance of Chanelle attaching herself to John like she had Brian, and have it not work out. When he said he would not be in the way and he planned on staying in a hotel anyway, she agreed.

The birthday party was perfect for a five year old. Cilla had brought a piñata filled with toys and candy. Tasha had pizza, cake, and ice cream. She had invited all of the children from Chanelle's Pre-K class, and some other children who lived in her apartment complex. John just sat back. He helped when needed but didn't try to bully his way into an authoritative position. He certainly didn't try to play daddy and Tasha was grateful for that.

As the children played, John noticed the trash was filled to the brim so he told Tasha he would take it out to the dumpster. On his way back into the building, he noticed a black car circling the building. When the car pulled up to him, he took a few steps back. The man rolled down the window and asked John if there was a party going on in 3B. He was hesitant but he said, "Yes".

The man leaned over in his back seat and pulled out a gift box, "Give this to the baby for me. Tell her daddy loves her."

John knew exactly who he was. "Sure, man."

He took the box and began walking in the building as the car sped off.

When John entered the apartment, Tasha noticed him carrying the box. He could tell by the way her eyebrows were squinted that she wondered where he got the gift. He walked over to her and whispered, "Daddy loves her."

Tasha took the box and chuckled as she hurled it into the corner.

By 8:00 p.m., Tasha was beat. Everyone was gone and she was now cleaning up the mess they left behind. Chanelle was sitting on the sofa with Cilla and John watching SpongeBob Squarepants. When John noticed Tasha on her hands and knees trying to pick something out of the carpet, he got up to help her.

"Go sit, I got it," she said looking up at him.

He paid her no mind. Instead, he got down on his knees and began picking up the tiny bits of paper. Tasha glanced over and noticed her mother looking at her. Cilla threw a thumbs-up and winked. Tasha chuckled, knowing exactly what her mother was saying.

By 10:00, Chanelle was asleep, Tasha and John had finished cleaning the apartment and Cilla had gone home. It was quiet and dark, and they sat on the sofa talking and periodically watching Saturday Night Live. When Tasha got up to get a glass of juice, she lost her balance and fell back into John's lap. They were face to face looking into each other's eyes. When she moved in to kiss him, he pulled back. She was so embarrassed that she jumped up.

"I'm sorry," she said hurrying into the kitchen.

When she returned, they sat in silence – only laughing at the crazy antics of the actors. As the credits rolled, John asked Tasha to call him a cab.

"I'll take you," she said putting on her shoes.

"I can't let you do that. Chanelle is sleep and I don't want you to wake her."

Tasha continued to dress herself, "It's no problem."

John grabbed Tasha's hand as she looked for her purse. "I don't want the baby out this late. Just call me a taxicab. Please."

She smiled, nodded her head, and grabbed the telephone book from her computer desk. As the cab drove away, Tasha yelled, "I'll be by at 9:00 a.m. to get you for church."

That Sunday was beautiful. The weather was well over 90, but the slight breeze helped alleviate the humidity. The service was blessed. After church, John, Tasha, Chanelle and Cilla all went out to dinner. They had a delightful time. At 5:00, Tasha brought John back to the hotel to get his things together. His plane wasn't scheduled to leave until 8:30 p.m., but she wanted to show him around the city and take him down to the boat docks for a

191

stroll. Chanelle had begged to go with Cilla anyway, so it worked out perfectly.

Tasha gave John a quick tour. They knew it would take more than the two hours they had to see the city, so they opted to head for the docks. As they strolled and talked, they stopped for a moment to watch the boat races. They walked down to the end of one pier. Taking their shoes and socks off, they put their feet in the water. They talked and watched as the sun began to dance. The haze was beginning to disappear and the mosquitoes were making their way out. By this time, Tasha knew it had to be after 7:00.

When they arrived at the airport, John checked in. Tasha asked if she could sit and wait with him – of course he said, "Yes." When his flight was called, they looked at each other.

"Well, I guess this is goodbye – again," Tasha said as they both laughed.

They put in a few more minutes of chit-chat before Tasha reached up to hug John. When they began to separate, he held her tightly. Looking into her eyes, he leaned down and kissed her passionately. Tasha was both shocked and excited. She melted in his arms. As he disappeared once again behind the closing airplane doors, he threw up the numbers 143 with his hand.

Tasha had been confused about the hand signals. She had no idea what John had tried to say. Later that night Tasha got a call from Lisa. It had been months since she heard from her cousin; especially since Lisa was now a senior at Bethune-Cookman College. Lisa had heard about Tasha's "new friend," so she had to call and get the first hand scoop on what was going on. While they talked and filled each other in on what was new, Tasha could hear music playing in the background. When Lisa asked her roommate to turn the radio down, Tasha asked what they were listening to.

"Musiq's first CD," she answered.

When Tasha heard the numbers "143", she asked Lisa to put the phone to the radio. As Musiq sang, "143 means I love you," Tasha began to laugh. When Lisa put the phone back to her ear, she asked Tasha, "So how you feel about this dude?" Tasha chuckled. *"I love him too."*

CHAPTER 41

Tasha was beaming. She had never felt like this before. Even with Curtis, it wasn't the same. She knew she had fallen in love with him because she had given him something no one else ever had – her body. But with John, it was different. There were no sexual emotions behind her love – it was strictly spiritual.

That mid-October, during one of their nightly conversations, John made a statement Tasha was not expecting, "Chanelle needs a father." Tasha remained quiet. She didn't know what to say after that. Sure it was true, but she didn't want to seem like she was trying to throw her responsibility onto him. It was obvious she had some reservations about that topic, so John threw in a joke to change the atmosphere. After the joke was no longer funny, silence filled the airways.

"When are you gonna come meet my family?" John asked.

"I would love to." Tasha was excited that John even mentioned it.

"When, was my question?"

Tasha smiled. "When can I come?"

"How about next weekend?"

"Next weekend!" Tasha asked, surprised.

"Not next weekend?"

"Sweetheart, you know I gotta study for midterms. This is my last year."

"How about the weekend after midterms?"

Tasha pondered it for a minute. She so badly wanted to say yes, even to the first date mentioned. "Okay, but I will have to ask my mom if she can keep Chanelle."

"No, I want Chanelle to come too."

Tasha's heart began to race. The thought of another man getting close to her child was frightening. She wanted to say, "No" but she knew it would send confusion to John.

When she didn't answer, he asked, "What's the problem?"

She paused. "Well…"

Knowing what kind of family John came from made her a bit uncomfortable. She did not want to be judged on the fact that she already had a child. She had been through the, "she's just trying to find a daddy for her baby" comments, and didn't feel like it again.

John interrupted her thoughts. "I know what you're thinking and my family is not like that."

She began to chuckle because once again, he was right – for picking up on her fears. "Plus, I have been bragging about you since I got home so they are expecting to meet you."

"Are you for real?"

"Look, I love you and everybody knows it – including you. I'm not ashamed that you have a child. Chanelle is a gift from God, and how many people do you know hide gifts?

Tasha could feel peace engulfing her soul.

"Just let me know, should I book the flight or not?"

Tasha laughed out loud. "Yes!"

*   *   *   *   *

John's face lit up when Tasha and Chanelle stepped off the plane. He was standing there with a bouquet of yellow, red, and white roses and a plush teddy bear. It had only been about five weeks since they'd seen each other, but it seemed more like five years. When Tasha walked up, she and John's lips collided. Chanelle was a bit hesitant when John bent down to give her a hug. Tasha had told him that Chanelle had been asking for Brian lately; that was the reason for Tasha's cautiousness. John wasn't overbearing; he just handed her the stuffed animal and tickled her. Her laughter broke the tension. As the three walked hand in hand Tasha felt total bliss.

"How was the flight?"

Tasha chuckled, "Thank goodness it was only an hour." John laughed and pointed towards Chanelle. "Yes."

When they arrived at the car, John opened the doors for both Tasha and Chanelle. The baby looked up and smiled – as if she knew he was supposed to do that. While driving, John talked with Tasha, but had more conversation with Chanelle. He asked her about school and her friends and what her favorite show was.

Tasha didn't interrupt. She was more impressed by the way John included her daughter.

"Is anyone hungry?" John asked.

Tasha said, "No," but Chanelle didn't answer; she was in the back seat playing with her new toy.

"Would anyone like to go to the zoo?"

In the rearview mirror, he could see Chanelle's eyes widen. "I do," she said enthusiastically with her hand raised as if she knew the answer to the question.

"To the zoo it is."

That night, after they were tired and smelling like animals, dinner was the only thing left to do. Tasha asked for the name and number to a hotel, but John insisted she and Chanelle stay at his place. It was only a one bedroom apartment, but he told her they could have the room and he would sleep on the sofa. After much toiling, she agreed. John wanted to take them somewhere nice, but Tasha was so tired that they decided to order Chinese and call it a night.

Chanelle fell asleep first. Thankfully, Tasha had already given her a bath and put her night clothes on. John lifted her limp body from the middle of the living room floor and placed her in the bed. He and Tasha stayed up a little while to watch TV and talk. After John cleaned up the leftover food, he returned to find Tasha sound asleep on the sofa. He didn't bother her. He simply laid a quilt over her, and laid one on the floor for himself.

*   *   *   *   *

"So this is Tasha?" John's mom asked, while shaking her hand.

"Nice to meet you, Mrs. Samuels."

"And who is this gorgeous little woman?" she questioned.

"This is Chanelle," Tasha added, "say hello."

The baby waved, then buried her head in her mother's lap. Everyone laughed.

"I have something for that shyness," John's mother said as she went into the kitchen and brought back a cookie.

John had told Tasha that his mother was going to prepare a dinner when she visited. And a dinner she had prepared: fried chicken, candied yams, macaroni and cheese and collard greens, and sweet potato pie for dessert. By the end of dinner everyone was stuffed and looking about ten pounds heavier. As they talked, a thin woman with a bandana tied around her head emerged from a closed bedroom door. Tasha knew it was John's sister, just from the pictures he had sent her.

"Hey sleepyhead," he yelled out.

"Hey everybody," she replied.

"Ruth, this is my friend Tasha."

Ruth's face lit up. "So this is the woman keeping that smile on my big brother's face?"

Tasha blushed. So did John.

While they all sat and got acquainted, Chanelle seemed to get antsy. Tasha noticed and tried to keep her still. Ruth noticed also, so she asked Tasha if it was okay to take Chanelle into her room to play with some of Ruth's stuffed animals. When Chanelle heard those words she got excited so, of course, Tasha said, "Yes." As Tasha, John and his mother talked, Tasha's fears began to subside. John was right – his family didn't judge her. Gloria, John's mother, asked if Tasha would be coming back for the graduation in December.

"I certainly hope so," John said looking Tasha's way.

"Only if you promise to come to mine in May?"

He smiled, "Bet."

The way the evening ended was a relief for Tasha. Her fears of not being accepted by John's family were put away, and her place in his life was made clear. When the three of them returned to the apartment that night, Chanelle was already asleep. She and Ruth were played out. She had even called Ruth "auntie" when they waved and hugged goodbye.

When Tasha put Chanelle to bed, she came into the living room to spend some quiet time with John. They had been eyeing each other all day. She didn't want to assume, but she could tell he thought about her in a more mature way – and she thought the same. As they sat on the sofa watching "Love and Basketball", John felt the sofa shake a bit.

"You okay?"

"Yeah, just a little chilly."

He got up and grabbed a blanket from the hall closet. "Here you go," he said laying it over her. "You want some hot cocoa?"

"That sounds great. Thank you, sweetie."

Tasha felt comfortable enough to start calling him pet names. He didn't seem to mind – especially since he smiled every time she said it.

Coming back from the kitchen, he held two jumbo sized mugs. He handed her one and carefully sipped on the other as he slid under the blanket she had thrown across her legs. She smiled.

As they watched the movie, they were silent; grinning at the parts that were romantic, and giggling at the scenes that were humorous. The scene when Monica asks Q to open the letter from the school, and she kisses him, made the room even quieter. Tasha could feel herself freezing up when John looked her way. They stared at each other for a moment before locking lips. Her body tingled when she felt his hand run across her shoulder. He placed the palm of his hand in the core of her back and pulled her closer. From the cold chill in the air and the heat from her body, her nipples began to harden. She closed her eyes and let the serenity of the moment carry her away. They kissed passionately – past the end of the scene of Monica and Q making love with Maxwell singing, "This Woman's Worth". Tasha could feel herself leaning back and John leaning forward. He softly kissed her lips and sensually licked down her neck. As she slid down the sofa, underneath him, she wanted so badly to feel him inside of her. With him on top, she could feel his bulge poking her. His strong hand gliding up her thigh made her even more aroused. Turning to kiss his neck, she saw Chanelle standing in the doorway. Immediately, she jumped up, "What's wrong sweetheart?"

The five year old stood there rubbing her eyes, "I'm thirsty."

After Tasha gave her daughter a glass of juice, she went right back to bed as if she never saw anything out of the ordinary. John had moved from the sofa, to a recliner over in the corner. Tasha could tell he was embarrassed by what had just happened.

"I'm so sorry," he said with the look of guilt in his eyes.

"Me too."

"We shouldn't have…"

Tasha stopped him when she walked over and placed her hand over his lips, "and we won't."

She left him sitting there as she went into the bedroom and closed the door behind her.

CHAPTER 42

"You finna go to Philly for Thanksgiving?" Tasha asked her friend.

"Nah. Since the doctor put me on bed rest last week, I'm not allowed to leave the state, so we're just gonna go over to one of my co-workers for dinner."

"How you been feelin'?" Tasha asked.

"I'm doin' alright – I guess."

"Are you still bleeding?"

"Nah. I've been taking it easy," Lee said.

"Mike gettin' on ya nerves yet? Doin' everything?"

Both women laughed. "Of course; you know how he is."

As the two friends talked, Tasha could hear the anxiety in Lee's voice – past the laughing and joking and even the cursing. Most people didn't know Lee worried because of her cool demeanor, but Tasha knew better. Talking about new cars and new houses meant nothing when it came to serious situations like this. Tasha tried to bring a more relaxed conversation when she told Lee about her weekend with John. While Tasha talked, Lee listened. She said, "Uh huh" and "what!", anytime Tasha got to a highpoint.

"So when is the ring coming?" Lee blurted out.

"What?"

"You heard me," she said with her almost lost North Philly accent.

"I don't think he's thinking like that just yet."

"Whateva! You know he can't wait to make you his wife!"

"I wouldn't say that," Tasha replied with hesitation.

"Well, I would."

Tasha got quiet. She had thought of being John's wife, but certainly didn't want to bring it up to Lee, and certainly not to him. A smile glided across her face as she sat listening to her best friend dream out loud. Finally being with him – for good; giving him babies and growing with the person you're in love with. What a wonderful thought that was. Mike's voice in the background broke her concentration.

"Hey, girl!"

"Hey, boy," she joked, knowing it was Mike.

"What's new?"

"Nothing much. I heard about your promotion."

"Yeah." He changed the subject as if it weren't important. "Did Lee tell you we been house shopping?"

"Yup. She also said ya'll saw one that ya'll really like?"

"Yes ma'am. We're gonna go talk to the broker Saturday afternoon. Hopefully we can settle before the baby gets here."

"Well, let me know what the verdict is."

"Will do. Here's Lee," Mike said handing the phone back over to his wife.

"Well girl, let me let you go. I got a few errands to run before I pick Nelly up from school." That was the nickname Mike had given Chanelle.

"Later!"

CHAPTER 43

"Why haven't you been cashing my checks?"

"Because I don't want your money!" Tasha yelled.

"It's not for you, it's for the baby."

"She's not a baby anymore. She's five years old!" Tasha said with rage in her voice.

"She's my baby!"

Oh no he didn't! Did he just say she was his baby? After five years and now this fool wants to claim somebody? He got some nerve!

Tasha just laughed. "Look Curtis, Chanelle has everything she needs. Why you want to start providing now is beyond me – especially when you denied her from the beginning."

"Ever since I saw that first picture you sent me, I knew she was mine; and I'm a man, so I takes care of mine!"

From the very first check Curtis sent, Tasha had been pondering whether to send the money back or keep it. She asked her mother and Lee what they thought she should do, and they both told her to put it into an account for Chanelle.

"I'm begging you; let me take care of my daughter."

Tasha could hear the pity in his voice. As cautious as she was, she couldn't refute the fact that he was her daughter's father – even if he originally denied it.

"Okay, Curtis."

As Tasha began ending the conversation, Curtis interjected, "I want to see her."

Panic and confusion quickly filled Tasha's mind. *"What was he doing? Why now? Why when she and John were getting so close did he want to come back into the picture?"* Tasha knew it, but she refused to admit that she had missed Curtis, and always wanted him in Chanelle's life. Now, he was asking. What was she to do?

She calmed her voice and said, "I knew this was coming."

"Well?"

"Curtis, I can respect the fact that you want to be a man now and handle your responsibility, but that doesn't mean I ought to jump when you want something. Yes, every child needs a father and before I say, "No" – which I want to say – I will pray about it and get back to you."

"Thank you Tash; that's all I'm asking."

With that said, Tasha hung up the telephone.

*　　　*　　　*　　　*　　　*

"Hello?" Tasha answered the phone with a groggy voice.

"The baby died," she heard a man say.

"Who is this?"

"Mike."

Tasha jumped up and looked over at the clock – 3:22 a.m. "Where are you? What happened?"

Nothing was said. She could tell Mike was crying but didn't want it to seem obvious.

"She started bleeding about five hours ago and I brought her to the hospital. By the time we got here, the doctor said that the baby was dead – that it had been dead about three days."

Tasha sighed.

"They made her deliver the baby anyway."

"Where is Lee?"

"She's in the room asleep. I'm in the hallway."

"Did you call her mother yet?"

"No, you're the first person I called."

Tasha wasn't sure of what to say as tears streamed down her face. "Sweetheart, I'm so sorry."

"My son!" Mike said, letting out a heaving sob.

Tasha cried even harder but covered her mouth as not to alert him of her grieving heart as well. "Mike, go back in the room with Lee. You have to be there in case she wakes up."

Tasha could hear Mike sniffling – getting himself together.

"I will catch the first plane out tomorrow morning and call you when I get to the airport."

Mike let out a sigh.

"Did you hear me?"

He cleared his throat, "Yes."

Tasha hung up the telephone and immediately called for a flight.

*   *   *   *   *

Walking into the room that early December afternoon, Tasha could feel death. She got the same feeling when her father had had the heart attack. The room looked different from when she visited her father, but it still reeked of ammonia. The walls were papered with bottles, safety pins, and rattles. A huge cherry oak dresser was neatly arranged in the corner with a matching book shelf. There was a lounge chair in the far left corner and a stretched sofa that lay with its back up against the large bay window. The curtains of the window were drawn but the Victorian lamps affixed above the bed were on. There were few machines – only an IV pole. This was the most comfortable delivery room Tasha had ever seen. She noticed Lee and Mike sound asleep on the bed – his arm wrapped around her still swollen body. She stood and stared for a moment. When she turned to walk out, Lee called her name, "Tash?"

"I'm here, sweetheart."

While Tasha tiptoed over to the bed, Mike sat up. Tasha hugged him first because he was closest to her.

"I'll go get some juice," he said, hugging her once more and whispering, "Thank you for coming," before leaving the two women alone.

Tasha could see the heartbreak in her friend's eyes. It practically crushed her but now was not the time to break down. Now, she had to be the strong one – the one who didn't react with fear or trembling.

"Ain't this some shit?" Lee joked before she burst into tears.

Tasha didn't reply. She simply walked over and got into bed – taking Mike's place with her arms wrapped around her friend.

Mike had taken a long time returning – probably giving the friends extra time to be together; but when he did, he found them laying in bed watching The Cosby Show on the TV affixed to the high left wall. Mike didn't ask for his place back nor did Tasha budge. He walked over and plopped on the couch. All three watched and laughed as Theo ranted about his Gordon Gartrell which Denise tried to copy. Tasha exhaled first when Lee squeezed her hand. That was her way of saying, "Thank you."

Tasha stayed for several more days. Long enough to attend the small burial for the baby – Michael Lamont Hopkins Jr. – and make sure Lee was comfortably back home. It was hard to leave her friend in such a depressing state; but she had to get back to Chanelle, school, work, and tending to her other daily routines. Tasha left Mike and Lee with five little words, "God's gonna make you laugh!"

CHAPTER 44

"You know the graduation is Saturday, right?" John asked.

"Yes."

"Are you still coming, because I haven't heard you say anything about it lately?"

Tasha didn't answer.

"Say something, baby."

"I wanted to talk to you about that," she started.

John could hear the "No" coming. "What's wrong?"

"I can't afford to come," Tasha said with remorse in her voice. "I used the money to go see about Lee and I..."

John interrupted her. "So you think I can't take care of my family?" He asked with a hint of frustration in his voice.

Tasha paused. Did he just say, "My family? What in the world was he talking about?" Tasha thought.

"Do you actually think I would make you pay for anything?" John questioned.

Tasha remained quiet. She knew she had paid for the last time she came to visit him, but didn't want to say anything and make it seem like he wasn't a man or that he was a liar.

"I just thought..."

Again he interrupted her. "I know what you thought sweetheart, and it's okay. Just let me know what day I should book you for?"

Tasha smiled, "How's Friday morning?"

"Friday it is."

"Am I..."

Again, John completed her sentence, "Yes, you are bringing Nelly."

Tasha laughed out loud. "How in the world do you know me so well?"

"Because you're my rib and I know my own body," John joked.

They both laughed.

"Can you book me a hotel too?"

"Actually, I was thinking that maybe you and Nelly can stay at my mom's house – get to know my family better? She has a spare bedroom, and Ruth would love to have the baby there with her; she hasn't stopped talking about Chanelle since ya'll left."

"Are you sure?"

"Yeah. I already talked to my mom, and she would be delighted to have ya'll there."

Tasha was so happy. "Okay, that's fine with me."

"Well, I guess I'll see you Friday afternoon."

"I thought you were gonna book the flight for the morning?"

"I am but I have to work, so I'm gonna send my mom and Ruth to pick ya'll up; and I'll be by the house after I get off. Is that okay with you?"

"That's fine, honey."

Before they hung up, John added, "That's what the check was for."

He said goodbye before Tasha could respond. Holding the receiver, her mind raced. *"What was the check for?"* she thought. Immediately, she began to laugh. She remembered that when she returned home from her previous visit with John, she found an envelope with a check stuffed inside her purse and a note that read, "Your money is not needed." John had refused to tell her what the check was for, but it made perfect sense now. The check equaled the plane tickets for her and Chanelle.

*   *   *   *   *

"Auntie," Chanelle said running and jumping into Ruth's arms.

Ruth hugged and kissed on Chanelle as if she were her own child. Tasha had worried the entire flight there. Even though her visit before was pleasant—she still couldn't be too sure how John's family would take to her, and especially Nelly. Seeing Ruth's reaction calmed her fears once again.

The four women went out for an early lunch. They talked about the graduation – how everyone was so proud of John. Gloria got choked up a few times when she spoke of his father. "He would be so proud," she said several times. John had told Tasha that his father died of prostate cancer when John was in the ninth grade and Ruth was in the fourth. Gloria had never remarried, although one of the deacons from the church wanted to court her. Tasha told them about her father as well; about their relationship and how she missed him so.

The conversation then turned to Ruth's health. Tasha had noticed that she had gained an easy fifteen pounds since they last saw each other. She looked great, Tasha thought to herself.

"Girl, that haircut is sharp," Tasha commented as they sat and talked. Her hair was growing back nicely – it had fallen out from the chemo.

After lunch, they returned to the house. There was a message on the machine from John. He was calling to make sure Tasha and Nelly had gotten there safely. Tasha called him back at work. "We're here, you can stop worrying," she joked.

"I can't wait to see you," he whispered.

Tasha chuckled.

"I'm on my way into a meeting right now, but I'll talk to you when I get there."

A smile engulfed her face, "Okay."

Just as they were about to hang up the telephone, John hesitated, "You and Nelly wear something fancy tonight, I wanna take ya'll out,"

"When should we be ready?" she asked.

"When I get there – about six."

"Yes sir," she joked as they ended the call.

*   *   *   *   *

Tasha's face lit up when John walked into the room. He wore a grey pinstriped suit with a cobalt blue silk shirt and tie to match. His shoes were polished to perfection and his hair and goatee were freshly cut – he looked delicious! When he walked over and hugged and kissed her on the cheek, he smelled even better.

"Where's my girl?"

Gloria began to laugh, 'She didn't want to go with ya'll so Ruth took her over to Brenda's house to play with the kids."

"That's fine. You ready?" he asked.

"Sure, let me grab my purse."

When they reached the car, he spun her around to get a good look. She wore a black wrapped fitted dress that tied on the side and ended at the knee. The plunge line was a bit low, but not too revealing. Her black strap-around-the-ankle pumps and hand-held purse added the finishing touches. Thankfully Jared had taught her to always pack something nice when she went away. That way, if anything came up, she would be dressed properly. Boy, was she glad she learned that lesson.

"Where are we going?"

"A guy I work with invited me to this restaurant/lounge where he does poetry; so I figured since we don't have the baby with us, we can swing by there. How's that?"

"That sounds great!"

When they arrived at the restaurant it was packed, with standing room only! John and Tasha knew it would be impossible for them to get a table anything short of an hour. Thankfully Maalik, John's co-worker, noticed him and offered them his complementary table. As they talked and ate, the announcement for the poet to begin shortly was made. John whispered in Maalik's ear as he headed for the stage.

As Maalik flowed, the room vibed. His words put stillness in the atmosphere. Every ear was tuned and receptive. Poem after poem, he captured the audience's attention. With his canny phrases and love prose, everyone was shell shocked. When Maalik mentioned he would be doing one more poem and dedicating it to all the loves in the house, John got up and excused himself from the table. While the words eased from the poet's lips, Tasha listened intently. She was that poem. Every word described her feelings for John; every motion of Maalik's hand swayed her. Even his pauses caused her to pause – to ponder her love for John. As her mind swirled with the words, she noticed John standing at the end of the stage. She had no idea what he was doing up there. As the people cheered and clapped for Maalik as he made his exit, John grabbed the mike. The room fell silent. Not even the rude people were talking.

"LaTasha Daniels, I am in love with you!" John started, "I have known it for quite some time and I can't keep it inside."

Tasha didn't move, she just listened.

"A few years ago, I asked God to send me what I needed. I thought he had done that, but I was wrong – until we met again in Jacksonville. That meeting was my birth and I have been living ever since. Now, I am sure he indeed does answer prayers."

The crowd began to clap as John paused. When he lifted his hand, everyone in the room gasped. He was holding a little black velvet box.

"Come here," he called out.

Tasha shook as she walked to the stage. Her knees felt like they weighed a ton and they would collapse at any time.

John grabbed her hand and got down on one knee. In front of the entire room he said, "I need you and Nelly in my life. You are my everything, and I would die without you. Will you make me the happiest man in the world and become my wife?"

The room was tranquil.

Tears streamed down Tasha's face, "Of course I will," she proclaimed as they embraced and kissed passionately.

CHAPTER 45

Tasha had been floating on cloud nine. It was only three months from the big June day, and the wedding plans were going well. John had gotten a promotion on his job – starting at six figures – and he was looking for a new house to surprise his bride as a wedding gift.

Everyone helped with the arrangements. Cilla and Lee helped with the bridal needs, and Ruth and Gloria helped with the groom's affairs. Cilla was a little sad because she knew Tasha and Chanelle would be moving away, but happy, nonetheless.

Finding the wedding dress was the biggest moment for Tasha. She had been looking since John proposed and had yet to find anything she truly liked. Lee offered to contact the bridal shop in Camden to see if the seamstress could be of any assistance. When Tasha received some of the patterns in the mail she wasn't very fond of any of them. "Let's give it one last shot," the owner said to her over the phone. When the new patterns arrived Tasha knew she had found her dress. It was classic but not traditional. It was egg shell with gold trim. The sleeves were sheer and flowing. The breastplate was satin with lace trim and the v-line plunged. The skirt was complete satin with gold intertwined throughout. It was absolutely beautiful! Tasha rushed over to her mother's. Cilla was sitting at the kitchen table with the look of death on her face, but tried to straighten up when Tasha walked in.

"What's wrong, Mama?"

Cilla cleared her throat and painted her face with a fake smile, "Nothing, sweetheart."

Tasha knew better. "Mama?"

Looking up, the older woman smiled at the younger one and blurted out, "Are you sick?"

"Sick like what?" Tasha was confused at what her mother was getting at.

"HIV?"

"No! Why would you ask me that?"

Cilla sighed. "A woman named Lola called here this morning looking for you."

Tasha sat down next to her mother.

"She said she was sick and that you might be infected too."

Tasha went on to tell her mother about the love triangle between her and Curtis and Lola back in school and the letter she had received over a year ago. She reassured Cilla that she had taken a test and it came back negative; and that she had not since been sexually active. Tasha comforted her mother with a big hug.

Cilla exhaled, "Thank you, Jesus! It's such a shame that that young girl's life is over," Cilla said.

"Did she leave a number?"

"As a matter of fact, she did." Cilla handed her daughter a piece of paper.

Tasha sat there in silence staring at the number.

Her mother interrupted her trance, "So let me see this dress!"

*   *   *   *   *

Tasha's heart raced as she dialed the number. After the third ring, she wanted to hang up but couldn't. Suddenly, she heard the voice of a tired woman, "Hello."

"May I speak with Lola please?"

"This is she."

"This is LaTasha Daniels, how are you?"

"I'm fine, how are you?"

"I'm blessed."

Silence engulfed the airways before Lola chimed in: "I spoke with your mother this morning, but I guess you already know that since you're calling me back."

Tasha wanted so badly to ask her how she was really doing but didn't want to seem insensitive. Lola's openness made the conversation much easier. As the two talked about the last few years, they focused on their children. Tasha was surprised to hear Lola say she had a fourteen month old son. *Why would she do that* Tasha wondered? Lola told her that's when she found out she was HIV positive – when she was pregnant – and decided to keep the baby after the doctors told her there would be a 70% chance the child wouldn't be born positive too.

Lola surprised Tasha when she asked about Curtis.

"He's trying to do the right thing but I'm getting married in a few weeks, and I don't want him to be a hindrance to my family."

During the conversation, Tasha had told Lola all about the reunion with John and their plans of marriage. She also told her about Curtis and where he now stood in her life. When Tasha said she had allowed Curtis to see Chanelle, and that he had asked for her to spend the summer with him; Lola interrupted. "I know that's your child and you can make decisions on your own, but be careful."

Tasha listened intently.

"Curtis could have changed over the years, but from what I've been hearing about him through David, his old roommate, he hasn't changed much. I used to be a snake, so I know how snakes live and move – be careful you don't get bit!"

Fear gripped Tasha. She knew nothing about Curtis' life now or what he was involved in. She was even more surprised to hear that Lola and David had kept in touch. The sound of a baby in the background let Tasha know her talk with Lola would soon be ending.

"That's my son waking up from his nap."

"Okay girl, I'll let you go," Tasha said trying to sound unfazed by the warning.

"It was really good talking with you and I wish you the best in everything."

"I know you have to go, but do you mind if I pray for you?" Tasha asked hesitantly.

"Not at all!"

As Tasha prayed, she blessed Lola's life. She asked God to protect her and her family and to give her strength and renewed health in the years to come. Tasha could tell Lola was crying. The harder she prayed, the harder Lola cried. When Tasha ended the prayer, she left her one time rival with four profound words, "Keep ya head up."

CHAPTER 46

The morning Tasha went to finalize the wedding invitations, she felt strange. Cilla had noticed she was a bit quiet but she just figured it was because of all Tasha had to take care of before the wedding day. Tasha had tossed and turned all night but was not sure why. This was a happy time for her, so why would she feel this way? After she dropped her mother off at work, she headed for her daughter's school. Whatever this feeling of uneasiness was, she knew it had to do with Chanelle. When she arrived, everything was fine. She talked with the teacher for a few minutes and didn't hear or see any signs of danger. When she left and headed for work, she laughed the feeling off, "*It must just be me.*"

That evening, after going to class and picking Chanelle up from her mother's, Tasha returned home. She had a message from John and one from Lee. She talked with both of them as she cooked. As she and Chanelle ate dinner, she realized she had forgotten to get the mail from her box when she came in. Exhaustion told her to wait until tomorrow morning but since she already had to take the trash out, she figured she would knock two birds out with one stone. Sifting through the pile as she walked up the stairs, she noticed a letter from the Florida Department of Social Services. Sitting on the sofa as her daughter watched "*The Proud Family*", Tasha began to read the letter. Her heart raced and she became short of breath as she read the letter:

Curtis Martin
—Vs.-
LaTasha Daniels

The State of Florida in conjunction with the State of California law 139-14C does hereby challenge parental guidance of one said minor listed below:

Chanelle Miriam Daniels

D.O.B.: 09/05/2

The date of this hearing is scheduled for June 16, 2008. Full or partial custody of the child so stated will be determined on this date. All parties are expected to be in attendance. Failure of either party will result in an immediate determination of favor for the opposing party.

"Was this a joke?" Tasha thought. By the way her hands shook, she knew it wasn't. Lola's warning rang back clearly – *"be careful."* Immediately, Tasha looked over at Chanelle. She was laid across the sofa with her hands planted firmly under her chin, legs in the air behind her swinging, and outrageously laughing at Suga Mama trying to steal a kiss from Papi. A happy, loved child was all she saw.

Tasha was pissed off! Not knowing what to do, she ran to her phonebook and retrieved Curtis' number. She dialed in haste. A woman answered the phone and Tasha didn't feel a need to be polite, "Where is that lying bastard!" she yelled.

"Who the hell is this?" the woman answered back.

"Tasha! Where is Curtis?"

The woman's voice calmed, "Honey, it's for you."

When Curtis grabbed the phone, Tasha let him have it.

"So I assume you got the custody letter," he said with ease.

Tasha caught her breath. She wanted to cry but refused. "Why?"

"'Cause she's mine too."

"I knew I shouldn't have let you see her!" she shouted.

Curtis sighed – not out of pity but out of boredom. "My wife and I will be there on the 16th."

"Your wife?" Tasha asked.

"Yes, the woman whom you just spoke with!"

Tasha shook her head. By that time Chanelle had come over to see what the matter was. She embraced her daughter in love, while hate and betrayal flowed through her heart.

"God will never let you get away with this."

"Yeah, yeah, yeah! I told you once, I handles my business!" He bragged as he hung up the phone.

For the next several hours, Tasha talked with everyone close to her – Cilla, John, Lee and Mike. Mike let her know he had some good legal connections in Florida and that he would find her the best attorney possible. John told her whatever the cost was, he would pay for it. Her mother said she would pray, and Tasha knew that was the best thing anyone could do.

While Tasha lay in her bed praying, she asked God, *"Is there ever any rest for the weary?"* He didn't respond. As she reread the letter over in her head a thousand times, it dawned on her that June 16th was the day before the wedding.

*   *   *   *   *

Tasha didn't want to eat, couldn't sleep, and didn't feel like school or work; but she knew she couldn't let the devil's plans get her down. Every day that week, she slept with Chanelle. During her prayer time, she constantly asked God why all of this was happening. Silence. After a week of pondering her options, a thought came to her. What was to be done was beyond her wildest thoughts – *"allow Brian to testify."* It was so farfetched that she knew God couldn't have said anything like that – that it had to be her. But, she had nothing to lose – she made the phone call.

When Brian answered the phone, her heart fainted. Never had she thought she would be in a situation like this, asking for his help. When she explained to him what was going on, he seemed uninterested. She felt like Moses begging Pharaoh to let God's people go. When he told her he could not help, she was crushed. Hurt later turned to anger; not towards Brian or Curtis, but towards God. She was beyond panic. But again, like so many other times, she had no control of the situation.

A week before the court date and the wedding, Cilla called Tasha early Sunday morning and asked her to go to church. Tasha was stressed because she had asked John to allow her to postpone the wedding, but he begged her not to. He said that everything would be alright. She agreed with him, but in her heart of hearts, she wasn't sure if it would be. The excitement of the wedding was the only thing that kept her sane.

A familiar place was exactly what Tasha needed. It had been years since she had been to church with her mother. Seeing all of the old saints brought a smile to her face. When the Pastor asked if she had any remarks, she simply asked everyone to pray for her.

The ones who knew Tasha was getting married expected to see her smiling happily, but she was looking the opposite.

When the Pastor ended with the customary benediction of "turn and hug your neighbor", everyone did just that. A few of Tasha's old friends ran over to say "Hello" and to ask her about the wedding; but were quickly halted when they noticed Sister Margaret making her way towards them. The older woman, now thinner and frailer, tottered over to Tasha.

"Suga, I just wanna see ya and that beautiful baby of yours," the older woman said.

Tasha smiled as she bent down to hug the mother. As she listened intently to the woman talking, her eyes began to water. The smell of Ben Gay seeped from the woman's pores. Tasha could also see the gray of her hair edges which the black wig she wore didn't cover. When Tasha noticed her mother waving to her to come talk to the Pastor; Sis. Margaret grabbed Tasha's hand. As Sis. Margaret continued to talk, she also began speaking in tongues. *"Not again,"* Tasha thought. Even after all of these years, Tasha felt the same way she had so long ago. The bustling in the church stopped as everyone focused on the two women. The older woman now grabbed both hands of the younger woman and stood face to face and began to speak: *"Fear not, fear not, fear not! For what I have given is a gift. And I, only I can withdraw my gift. Isaac was not only a gift to Abraham but a promise and I, even after the test did not remove the gift. Fear not, fear not. My gift was for you and is for you."*

Tasha broke down and began to cry. Her tears quickly turned to praise. She knew that was the answer she had been waiting for! When Sister Margaret began to walk away, Tasha grabbed and hugged her tightly.

"Thank you, thank you!"

Only Tasha's mother knew what the thanks was all about.

CHAPTER 47

The Tuesday before the wedding, John and all of his family arrived from Raleigh. Seeing him walk off the plane, made Tasha want to melt in his arms. His hug let her know he would handle everything. Chanelle ran and jumped in Ruth's arms, and Cilla finally got to meet Gloria. It looked like one giant family reunion in the terminal, especially when Lee and Mike's plane landed an hour later.

After everyone was settled in the hotel, John and Tasha decided to go for a drive. She had told him about what happened at church, but wanted to tell him the story again. They both wondered how God would handle things, but it didn't make much difference – as long as it was handled.

The next day, while Tasha, John, and Mike met with the attorney to finalize all the necessary paperwork for Friday, Cilla, Lee, Gloria, and Ruth finalized all of the wedding arrangements. Tasha knew she had great women supporting her, so she didn't feel at all nervous to see what final changes they would make.

Later that night, Cilla asked if anyone wanted to go to bible study with her. She was surprised when two people jumped up.

"I would love to go," Lee said.

"So would I," Mike added.

Tasha smiled brightly.

"Do they still have prayer before the study?" Tasha asked.

"Yes."

She didn't say another word. She just grabbed her purse.

Prayer was exactly what she needed. Gloria decided to go as well. John stayed behind to keep an eye on Chanelle and Ruth – she had not been feeling well since the flight.

The prayer and the study were excellent. Afterwards, the Pastor came over to meet the new family and friends. Mike and Lee both thanked him for explaining the scriptures so vividly. They had never heard anyone talk about the Bible as if it were actually true. In the middle of their group conversation, Tasha spotted Sister Margaret making her way across the room. She was both nervous and excited. *"Was the old woman going to prophesy or was she just coming over to say hello?"* Tasha wondered. The Pastor also caught a glimpse of the woman and signaled for his wife to deter her. He was not going to allow this – not tonight.

*   *   *   *   *

There was no way to have a rehearsal dinner that Friday night before the wedding with so much happening earlier that day, so Cilla decided to have it Thursday night at her house. She, Gloria, Aunt Viv, and John's Aunt Charlene spent all day preparing a feast. Everyone close to Tasha showed up. She even invited Nicole and Marcus, despite what happened between her and Brian. They had a great time. Tasha laughed as much as she could, just not to think about what the next day would hold.

Everyone was dressed and ready to go to the courthouse by 8:00 a.m. The hearing wasn't until 11, so they decided to have breakfast. Tasha didn't want Chanelle to witness what would happen, so Ruth and Lisa decided to take her to the zoo.

Walking into the courthouse holding John's hand, Tasha spotted Curtis and presumably his wife standing by the water fountain. She was pretty and obviously pregnant. He looked almost the same from the last time she saw him a year ago except for the full beard he now wore. Her heart began to race. Not because she still had feelings for him, but the adrenaline of anger caused the feelings. *"How could he try something like this – even after I allowed him to meet Chanelle?"* she thought, walking by. They just stared at each other – not saying a word. When she entered the courtroom, she felt like a child – small and scared. She was happy she was not alone; the grip of John's hand let her know that.

As the proceedings began, both attorneys began arguing their cases. Tasha felt numb. She periodically looked over to see how Curtis was responding; he never once looked her way, keeping his head straight. Each attorney began calling witnesses. When Curtis was called, he brought up the fact that he had been sending her money – alleging he has been taking care of her and that Tasha allowed him to meet Chanelle – lying before the judge, saying she

- 218 -

offered to give him the baby so she could go on with her life. Tears welled up in her eyes as she listened. "How could he?" she mumbled. She knew he would use those two tactics to fight. Luckily, she took the attorney's advice and brought a statement of Chanelle's bank account with every penny he ever gave her accounted for. Both teams went back and forth, debating the truth. When Cilla began to noticeably cry, the judge called for a fifteen minute recess. Tasha begged Lee not to say anything, but she had to.

She walked over to Curtis and spit in his face. "You lying bastard!"

He didn't move, he just pulled the handkerchief from his lapel and wiped his face.

"And you wanna be attached to a man like this?" she said looking the wife in the face. The wife's response was a bit more respectful – she put her head down.

In the hallway, everyone stood around talking. Curtis and his wife went outside to get away from Tasha and her family. When the attorney motioned for everyone to return to the courtroom, Tasha held up one finger – alerting them she needed one more second. She ran over to the water fountain and took a sip. Instantly, she felt a tap on her shoulder. When she turned around, Brian was standing there. Her eyes widened but she didn't speak – neither did he. She looked over at John standing by the courtroom door. He smiled; so did she. She turned back and looked at Brian. Her eyes softened. Neither said a word. They just walked into the courtroom.

When Tasha's attorney called for Brian to testify, he stood up and headed for the bench. Tasha couldn't negate the fact that he was a handsome man; tall and burly – smooth as ever and most of all – confident. She knew that's what attracted her to him in the first place. Everyone noticed a television positioned in the middle of the courtroom that was not there before the break. The attorney asked his first question, "Can you tell the court who you are?"

Brian looked over at Curtis and confidently said, "I'm Chanelle's father."

Tasha's eyes widened. Cilla and Lee looked over at her but didn't say a word.

Brian then began explaining what qualified him to be Chanelle's father. No, he was not the man that helped create her, but he was the man that loved and protected her. The bailiff walked over to the television and hit the start button. On the screen was a home movie of Chanelle's first birthday. Brian was there – being daddy. All through the video tape were scenes of Chanelle, Brian, and Tasha – at the zoo, at the park, in the house playing, her second birthday party – Chanelle calling him "Daddy" the entire time. At that moment, Tasha knew why the Lord had told her to call Brian; he would be the one to save her child. Curtis' attorney tried to cross examine Brian, but what could he argue? The tape spoke for itself. Brian added another low blow to the plaintiff's case when he pulled a framed picture from his suit pocket of him and Chanelle that read, "Daddy's Little Girl."

Right before the judge made his ruling, he asked if either party wanted to make any last comments; Tasha stood up. When the judge gave her the floor ,she turned and looked at Curtis and Brian, and then at John. Every man that she had ever loved was assembled in the same room. At this moment it was not about Chanelle – she already believed what the Lord had told her – but it was about the steps of her life. It was about the plan God had for her. It was about closure.

Her heart began to race when she looked over at Curtis and began talking. "Thank you for my child. She is the most wonderful thing that has ever happened to me. For so long I asked God, why you? He never answered, but now I know why you; because if it were not for you, there would be no her."

She smiled and focused her attention on Brian.

"Thank you for helping me raise her. You were exactly what I needed – at the time. Your love and protection was exactly what we needed – both me and Chanelle. You can't know what that means to me and I love you for that."

Her eyes welled up as she turned to John; her face soft and loving. "Tomorrow we become one. You are the man God originally had for me; and now His promises will come to pass; and I know – with all my heart – you are what we need. Thank you."

When Tasha took her seat there was not a dry eye in sight. The judge asked once again if anyone had anything to add. Curtis jumped up.

"Your honor, my wife and I have decided to forfeit our case and waive any parental rights we may have."

Tasha let out a huge sigh as the rest of her family went up in a cheer.

The judge tried to get order by hitting his gavel. "Are you sure, Mr. Martin?" he said. Curtis looked down at his wife, "We're sure."

The judge pronounced the child to remain in the custody of her mother holding full guardianship.

The case was closed.

*   *   *   *   *

Lying in her bed that night, Tasha stared up at the ceiling, still excited from the day's events. She remembered so many other times she lay in that position, but those times were different - mostly wearisome. This time, she stared in joy and not anger. This time, things had worked out. This time, she was smiling and not crying. She was not questioning God, but thanking Him. Lying there, she basked in peace until she fell asleep.

CHAPTER 48

Early the next morning, Tasha was awakened by the smell of bacon and the gleam of the sun shining through her window. It instantly took her back to Easter mornings when she was a child. How her mother would get up at 4:30 a.m. to make breakfast so they could be at Sunrise Service by 6:00. Those were happy times for Tasha and today, she had the same feeling – knowing she would get to wear a beautiful dress, get treats, and enjoy the company of her family. With her joy, sadness crept in. The only thing missing was her father. She always knew he would be the one walking her down the aisle, but today that wasn't possible. Her mind began to wander as she thought of what it would be like if he were there. A slight tap on the door broke her trance.

"Are you awake?" her mother asked as she peeked into the room.

"Yes."

Cilla walked in carrying a black velvet box. Sitting on the edge of the bed, she looked at her daughter. The love of a mother to her only child flowed between the two of them. Tasha sat up, outlining the contour of her mother's brown face, seeing the age that was now obvious but still beautiful. Tasha noticed the gray of Cilla's hair, although the pink sponged rollers she wore hid most of it. While Tasha always knew she looked like her father, she increasingly realized just how much she resembled her mother, and just how much Cilla resembled Marlene. The beauty, spirit and strength of the generations had been passed down.

"Thirty-eight years ago my mother walked into my bedroom and sat on the edge of my bed – just as I'm doing. She pulled out this same box and opened it before me – just as I'm doing. Then she gave me a few words of wisdom – just as I'm about to do."

Tasha could see love in her mother's eyes, love she had never recognized, but that had always been there.

"I thank God for you. You are the best thing that has ever happened to me. Sometimes, God allows us to wait for the promise – just like he did Sarah, but the first look into Isaac's eyes made her forget why she had laughed at God in the first place."

Tasha smiled, knowing exactly what her mother was saying.

"Now that you're a woman – and a fine one – I have totally forgotten why I laughed at God."

Both women chuckled.

Cilla's eyes stiffened for a moment when she grabbed Tasha's hand. "Your father would be so proud. He loved you with all his heart. I would give anything to let him see you today."

The tears that filled Tasha's eyes spilled onto the velvet box she was now holding. "He sees."

"I know baby, I know."

They embraced each other, finally grieving the lost of Jared – together.

Grabbing the box of tissues from the night table, they wiped each other's tears. Instantly, they both broke out into laughter.

"Okay, back to my original spiel," Cilla said.

Tasha's face straightened up.

"I'm gonna leave you with the only three words my mother told me that made the most sense – Love your family."

Tasha's face remained calm.

"No matter what, love them."

Tasha began to nod her head, as if the light bulb came on.

Cilla motioned for Tasha to open the box. The most beautiful string of pearls Tasha had ever seen was before her.

"These were my mother's and her mother's and her mother's, and now they're yours." Tasha hugged her mother – so proud to be of a blessed people.

*   *   *   *   *

The house was busy but peaceful, with everyone running around trying to get dressed. Lee and Lisa helped Tasha get dressed as Ruth looked after Chanelle. Cilla and Gloria tried to keep order, but it was almost impossible with constant movement throughout the house.

When the Rolls Royce showed up in front of the house, Chanelle ran into the room with her mother.

"Oh my goodness, sweetheart, you look so pretty," Tasha said hugging her five year old.

"You too, Mommy."

The little girl handed her mother a medium sized gift wrapped box with a card attached to it, "Daddy sent this for you."

Tasha was so happy to hear those words come from Chanelle's mouth – knowing she was speaking of John. Tasha shook the box. From the echo, she knew it was either something glass or something with a chime. She removed the card and handed it to Lee who opened it and began reading:

Last night I prayed
I asked God if he would keep me in perfect peace
I asked if you would love me forever;
to live in the beauty of holiness

I thanked him for grace and mercy which was given as an incentive
I asked that despite our shortcomings he would forgive us
In spite of our selfish ways he would bless us
Despite our fleshly desires he would heal us
And besides our sin sick soul he would save us

Last night I prayed
I asked God if he would bless our union
coming together as one from two different perspectives
That we would love when we are unlovable
And be patient when tolerance has been crushed
I thanked him for commitment and trust was added
I asked that we would serve with a humble heart
and give of all that we have

Last night I prayed
I asked God if I could assist with your dreams
and comfort you when you feel alone
I thanked him for wisdom and knowledge was acquired
I asked that I would support when I don't understand
and listen when nothing is being said

Last night I prayed
I asked God for all of these attributes
That he would equip us with his word and power
I asked him for the privilege to be an example

Last night I prayed
and before I could say amen
he replied
You have been blessed with time
 use it effectively
not wasting it on idle chat or self-indulgent thoughts,
but, always giving glory to him through our lives

Last night I prayed
and before I could say amen
He replied
It is done

There was not a dry eye in the room.

"Mommy, why are you crying?" Chanelle asked.

Everyone began laughing. The five year old looked around in confusion.

"'Cause I'm happy, sweetheart."

The child began to laugh, not knowing why; but also growing impatient while waiting for her mother to open the enticing box. Tasha could see the eagerness on her daughter's face. "Here honey, you open it for me."

Chanelle tore into it as if it was Christmas morning. She gave no regard to the lavish bow or the satin trimming hanging – she just ripped. Inside were a set of keys and a picture of a house. Tasha flipped the picture over and on the back it read, "Welcome home."

Her mouth fell open as everyone in the room "ooh-ed" and "aah-ed."

*   *   *   *   *

Arriving at the church, Tasha was at total peace. She had never thought anything like this would happen for her – but it was. Sitting in the pastor's chambers with the bridal party, she could hear the organist playing her father's favorite songs. It brought tears to her eyes.

"We won't be having any of that," Lee said grabbing for tissues.

Cilla just smiled, she knew what the tears were about.

The women sat and talked for a few minutes, until the usher came in and told Cilla it was time for her entrance. Gloria had already left to see about John.

"Well girls, see ya when I see ya."

Everyone laughed, knowing Cilla never used young people's slang. When she opened the door, Sis. Margaret was standing there – about to knock. She didn't acknowledge Cilla; she just walked right past her as if she weren't standing there. The old woman walked over to Tasha.

"You look so pretty," she began in her country accent.

Tasha just smiled, waiting for the next thing to come from her mouth. Without warning, she looked over at Lee.

"Hi, suga."

Lee quickly looked at the old woman, then at Tasha.

"Hello, Mrs.," she replied.

Cilla stood there, the usher waiting for her to move; but she couldn't. She had to see what was going to be said or done.

"I tried to come over and see you at church the other night but the first lady needed to talk to me. With me being so important to the ministry, she consults me about a lot of stuff."

Tasha chuckled to herself. She glanced over at her mother who was also chuckling and shaking her head.

The old woman began rambling about her position as head usher and a member of the deaconess board. Tasha cleared her throat to try and bring the elderly woman's attention back into focus. Lee was great; she just stood there listening, not really sure what else to do.

"But anyway. The Lord told me to tell you that your heart was broken but he is mending it now," as she placed her hands on her chest.

Tasha's eyes widened. She hoped Lee wouldn't react – and she didn't. The elderly woman's wrinkled hand moved from her heart down to her belly. "This is the product of a mended heart."

Tasha put her hands to her face in surprise. She looked at her friend who was looking back at her, and shook her head in agreement to what Sister Margaret was saying.

Lee began to laugh. Tasha looked over at her mother with a humongous smile. Cilla looked back, shaking her head. Tasha wasn't sure if the laugher offended the elderly woman or if she was finished delivering the word, because she gave Lee a fake grin and left the room. Cilla followed her out without saying a word; and neither did Tasha speak because she knew at that moment her friend was already pregnant.

Within minutes, the usher returned to the room and announced they were ready. As everyone exited the room and headed for their positions, Lee held Tasha's hand. This was the first time she didn't have anything to say, but Tasha did.

"Didn't I tell you God was gonna make you laugh?"

They looked into each other's eyes, not saying another word, just smiling. That was all they usually needed to do.

When she left, Tasha stood there all alone. Glancing in the mirror, she could see the reflection of both her dad and her grandmother glaring back at her. She knew tears were not appropriate for the moment – a "Thanks" was.

She threw up her hands and whispered into the air, "Thank you, Lord."

She never heard the door open up. She just heard the usher say, "They're ready for you."

When the double doors were swung open and Tasha saw John standing there with a smile on his face and a tear in his eyes; she knew that *rest had finally come to her weary soul*.

...About the Author...

Janene was born and raised in the hard streets of Camden, New Jersey. In the 4th grade a reading teacher stood at the front of the classroom holding a book which he proclaimed, "would introduce us to a world we've never known." That book was Edgar Allen Poe's <u>Poetry and Short Story Collection;</u> the first poem he read was "The Raven". Instantly, Janene was in love. Being a journal keeper and an avid reader; and loving to listen to her mother tell folk-tales, she began writing short stories secretively. In high school Janene was persuaded by a teacher and friend to enter her first short story contest.

It was a no-brainer for Janene to pursue writing in college. She graduated from Rutgers University with a Bachelor's of Arts degree in English-Literature, with an emphasis in Pre-Modern Day Era Literature and Creative Writing. She also earned a Master's of Science degree in Christian Counseling from Philadelphia Biblical University. Janene plans to further her education with another Master's degree in Fine Arts in Creative Writing and a doctorate degree in Urban Studies.

Janene has won numerous writing contests and has had several of her short stories and poems published in local print magazines, online magazines and periodicals. Janene gains a lot of her inspiration for writing from just observing life; and several of her writing heroes, namely J. California Cooper and Edgar Allan Poe.

Janene lives in New Jersey with her teenage daughter.

www.ingramcontent.com/pod-product-compliance
Lightning Source LLC
Chambersburg PA
CBHW050516260626
47157CB00004B/1353